"What is it, Patrick? Do you want something?"

He held her tighter. "I want you. I need you tonight, Briony. Love me."

His mouth was demanding as it played against hers, his tongue insistent and probing, hungry for what she had to offer. His fingers, which so often served as his eyes, traced patterns over her supple skin, stroking her with heavenly eloquence until Briony's nipples hardened under Patrick's sensitive touch. Slowly he caressed the peak of one breast, catching it between his thumb and forefinger, putting flame to the delicate tinder of Briony's passion and setting loose a wildfire....

Dear Reader,

It is our pleasure to bring you romance novels that go beyond category writing. The settings of **Harlequin American Romance** give a sense of place and culture that is uniquely American, and the characters are warm and believable. The stories are of "today" and have been chosen to give variety within the vast scope of romance fiction.

As in her first book, *Dark Star of Love*, Elizabeth Glenn again explores the problems and obstacles of the disabled through her hero—a blind professor. His courage and determination will inspire you.

From the early days of Harlequin, our primary concern has been to bring you novels of the highest quality. **Harlequin American Romance** is no exception. Enjoy!

Vivian Stephens

Vivian Stephens
Editorial Director
Harlequin American Romance
919 Third Avenue,
New York, N.Y. 10022

Taste of Love

ELIZABETH GLENN

Harlequin Books

TORONTO • NEW YORK • LONDON
AMSTERDAM • PARIS • SYDNEY • HAMBURG
STOCKHOLM • ATHENS • TOKYO • MILAN

Published December 1983

First printing October 1983

ISBN 0-373-16036-4

Chapter One

Briony watched the man walk across the airport lobby, his head up and his shoulders squared in that alert way of his that she remembered so well. His gait was deceptively casual. His green eyes, apparently fixed with thoughtful concentration on the floor far ahead of him, didn't notice the admiring looks, both surreptitious and frank, that he received from passing females of all ages.

Briony's thoughts echoed their admiration. At thirty, he was still by far the best-looking man she had ever seen, his thick and almost curly hair only slightly darker than the golden tanned skin tones of his strong face. It was hard to say just what it was about that unconventional face that was so arresting. It was well-shaped, true enough, but the chin was stubborn and the jaw obstinately square, and the nose—poor nose, had he broken it again? It was somewhat crooked, and that fact plus his tall, broad-shouldered build contributed to the mistaken first impression that he had been a college football hero.

No doubt, though, it was his eyes—wide-set, dark-lashed, beautiful green eyes that seemed to have captured the sun forever in their depths—that fascinated people, that made them look a second time and often a third. Briony found herself staring at those eyes now as he walked in her general direction, willing them to glance up and see her, to recognize her. Because it was a futile wish, and a dangerous one, she felt her heart give a painful twist and thought for a moment she might cry. Instead she blinked furiously and moved forward, glad that the lobby had almost emptied of travelers by now.

He had stopped near the ticket counter and stood, half-turned away from Briony, but at the sound of her approaching footsteps he swung around, a frown worrying his usually straight fair eyebrows. He said nothing, seeming to watch her legs as she crossed over until she was close enough to reach out and touch him. Now those sexy eyes with their slightly lazy look appeared to be dwelling far too long for politeness on her breasts, firm and upthrust beneath her powder blue silk blouse with its matching linen skirt. Indeed, if he had been anyone else, she might have slapped him, or at least verbally remonstrated him for taking such liberties.

As it was, she stood where she was and enjoyed the chance to study him close up again after five long years.

She watched him frown, considering, and sniff her perfume, and then his mouth with the full lower lip opened a little and he said doubtfully, "Briony Hammond?"

"As I live and breathe," she murmured softly, "if it isn't Patrick Donahue."

The frown disappeared, the eyes lifted to the height indicated by her voice, and an expression of pleasure spread over the uniquely attractive features. "Little Briony," he exclaimed, propping the long white cane that he carried against the ticket counter and holding out both hands toward her. "Can I claim a hug as an old friend?"

She giggled with delight as she grasped his hand and

let him pull her into his arms, knowing his sense of touch would now tell him what his eyes could not. "Hey," he reproached her when his arms had closed around her. "You grew up when I wasn't looking."

For a moment Briony was too overcome with the joy of his proximity to answer. So many times over the years he had been away she had fantasized about this happening, had pictured him strolling back into her life, looking every inch the handsome college professor in his white button-down shirt and red-striped tie, corduroy sport jacket and slacks, embracing her hard and tight like this, and kissing her full on the lips.

Briony drew a shaky breath, her cheek crushed against his collarbone. "I'm five-six. I haven't grown an inch since you left Austin, Patrick. You've just forgotten."

He laughed deep in his throat and drew back to run both hands down her sides, making sure of her curves, his fingers searing her skin through the thin material of her blouse. "Oh, you've grown, all right, and in all the right places. I seem to recall Steve telling me you won a beauty contest of some kind."

"Oh, that." She carelessly dismissed the fact that she had been crowned the most beautiful young lady in the state. "That was four years ago, and besides, it was nothing. I'd much rather have gotten my doctorate like you did." She was happily aware that his hands still rested on her waist, as if to be sure she didn't move out of his reach. "After five years, don't you think you can at least kiss me hello?"

Here it came now. The best part of her fantasy, where bells rang and sparks flew and he became brilliantly aware that he loved her, had always loved her, and would love her until they were parted in death. Lovely improbable fantasy.

Patrick pressed his sensual lips to her forehead and murmured against her hair, "I'm glad to oblige."

"No, no, no," Briony scolded him, bringing her hands up to his face and drawing it down. "Like this." Still framing his brown cheeks with her palms, she kissed him on the mouth warmly, lingeringly, and for her the sparks flew, just as she had known they would. His breath tasted fresh, and he smelled so good she felt an exciting ripple of desire shoot through her.

He returned her kiss for a moment and she thought he was enjoying it too because his hands tightened on her waist. When he finally lifted his head, it was to give her one of those engaging grins that lit his whole face, even his eyes, and made it impossible to believe he was blind.

"I'm shocked at you, Briony. That was a very adult kiss."

"Of course it was. I'm very adult."

"Mmm-hmm," he mused. "Four years younger than Steve and me. That makes you twenty-six."

"Correct."

"Twenty-six years old. That's incredible. I remember you as you were the last time I saw you—no, I mean *really* saw you. Golden ringlets, a chubby little thing in a pink-and-white pinafore, begging us to play catch with you. But we were getting warmed up for the big game, so we didn't have time for you and you started crying. Your eyes were enormous. What color are your eyes, Briony?"

She could hardly breathe for the pain that came over her when he spoke of that time long past, that summer day just before he was blinded. As if it were yesterday, she recalled the scene: the Little League ballpark with the stands full of cheering parents and friends. Briony sitting between Patrick's father and her own, watching the boys during their turn at bat. The brilliant sun... the gay atmosphere... the grape Popsicle that had been dripping down her chin. The sudden horrible tragedy that had dropped like a black veil over all of them and blocked out Patrick's sunlight forever.

She swallowed with difficulty and steeled herself. "My eyes are green, like yours," she managed to answer him. "People say you look more like my brother than Steve does. It's our hair and eyes, I guess."

Patrick moved one hand up from her waist to her face and cupped her cheek. To a passerby he might have seemed to be studying her, but of course he was really analyzing her mood in that uncanny way of his, sorting out the emotions she hadn't been able to keep out of her voice. She wondered what interpretation he was making, and felt ninety-eight percent certain that he knew what had upset her, because Patrick had been astonishingly perceptive for as far back as she could remember.

And when he had figured out that her anguish was for him, it was characteristic that he remind her he didn't want pity. "Well, little sister," he teased her at last, "I hope you don't mind if I bring myself up to date on how you look. It's disconcerting to get a kiss like *that* from a girl I can remember best as a six-year-old." He raised one eyebrow at her, waiting for her permission.

Briony didn't care that they were still standing beside the airline ticket counter and that people were coming and going around them, the bustle increasing as it came closer to time for another arrival.

"Go ahead," she whispered shakily.

He used both hands and the lightest of touches, his

experienced fingertips moving over her high cheek-bones and down the curve of cheek to her generous mouth and uptilted chin. They slid up her fragile jawline, over her small ears, and then explored her forehead under the heavy gold-and-silver streaked bangs that swept down and back in the latest cut. One index finger traced each eyebrow and the somewhat deep-set eyelids before examining the long thick fringe of dark gold eyelashes that feathered onto her cheeks. He gently tweaked her straight little nose.

From there his well-shaped hands with the long tapering fingers rose to the top of her head. His thumb and forefinger tested the silky texture of one strand. Gravely he slid both hands beneath the smooth golden bell to caress her slender graceful neck, seeking out the hollows of her collarbone just inside the opening of her blouse.

Briony stood quite still as he satisfied his mind's eye. His touch tantalized her, lit fires throughout her body, set her heart racing with delight. If she could have, she would have made the moment last forever, asking nothing more of life than to spend it like this, burning beneath Patrick's fingertips.

But in a minute he had finished and was withdrawing his hands and smiling to himself. "Thanks," he said casually. "I can see now you're not at all six years old."

She was silent, wondering if he liked her face, but he didn't volunteer the information and she was too proud to ask. In another second, a stewardess in a smart red uniform came up with clicking footsteps that caused Patrick to raise his head alertly. "Here you are, Dr. Donahue. You deplaned before I had a chance to say good-bye, and I was afraid you might have gone already." The woman glanced at Briony briefly and turned to survey the lobby. "Still waiting for your father?"

"Sorry, Patrick," Briony interjected before he answered. "I forgot to tell you, Uncle John couldn't make it so I came instead. My car is at your disposal and your wish is my command, sir."

He nodded and extended his hand to the lovely stewardess, who took it immediately. "Thanks for all your help on the flight, Patty. Thank you especially for your company on the layover. Airport newsstands are sadly lacking in braille reading material, and I'm not very big on sight-seeing."

Patty chortled and gave him back his hand with obvious reluctance. "I enjoyed it, Patrick." She flicked another appraising glance at Briony and added, "Don't forget, I'll call you when I'm back in town on Friday. I'm really looking forward to dinner with you."

"I'll see you then." He smiled and waved her off, and turned to Briony. "So you're to be my chauffeur, hmm? That's just my luck. Miss Texas announces that she's at my service, and I can't see her." He grinned suddenly, wickedly, reaching for her waist again. "How about another 'look'?"

"I think not," she said snappishly, peeved that he had made a date with the stewardess. "We'd better gather your luggage and leave before my car gets ticketed."

Obligingly Patrick retrieved his cane, took her elbow, and walked beside her as they made the necessary arrangements for a porter to carry his three big bags to Briony's new Thunderbird.

We might be any couple, she marveled as they went out into the bright, late October sunshine. A handsome man holding a pretty girl's arm, a somewhat subdued look on his face, only his cane alerting everyone to the fact that his clear green eyes couldn't see.

"We're at the curb," she said, slowing her steps.

"You always were good at this," he observed as he opened the car door for himself. He kept a hand on the top of the doorframe as he got inside to be sure he didn't hit his head. "Have you been guiding someone else around while I've been gone?"

"Certainly. I had to keep in practice, didn't I?" Briony made sure his fingers were safely inside before slamming shut the door.

"Anyone I know?" he asked when she had gotten in the driver's seat.

"Pardon?"

"Your blind friend."

"Oh. No." The car slid easily out into the light traffic. "Once in a while I go over to the School for the Blind to help out, and I got to know a couple of the students. Before they graduated, we went shopping together sometimes, and they came to the house to visit."

Patrick grunted, and she wondered what he was thinking.

She could have told him she only did it for him, to learn about new aids for the blind and as a means of feeling connected to him despite the many miles between them. She could have told him that, but she didn't. As well as she had once known Patrick Donahue, she hadn't seen him in five years, with only an occasional letter to let her know he remembered her, and she had no earthly idea how he would react to a declaration of her undying love.

"Briony"—he broke suddenly into her thoughts— "how's Dad?"

She had been dreading the question, and she glanced at him nervously. His head was turned toward her, waiting for her answer, his eyes hitting her chin. As usual, that slightly unfocused look of his brought a lump to her throat.

It took her so long to answer that he furrowed his brow. "Briony? What's the matter?"

"It—it's just that...Uncle John isn't feeling well these days." That was an understatement. Some days when Briony looked in on him, she found him gasping for breath and in unbearable pain.

"I know. He's going into the hospital for tests. That's one reason I felt it was important to come home just now."

Watching the road, she reached over and put a comforting hand on his where it lay on the seat between them. "No, Patrick, he's already in the hospital." Although she gave him the news as calmly as she could, she felt his hand become tense. "He had a spell with his heart yesterday evening and the nitroglycerin didn't help at all. I called Dr. Hayes, his cardiologist, and he ordered me to bring him straight to the emergency room to be admitted."

He turned his hand palm up and laced his fingers through hers. His face had gone taut and a little pale. "Was it a myocardial infarction?"

Heart attack? Of course Patrick would use the correct term and expect her to know what he was talking about.

"A mild one," Briony responded. "He's doing better today. Poor dear, he's been so thrilled you were coming and he's crushed to have you see him first in Cardiac Care, but that's where he is for the time being."

Patrick nodded shortly, not speaking, and she respected his silence as she drove the rest of the way to the medical center where John Donahue was under treatment. He didn't release her hand but held on to it as if it anchored him to something safe. Looking over at the profile she had seen in dreams for half a lifetime, she wondered for the thousandth time how he had gotten the nerve to leave the familiarity of Austin, to venture out into the unknown, unseen world and make his way there. For her own sake, she would rather he had spent the past five years here, where she could be with him. For his sake, she was glad he had proven to himself that he could do it. Her admiration for his courage swelled within her and her eyes shimmered with tears.

Walking beside Briony up the front steps of the hospital and through the busy reception area, Patrick seemed to have recovered from the shocking news about his father and looked his old alert self. His nose twitched and he scowled his displeasure as they passed the cafeteria, which smelled of cabbage and tuna, and again on the third floor, where alcohol and disinfectant fought for supremacy.

The CCU waiting room was jammed with relatives awaiting the ten-minute visitation period that was due in half an hour. As the seats were all taken, she suggested that he stand back against the wall in the corridor and wait while she hunted up Dr. Hayes.

"Whatever you do, don't wander around," she said in a low voice, eyeing with concern the furniture, water fountain, phone booth, and assorted protruding legs and feet that he might trip over.

"Afraid I'll get lost?" he drawled. He had left his cane in her car.

"More afraid you'll break your neck," she shot back.

"It would probably be my nose I'd break," he muttered, rubbing it ruefully, and she grinned at him even though he couldn't see her grin.

Dr. Hayes happened to be at the nurses' station on CCU when Briony stepped inside to ask for him, and the stocky bald-headed physician immediately procured a small office nearby where he could talk to Patrick.

"He's on the shortish side," she whispered as she walked Patrick back to the office, and when she stopped, putting him directly opposite the white-coated older man, Patrick stuck out his hand at just the right level.

"Dr. Hayes?" he said politely. "I'm Patrick Donahue."

"I'm so glad to meet you at last, Dr. Donahue," the man enthused as they shook hands. "Your father has told me a great deal about you during the three years that he's been my patient. I guess you know how proud he is of his college-professor son."

"His only son," Patrick added dryly. "Yes, Dad has been known to bore audiences on the subject of the remarkable Patrick Donahue."

"Oh, I assure you, I wasn't bored. Matter of fact, I'm something of a history buff myself. John tells me your speciality is the Civil War. Haven't you got an article coming out soon?"

"That's right. It's on the aftermath of Gettysburg. If you like, I'll send you a copy of the journal when it's out next month."

The doctor looked pleased. "That would be marvelous, thanks." He sobered up. "Well, shall we sit down and have a little talk about your father?"

With pressure on his arm, Briony indicated for Patrick which way he should move, and guided him so unobtrusively to the sofa that he turned and sat with a complete lack of the awkwardness she had seen in many of the students at the School for the Blind. She thought that part of his unhesitant movement had to do with the way he trusted her to lead him with absolute care, and that realization made her proud. When she sat down next to him, he took her left hand and squeezed it, sending a crooked smile her way.

"Now, Dr. Donahue," the cardiologist began, and Patrick turned his head toward the voice. "I'm glad to have this opportunity to talk with you before you see John. Otherwise you might be quite alarmed at how he looks. And well you might, because his condition has deteriorated since you last saw him— When was it?"

"He flew to Boston to see me in the spring."

"Ah, yes, I remember. I objected to the trip strenuously."

Patrick frowned. "I had no idea."

"No, I'm sure he would have kept my objections from you. He was determined to hear you give the commencement address at your alma mater, and of course I recognize what an honor that was for one as young as you. But did you notice then that he couldn't walk far, that his color was bad?"

"We didn't do much walking," Patrick said after a brief pause. "You're saying he's gotten much worse since then?"

"Appreciably so. His circulation is poor, which accounts for the pain in his legs and his heart."

"Has he been in a lot of pain?"

"Yes, Patrick," Briony put in quietly. "He hasn't complained, but he gets all ashen and perspires until he needs to change clothes and he just doesn't have the strength."

Patrick had gone rather white himself. "Why the hell didn't someone tell me? You've written me," he accused Briony. "Why didn't you make it clear to me how badly he's doing? All you ever did was allude vaguely to his being under the weather."

"I wanted to tell you more than once," she apologized, "but Uncle John wouldn't have it. He's usually gentle as a lamb, but he became agitated when I tried to persuade him you ought to be told. He didn't want to worry you, and I was afraid if I insisted it would bring on a heart attack."

Patrick shut his mouth at that, but from the grim line of his lips Briony realized he was unhappy about it. "Exactly what is the situation with my father?" he asked, and Dr. Hayes leaned forward and laid it on the line bluntly.

"He is in dire need of surgery. His arteries are so clogged with plaque that his heart is dying from faulty circulation. I've been trying for a year to get him to consent to bypass surgery, because he's doomed without it, but so far he's resistant. God knows why."

Briony knew it was because the old man feared dying on the operating table, not for his own sake but for his son's. Although Patrick had lived in complete independence for years, John Donahue worried that after he died Patrick might need someone and be alone. The information, however, was not something she could tell the rigid stony-faced man beside her.

"He'll have the surgery," Patrick said with conviction. "I'll talk some sense into him."

Dr. Hayes looked dubious. "I don't know. He's been immovable on that one subject. Besides, I must warn you that he's waited so long there's a very good chance he won't survive the operation. This infarction he had yesterday made the outlook much less optimistic."

Briony gritted her teeth to keep from crying out as Patrick unconsciously crushed her slender hand in his. "What do you suggest, then?" His voice was low and almost shaky, but his green eyes met the doctor's steadily.

Dr. Hayes sighed. "He isn't in an enviable position.

To refuse surgery is to guarantee a short life expectancy—just how short, I can't say, because it depends on how soon the blood flow to the heart shuts down or how soon he has a fatal heart attack from the strain. If he survives the surgery, he has a chance for another few years, hopefully *good* years. But his chances of surviving surgery are decreasing all the time."

Patrick didn't bother asking what the odds were, probably realizing as Briony did that life wasn't usually predictable. He sat without moving or speaking for a moment, and when he had considered the doctor's words he stood up, pulling her with him. "I'd like to see my father now."

Dr. Hayes rose too, gazing up at Patrick with a worried expression. "How do you plan to advise my patient?"

"I want Dad to live as long as possible, if the quality of his life is...acceptable to him." He didn't look happy with that phrase, but he didn't change it, either. "I want him to live, but I'm not going to tell him what to do. He's risking it, whatever he decides. I'll support him in whatever decision he makes."

Briony couldn't tell if Dr. Hayes approved of Patrick's choice. He merely gave a neutral nod. "I see. Fine. Well, let me ask that when you see him now, you don't let on how shocked you are at his condition." He put out his hand, but Patrick was already turning toward the door.

"Dr. Hayes wants to shake hands," Briony informed him softly, and he turned back so abruptly that he bumped into the smaller man, nearly knocking him down.

Briony put her hand on Patrick's sleeve to steady him, and the doctor recovered his balance, apologizing profusely, a look of disbelief on his face at the realization of Patrick's blindness.

Briony paused in the wide open doorway to John Donahue's room in Cardiac Care. Patrick naturally wondered at her hesitation, but knowing his father was nearby, he didn't question it aloud.

The old man lay with his eyes closed, a tube down his nose, an I.V. attached to his hand, and wires running from the bed to the built-in machines behind it. The machines monitored his vital signs through leads that were taped to his chest. A video camera on the opposite wall relayed the patient's every movement to the nurses' station just outside the door. For once Briony was almost glad Patrick couldn't see, because the sight of his vigorous, dynamic father so shrunken, still, and deathly pale would have appalled him as surely as it appalled her.

"I think he's asleep," she whispered.

"Who's that? Patrick?"

John Donahue croaked the words weakly and made as if to raise his head from the pillow, bringing Briony hurrying forward, dragging Patrick after her since he was holding onto her arm. They came right up to the bedrail before she stopped and bent over to give him a tender kiss on the forehead.

"Yes, Uncle John, yes! Be still," she soothed him. "Here's Patrick. I brought him to you all safe and sound, didn't I, just as I promised you I would. Now you lie quietly and look at him. Goodness knows you've been waiting long enough for today to arrive." She reached for Patrick's right hand and placed it on his father's, on the cool sheet.

"Hello, Dad," Patrick said huskily. She watched his big strong hand close over the wasted hand beneath it, and tears sprang to her eyes.

"Patrick. Patrick, son." Uncle John repeated the name over and over, staring up at his only child with tired pride. "My God, but you look good."

Always before, Patrick had answered that compliment with the same: "You're looking good too, Dad." It was a gentle kind of humor that helped to ease the father's agony over the son's darkness.

Now Briony saw Patrick's throat work, his mouth open and close, but he couldn't get the words out, and the silence stretched, becoming awkward for them all.

"Isn't he looking good, Briony, my girl?" the old man demanded, sending her a pleading look that tore at her heart.

"Uncle John, your son is the handsomest man in the world next to you," she assured him solemnly, leaning over to kiss Uncle John's cheek this time. "He's looking better than I've ever seen him look. Better than anything I've seen in a long, long time. I love him dearly."

And he did look good. Seeing him here, beside a sickbed, she became more aware than ever of Patrick's tanned good health, the strength in his long arms and legs, the golden sheen of his hair, and the shining green eyes that seemed so far-seeing and full of life. More aware that she wasn't joking when she said she loved him.

"You two watch that kind of talk," Patrick finally managed with a semblance of lighthearted banter. "It's liable to give me a swelled head, and think of the problems I'd have navigating *then*."

At least it made Uncle John laugh, although the sound rattled in his chest.

Somewhat encouraged, Patrick laughed a little too, his left hand moving up to inch through the bars of the safety rail and grope cautiously until it located his father's shoulder. He touched the older man and smiled in his direction.

"Dad," he announced, "it's good to be home."

John Donahue tried to clear his throat and succeeded only in growling. Briony sniffed, unable to stop herself, and because he sensed that all three of them were approaching a dangerous level of sentimentality, Patrick forced another laugh. "I liked your Dr. Hayes," he said, "but I think meeting me was quite a shock for him. Dad, why didn't you tell the man about me?"

"Tell him about you?" John echoed.

"You know damned well what I mean," Patrick chided him gently. "You never mentioned to him that I'm blind, did you?"

Briony was the only one who saw the mist in Uncle John's eyes. "I told him all the significant things about you. He knows about your Ph.D. and those four history books you've written and that full professorship you've got there in New Hampshire."

Slowly, carefully, Patrick's left hand moved up to stroke his father's gray hair. His expression affectionate, he teased the old man. "Some people might not agree that blindness is insignificant."

"Hmph," Uncle John snorted and broke into a spasm of violent coughing. Hastily Briony brought his glass of water from the nearby nightstand and put the straw to his lips. When he had sipped at it a moment, the coughing stopped, although Patrick continued to look alarmed.

"Hmph," Uncle John repeated, his tone subdued to a raspy near-whisper. "On you it looks damned insignificant, boy." As if that reminded him of something else, he lay looking at his son thoughtfully for a moment. "I saw Tom Clayton the other day," he said at last.

Tom Clayton. The name was familiar to Briony. Probably one of Patrick and Steve's childhood friends.

Patrick tilted his head sharply. "Really? What's he

up to these days?" There was intense interest in every detail of his voice and manner.

And it was at that moment that Briony placed the name, put it together with a freckle-faced, red-haired little boy, and recalled just exactly how important Tom Clayton had been in Patrick's youth.

"He's with the Austin Police Department," Uncle John explained. "A criminal investigator."

"A detective?"

Briony watched Patrick smile over the discovery and wondered at his seeming composure. Inside she was seething with the emotions that filled her whenever she thought of Patrick's accident, and his bravery only brought her that much closer to tears.

"I told him"—Uncle John paused for breath—"I told him you were coming home. I said we'd like him to come by to see us while you're here."

"Sure," Patrick agreed, his hand straying to his father's shoulder again. "Dad, you're tired. We'd better let you rest."

"I'd rather see you than rest," the older man muttered petulantly, but Briony thought he did welcome the idea of sleep. "Patrick, you'll be nice to Tom when he comes over, won't you?"

"Have I ever not been nice to Tom?" Patrick countered lightly. "Of course I'll be nice, if I should happen to see him."

"Maybe you could call him," Uncle John fretted, clinging to Patrick's hand with persistence.

"Maybe so," Patrick murmured, not committing himself fully.

Briony thought it was time to end the visit, before the patient was completely worn out. She had let it go on too long as it was, she suspected from the film of perspiration on Uncle John's forehead and the tightness around Patrick's lips, but it had been so long since the two had seen each other.

How much of Patrick's tension was caused by concern for his father, and how much by talk of Tom Clayton? she asked herself.

"Darling, we're going to go home now," she spoke up with pretended gaiety. "I'm taking Patrick home to eat, and if you're very good and sleep a lot, he'll come back to see you for a few minutes this evening."

He couldn't seem to take his eyes off the younger man. "Thank you, Briony, for being so good to me and Patrick. You won't let him get lonely, will you?"

"I should say not. He's staying with the Hammonds as long as you're in the hospital. Just let him *try* to get lonely."

"Good girl." Uncle John sighed and closed his eyes, and Briony gently drew Patrick away.

Now he seemed almost stunned by the realization of his father's tenuous hold on life. She noticed that he was letting her lead him numbly, without his usual attention to his surroundings. After a few minutes she dared to put her arm around his hard waist, walking close beside him, and his arm settled around her shoulder in response. Briony hoped he received in return at least a fraction of the comfort that she got from his body warmth and nearness.

In the car he might have been staring through the windshield. "He's dying, Briony," Patrick said, sounding dazed. "It's not just my imagination, is it?"

No, it wasn't his imagination. It was the truth, but she didn't know if he could bear having it confirmed right now, so she just patted his hand and kept silent. But he persisted, turning to face her. "Don't try to spare me in this, Briony. He has all those tubes and wires hooked up to him—"

"How did you know?"

"I've been in hospital rooms before, and besides, I heard the beeping. He's like a ghost of himself."

She nodded unhappily and then reminded herself that he needed more than a nod. "He's just a shadow." There were tears in her voice where she couldn't hide them, and she had wanted to be strong for Patrick, because he was always so strong.

He reached for her now, grasped her wrists and pulled her over against him to put his arms around her. She fit right against his chest, her soft cheek pressed to his close-shaven one, her hands going around his neck to lock there while she and Patrick held each other, mute with sadness for the man they both loved. In sharing that long tight embrace, Briony did feel stronger, somehow restored. She hoped Patrick felt it too, and when after some minutes he stirred and pulled back, she thought his face looked less desolate.

"Okay," he spoke evenly, "we've cried now." She looked at him wonderingly. Had he cried? His eyes were half closed, aimed at her chin, and she fought down the urge to kiss his eyelids. "We can't cry anymore or he'll know we're grieving for him. There's time enough for grieving after he's gone."

She shook her head. "No more tears."

"Good girl." He echoed his father's praise of her and added his own reward, a kiss that landed on the side of her nose. He smiled wryly as he let her go. "I missed."

She started to suggest that he try again, with her help this time, but he was already inching away from her on the seat, almost seeming to want to put as much distance between them as possible. It seemed to her that a change of subject was in order, and there were questions in the back of her mind, nagging thoughts that she wanted to explore.

She broached the topic in her usual straightforward way. "Uncle John mentioned Tom Clayton earlier. Isn't he the boy who—"

"Yes." Patrick cut her off in a calm but clipped tone.

"Well...." She looked at him helplessly. "Why... I mean, do you plan to call him?"

She searched his face for bitterness, anger, hatred, but saw no recognizable sign of any emotion. "I don't know," he said.

"Your father thinks you ought to."

He nodded but didn't answer. Briony wished she knew what they were about, the undercurrents that charged the air around them. All she knew was that if she were Patrick, Tom Clayton would be the last person she would consider contacting.

"I don't think you should," she decided, thrusting out her chin. "I don't see how you can stand to talk to that—"

Patrick turned and silenced her with a remarkably well-aimed scowl. "It was an accident, Briony."

"I know," she whispered, "but—"

"No." He was shaking his head. "It was an accident."

"A stupid, careless, senseless accident!" she insisted.

"Aren't all accidents senseless and stupid?" he asked dryly. "And what's the sense in placing blame? Where's the wisdom in that? Will it make me see again?"

She had never wanted to howl with pain as much as she did right then, nor to enfold him in her arms and kiss him, but she didn't even touch him. "So are you going to call him?" she asked instead.

"I don't know." Patrick leaned toward her, found

her cheek with his palm, and stroked it. "Forget it, Briony." His forefinger touched one side of her mouth and his thumb the other, nudging the corners up to form a smile. "I can't have my beauty queen developing wrinkles from worrying, can I?" He grinned, and she smiled in spite of herself, reluctantly getting down to the business of driving them home.

As she drove she tried to steady her breathing, to slow down her heartbeat, to discipline the wonderfully alive feeling that she derived from just sitting next to him. She remembered his hand on her cheek, his kiss on her nose, and somehow the memory seemed to put her at a tremendous disadvantage. If she could have, she would have controlled the tingling awareness of him that coursed through her body. She hadn't felt this good in all the years he'd been away.

Her thoughts skidded to a halt when she glanced sideways at Patrick and saw what he was doing.

With his long well-shaped fingers, he was studying the interior of Briony's car, and the sight of his silent, almost furtive exploration made her swallow with difficulty. She had forgotten how he liked to acquaint himself with his surroundings in the most natural way available to him. The fingertips of his left hand slid over the expanse of blue leather between them, examining the regularly spaced indentations and the stitching, assessing the width of the seat. At the same time his right hand flattened against the door panel and inched across the surface of the upholstery, finding the arm rest and door handle and window crank.

Frowning a little in concentration, he extended both arms to brush his fingers over the padded dash. Briony shivered at the thought of what his sensuous touch would be doing if that were her skin he was touching.

The thought made her grin. Imagine being envious

of an automobile dashboard, just because it was fortunate enough to be caressed by Patrick.

Still smiling, she kept half an eye on him, watching him identify the air conditioner vents and glove compartment, his fingers lingering over the various knobs of the radio and tape player.

"Want some music?" she inquired.

Even though her voice was quiet, he started and jerked his hands back, and she wished she hadn't spoken.

A second later he shifted on the seat and turned a sheepish face to her. "You caught me." He laughed. "No, I don't want music. I just like new cars." Drawing in a long breath, he sighed. "What a terrific smell."

"Isn't it?" she agreed. "Too bad the newness won't last." She wondered if the wistful note she heard in his voice had anything to do with the fact that he had never driven a car.

She suspected she was right when he changed the subject abruptly. "I was surprised when you wrote me you were going to start teaching sociology at the college last fall. Weren't you the one who hated the very thought?"

She couldn't help laughing. As a teen-ager she had protested loud and long against school, teachers, and education in general. "What did you expect, with a mother who was dean of students and a father who was president of a college? I was determined to be a rebel."

"What happened to make you capitulate and earn your master's?"

You, she thought. Becoming a teacher was just one more way of hanging on to Patrick Donahue.

"Oh," she evaded lightly, "I've grown up and put away my childish notions. If you don't believe me," she invited, "I'll be glad to stop the car and give you some convincing evidence."

"Mmmm... thanks, but I have all the evidence I need. Tell me about your fiancé."

Briony turned to gape at him. "Who told you about Dennis?"

"No one told me about Dennis. You're wearing an engagement ring, aren't you?"

Ye gods, did *nothing* escape him? "Yes," she said slowly, and then remembered the way he had held her hand while they had talked to Dr. Hayes. Was that how...?

"Well?" he prompted, leaning back in his corner and showing her an expectant face. "Tell me about Dennis."

She hadn't thought it would come up so soon in the conversation. "Oh, what's to tell?"

He lifted a fair eyebrow at that, and she thought how odd it must seem, to dismiss one's fiancé so casually.

"I mean," she amended hastily, "he's, er, nice. Very nice, in fact. Charming. That's Mom's word, not mine."

She paused to see how he was taking the news and found that he wore a mildly amused look. "You're doing fine so far, Briony. Tell me more."

"Well, what would you like to know?"

"For starters, his name. Surely he has another names besides Dennis?"

"Of course. He's Dennis Phillips. You want his statistics? He's twenty-five—I *know* that's a year younger than me so you don't need to tell me—and he's... oh, I think 'cute' is the best way to describe his looks."

"Very graphic," Patrick drawled.

She ignored that. "He's a little taller than I am, and he has curly black hair and brown eyes and a dimple.

He's almost pretty. Which is a sore spot with him, by the way. You can call him handsome all you like, but don't call him pretty."

"I'll remember that. You can count on me not to comment on his looks at all."

"Damn you, Patrick, you asked, and I'm telling you," she flashed, and then she saw his mocking grin and calmed down. "Okay. What do you consider vital information? He coaches baseball and track at Churchill High and teaches math as well. He's the oldest of three brothers and his family lives in Corpus Christi. He went to the University of Texas. That's where we met two years ago. We were both jogging over at Memorial Stadium. He's a gourmet cook and he coaches a Little League team at the Y. He doesn't drink, smoke, or swear."

He let out a low whistle. "I'm impressed. I'd hang on to old Dennis if I were you. He sounds like a prize catch."

She didn't answer, pretending to concentrate all her efforts on driving, but after a minute she muttered without looking at him, "Your turn now. Tell me about your woman."

"My woman? Singular?"

"All right, then, your women. You're not engaged, or otherwise taken?"

"That depends on what you mean by taken," he said, and then, looking as if he regretted that suggestive statement, added, "No, I'm not taken."

She wondered, though, a thin sliver of fear stabbing through her at the idea of Patrick settling down with one female.

"I've known lots of women," he admitted. "I don't possess any of them, so I guess I'd have to say none of them is mine."

"Are there any special ones?" she ventured.

"Oh, there are special ones, all right." He was smiling at the windshield. "There are great volumes of special women in my life, but I won't bore you with the details."

"Are they all pretty?" she asked wistfully, and then immediately blurted, "Forget I asked. That was a dumb question."

"Why?"

"Because...I don't suppose you know if they're pretty."

He laughed. "You're joking, aren't you? I can't see, Briony, but I'm not stupid. It doesn't take 20-20 vision to know that men treat a pretty girl differently than they treat one who's ugly. To answer your question, no, not all my special women are pretty. One of the brightest stars in my galaxy is a nice old grandmother who lives in my apartment building and has sort of adopted me, and I don't believe anyone wold call her pretty. And as for girl friends, in the past I've been involved with more than one lady who assured me she was hopelessly plain, and I've enjoyed those ladies every bit as much as the beautiful ones. There has been at least one time that I stopped dating a real beauty because she used my blindness as an excuse to get sloppy. I care how a woman sees herself, and I damned sure care how she feels to me when I hold her."

He reached over and stroked Briony's blue silk sleeve, sending a shiver up her arm. "Clean, soft, and sexy," he murmured, smiling very deliberately in her direction, and her heart was pounding so hard she thought it was a good thing they arrived home just then.

Chapter Two

The Hammonds had lived next door to the Donahues for longer than Briony's twenty-six years, in a neighborhood that could best be described as genteel. The houses were all big and old and lovely. A retired businessman, John Donahue lived alone now in his imposing red brick Georgian Colonial that was covered with ivy and shaded by tall elms. Dr. Ryan Hammond and his wife Esmé presided over Dreyfuss-Bartholemew College, a small private liberal arts institution, from their English Tudor house with its diamond-pane windows and exposed half timbers. Most evenings found several students or faculty members dropping by for an informal chat with either the president or dean of students, and all were made equally welcome by the gracious, still-youthful couple.

Patrick Donahue had spent as much time at the Hammonds' as he had at his own home during his younger years. He was an only child, being raised by an only parent, his mother having died in a car wreck when he was three. His father was busy amassing a fortune by bottling and distributing a popular soft drink. At first, John Donahue used his work as an analgesic to the loss of his wife. Later, after Patrick's accident, he seemed obsessed with ensuring a secure future for his son, whose life was turned upside down in the space of a few seconds on a brilliant day in June.

Briony supposed that as long as she lived, she'd never forget that deceptively beautiful afternoon. Most of it was still fresh in her memory, despite the twenty intervening years, although she had blocked out segments that in retrospect were simply too hot to handle.

Steve and Patrick's Little League team, the Pirates, had won all their games so far and were up against their longtime archrivals, the Cardinals, that day. The coach was having no trouble psyching the boys up for *this* game; in fact, if anything he was kept busy calming them down.

When little Briony wandered down to the diamond as the teams warmed up and asked her two boys—she was quite possessive of both Steve and Patrick—to pitch her a ball, she received a prompt set-down. Big brother Steve glared at her and ordered her back to their parents in the stands, whereupon she burst into tears.

With his usual kindheartedness, Patrick took her aside and told her she might get hurt down here with all the baseballs whizzing around and would she please go sit with Uncle John and keep him company.

"But Daddy and Mommy are with him," she pointed out, still sniffling.

"I know, but he'd rather have you," Patrick reasoned with tact. "You try to stop him from getting too upset over the game, okay? He likes to yell a lot, and that's fine, but sometimes he gets mad if we're behind. You're his favourite kid, Bri. You go take care of him and let him buy you a snow cone or something, so all I have to worry about is the game. All right?"

"But I want to play too," she pouted, blinking her

big green eyes up at him. At the age of six, she already knew that her tears gave her some special kind of power over Uncle John and daddy, and she hoped that maybe Patrick would be susceptible too.

But he wasn't, and his patience was wearing thin. "Look, Briony, you can't play. I'm really sorry, but you might get hit by a ball. Now go on over and sit with my father before I paddle your bottom." His voice was very firm, giving her no choice but to obey him.

Much later she went through a period of being unreasonably mad at him because of his warning that she might get hurt. It had implied that he was safe, that he couldn't possibly be hurt. And he had been. He had lied, and he had been hurt, so awfully hurt.

It happened in the eighth inning, while the Pirates were at bat. The bases were loaded, and the Pirates needed two runs to take the lead. That red-haired boy Briony had almost managed to forget, Tom Clayton, had two strikes and Patrick was on deck, waiting for his turn. Maybe he was a little too close to home plate, but at the time he hadn't seemed close enough for anyone to take notice. When Tom swung at the next ball and missed and the umpire called him out, he lost his temper. Turning in unseeing rage, he flung the bat away from him, catching Patrick square in the face with the wide end. The sharp crack of the impact was audible to everyone in the stunned silence of the grandstands.

Did Briony actually see the accident occur? She honestly couldn't recall. Possibly she had only heard about it from everyone else so often that it was indelibly etched in her mind. She had a vivid mental image of Patrick lying on his back in the grass, unconscious, his baseball cap knocked aside and his hair shining like white gold in the sunlight. There was blood on his face and on his blue pin-striped uniform, and she thought he was dead.

A moment later it seemed that half the adults in the ballpark had converged on the comatose Patrick. A couple of them were doctors, who were there in the capacity of parents, and they took charge of him until he could be rushed to a hospital.

At the medical center X rays revealed that the one heavy blow had done extensive damage, fracturing his skull, his nose, one orbital socket, and one cheekbone. What really concerned the doctors, however, was his state of unconsciousness, which didn't lift until late that night.

And then, when he finally woke up, they realized that they had other things to worry about, because the ten-year-old boy with the bruised and swollen face couldn't see a thing. Of course, it might only be a temporary result of the brain trauma, the physicians told John Donahue, but they were calling in an eye specialist just to check it out. Using an ophthalmoscope, this doctor would look into Patrick's eyes and see if he could locate the problem.

Briony remembered hearing her parents talking to Steven the next day, trying to explain it to him. "The blow to Patrick's head was so hard that it caused the lining of both eyes to tear loose," Ryan said quietly, sounding very grave. "The condition is called bilateral retinal detachment, and it's serious."

Steve didn't say anything for a while. Briony saw him swallow hard, and she thought his dark eyes looked unusually bright. Finally he asked, "Can they do something to make him see again?"

Briony wondered what Steve meant. Make Patrick see again? Patrick could see just as good as she could.

"Honey, they're going to try," Esmé answered

huskily, hugging her shaken son to her. "They'll operate on both eyes to reattach the linings so he can see again, hopefully."

The whole thing confused Briony, but Steve started to look more cheerful after that. He was even allowed to go with his father to visit Patrick at the hospital. He reported to his mother later that the doctors were insisting that Patrick lie completely still and not move his head, to prevent any further damage. After the surgery Patrick's movements were restricted for several more days, until the bandages were removed, and then there was no more point to it because the surgery had failed.

Briony didn't know the significance of it yet. She only knew that Steve cried for days on end and kept asking why. No one could give him any good answers. "The surgeon said both the linings were too badly torn," Ryan told him, looking angry with himself for being so helpless to do anything about this situation. "He knew from the start that the surgery probably wouldn't work, but he felt he had to try anyway."

"But why, Dad? Why Patrick?"

And Ryan finally understood that Steven was not asking for a medical explanation. He just wanted a reason he could live with, a reason that this awful thing had happened to Patrick rather than himself or someone else.

"I don't know," Dr. Hammond admitted sadly.

Soon after that they took Briony, after much begging on her part, to the hospital with them, and she had her first contact with the blinded Patrick. Besides the fact that his face was still unfamiliar and discolored from all the bruising, and that he couldn't see her anymore even though his eyes were open and fixed almost right on her, he didn't feel very good that day, and he didn't want to talk to her. For the first time in her young life she saw him cry then, bitter tears of fear and fury over his loss, and it frightened her to see him like that. That was when she got mad at him for being hurt. She told her parents she was glad she didn't get to go back to see him again at the hospital.

Of course her anger didn't last. When Patrick came home, his mood lifted and he started to laugh again and to tease Briony. Now that his activities were so limited, he was more willing than he had been in the past to spend time with her, to her utter delight. She wanted to do things for him, wanted to be with him every waking minute, and Steve grudgingly allowed her into their charmed circle because he saw that Patrick really needed her at times.

If the accident recharted the course of the ten-year-old's life, it also changed the purpose of John Donahue's. He continued to work long hours, multiplying his assets until Patrick's future was guaranteed to be free from financial worry, at least, and he could easily have moved them to the wealthiest section of Austin. He chose, however, to remain where he was, recognizing that his child was getting something from his friends the Hammonds that he might not find in a new neighborhood: complete acceptance in spite of his rather awesome handicap.

It was Steve Hammond who undertook to help Patrick regain his independence. For three years he attended a private school for the blind out of state, but after that, with Steve's assistance, he lived at home and went to the local public schools. The two boys' schedules were arranged so they had the same classes and could study together. Since cassette recorders had not yet been refined, and reel-to-reel tape recorders proved too clumsy to be moved around at school, Patrick perforce resorted to developing his memory to an incredible degree of reliability. He learned his way around the house and neighborhood and school until he walked freely, often without even a cane, only occasionally colliding with an unexpected obstacle, or with someone who didn't realize the handsome young man couldn't see him coming. His face looked perpetually battered for a while and his nose was bloodied and broken numerous times before he reached his current state of apparently casual movement.

Because Patrick could read only braille now, Steve learned it and gleefully used it to send "secret" messages to his best friend. That, among other things, prompted Briony to learn braille as well, so she could decode those secrets. It was only one step further for the Hammond family to obtain a braille writer just like the one at the Donahue house. During the past five years, Briony and her parents had used it sometimes to write to Patrick in the New Hampshire college town where he lived and taught. Other times they recorded their letters to him on cassette tapes, which was how Patrick corresponded with his friends who didn't know braille.

Looking back on it, Briony saw that Patrick hadn't been the only one who had to adjust to his blindness; his father, Steven, Briony herself, and Dr. and Mrs. Hammond had all felt the effects of his accident. They had suffered with him when he stumbled and fell and hurt himself, and then had to watch as he picked himself up again and tried to get reoriented, to find his way in the dark. It was amazing that he had kept at it all these years. Come to think of it, both families had come through it remarkably well, all caring deeply for each other, none of them especially neurotic or hung up about Patrick's handicap. In John Donahue's words, Patrick managed to make blindness seem damned insignificant. Sometimes, she thought wryly, they even got to believing that it *was* insignificant.

The moment Briony brought him in the front door this evening, Patrick was enveloped in a cloak of love so genuine, so strong, he had to feel it. Ryan and Esmé hugged and kissed him without restraint or embarrassment, ushered him into the study, which was the heart of the household, and sat him down to query him extensively about his writing and teaching, his health, his political views, and his philosophy. Was he happy in his work? Did he have someone to come in and take care of him? Did he eat enough? What sort of cultural activities were available near his home? What did he do just for fun?

All were questions she had wanted to ask and was glad now she hadn't, because she thought he tolerated them better from her parents. His answers were respectful and often humorous, making light of any difficulties he may have encountered in adjusting to apartment living on his own. His coat cast aside, he relaxed on the sofa, loosening his tie and sipping at a Bloody Mary until dinnertime.

"Tell me about this sabbatical you're taking," Dr. Hammond said when they had moved to the dinner table. "What is this book you're researching?"

"Not now, dear," Esmé said firmly. "Patrick is going to be here for a nice long visit. Just now let him concentrate on the sweet and sour chicken." Then, as if she did this before every meal, she described for him the location of the food on his plate, the hot mustard and sweet sauce in their little crockery pitchers, his water and iced tea glasses, and the sugar.

It was a tactful and typical thing for her mother to have done, and it reminded Briony of the way her parents had determined from the very first to help Patrick refine his social skills after he was injured. John Donahue was too busy with his work, and besides, the need would never have occurred to him, but it occurred to Esmé and Ryan. The two of them worked with consistency and diplomacy to assure that the motherless boy next door should never find himself embarrassed by a lack of table manners or by the habits he might have unknowingly picked up in his blindness. With Esmé's guidance, he learned to eat neatly and carefully with a minimum of help, and to stand up straight and tall rather than slump like so many sightless people did. She was the one who first informed him that his eyes looked perfectly normal—quite extraordinarily handsome, in fact—and that she wanted him to look at her when he talked to her. He had nothing to be ashamed about. Ryan worked with Steve and Patrick together, instilling in them a sense of conservative good taste in clothes and educating them on the subject of how to treat a lady on a date.

Thanks to Briony's understanding parents, Patrick could hold his own with confidence in any social situation. Feeling warm with gratitude to them, Briony gave Ryan and Esmé a wide smile, which only her father returned.

Esmé Hammond's thoughtful frown brought to mind what the older woman had said to Briony that morning: "I hope you're not pinning too many dreams on Patrick's visit home, darling."

"Dreams?" she had asked innocently. "What are you talking about?"

"You know, Briony. I don't think anyone but Patrick is unaware of your vulnerability to him. If he could see your face when you talk of him, you couldn't keep it a secret from him, either."

"You mean that I love him?"

A look of pain had crossed Esmé's face. "Darling, don't be so free to tell it. Remember that you're engaged to someone else, and Patrick is just coming home on a visit, after all. He'll be going back east one day. I don't want to see you, or Dennis, or Patrick, hurt."

"Mom," Briony had said, intoxicated by the knowledge that Patrick would be there in a few short hours, "please don't worry. I have no intention of hurting Dennis, and I'd sooner die than hurt Patrick."

Esmé had nodded. "I know. But it's really you that I'm most worried about, because although I love Patrick as a son, he's not going to be the one who gets hurt. I'm afraid the anguish will be reserved for you, my dear daughter."

Evidently her mother's thoughts were running parallel to Briony's, because she spoke up now. "Is Dennis coming over to see you tonight, darling?"

"No, I told him I'd be busy," Briony replied. "Patrick and I are going back to see Uncle John this evening."

Esmé bit her lip at the announcement, then brightened. "Why, I'd be delighted to drive Patrick over to the hospital. I haven't seen John since he was admitted—"

"No," Briony snapped, jealously guarding the right to chauffeur the returned hero. "I promised Uncle John I'd come back, and besides, you know you have that lecture to prepare for Dr. Ramsey's class tomorrow."

She saw that Patrick's head had come up and that he was listening alertly to their discussion. In a moment, she feared, he would offer to take a taxi to the hospital. "Dennis had some sort of P.T.A. meeting to attend," she threw in for emphasis, "so we couldn't have gotten together anyway."

Although her mother gave in with good grace, Briony noticed her silent sigh. Thankfully, Patrick resumed eating without making any comment on the arrangements, and everyone seemed quiet as they finished the meal. While the other three retired to the study to visit some more, Briony cleared away the dinner things, put the dishes in the automatic dishwasher, and ran upstairs to freshen up a bit.

Remembering what Patrick had said in the car about liking his women "clean, soft, and sexy," she took a little extra time to change into a cashmere sweater and flannel straight-legged pants in a shade of lime that complemented her blond hair. For the final touch, she applied a dab more of the tantalizingly delicate perfume she had favored for years.

Downstairs she found her parents engrossed in their own things, Dr. Hammond's big iron-gray head buried in the evening newspaper, her fair mother bent over the desk, making notes.

"Where's Patrick?" she asked.

"Washing up in the downstairs bathroom," Esmé raised her head to answer, her pretty face solemn. "You look lovely in that outfit, Briony. It's new, isn't it?"

Briony nodded. She had bought it, and quite a few other new things, in honor of Patrick's homecoming, but she had hoped her mother wouldn't remark on that fact.

"Give John our love. I hope he's doing better tonight" was all Esmé said before she went back to her writing.

Briony waited in the hall for Patrick, and after a minute he opened the door and stepped out of the bathroom. His coat lay on a chair nearby, and he retrieved it unerringly and slipped it on, then turned and stood still, a faintly uncertain look about him. "Briony?" he called out softly.

"Here," she answered, going to him and reaching for his tie. "Let me just straighten this a little." As she did so, she felt the warmth of his chest through his shirt, smelled the musky after-shave he was wearing, looked up at his cherished face, and her senses felt suddenly overwhelmed.

Flushing with emotions, she wanted more than anything to embrace him right now, to press against his long muscled body and feel his arms and thighs return the pressure. It didn't take much effort to imagine how heavenly that would be. Briony's eyes roved over his length, while she wished with a sweet ache in the very bottom of her stomach that she could explore him with her fingertips until she knew him completely, because she already knew she would like what she found. But she couldn't do that with her parents just down the hall.

Breathing rapidly, struggling to maintain her equilibrium, she withdrew her hands quickly and stepped away from him.

He gave her a small grin. "My tie looked straight to me."

She tried for a laugh and pulled it off, if somewhat shakily. "Oh, it *was* straight. That was just an excuse for me to touch you, couldn't you tell?"

"Was it?" Unaccountably he looked bothered by her words. "Actually I couldn't. Blind people miss out on a lot of clues that are obvious to others, you know."

That was so totally out of character that she could only stare at him for a shocked second, but then she refused to take it seriously. "Not you!" she asserted, tucking her hand through his arm and walking him slowly down the hall. "You don't miss out on a thing that matters. Now, do you remember our house, or should we take a quick tour?"

"That depends on whether you want me to decorate the place in Early Disaster the first time I'm turned loose in here alone."

"Okay, a tour," she agreed and spent half an hour escorting him around each room, letting him count the steps and touch the furniture. When he told her he liked the feel of the polished oak dressing table in her bedroom, she got down her little Hummel figurines from the wall shelf and placed them one at a time in his hands for him to enjoy. As soon as his sensitive fingers had traced lightly over each expensive miniature, she demanded that he describe the character he had just examined. To his smug satisfaction, he gave an accurate account of every single one.

In the bedroom that used to belong to Steven, he stood still, his head tilted as he listened to the sound and inhaled deeply the smell of the room. Grinning at what must have been a flood of happy memories, he wandered over to the bed and sat down, bouncing a little as if testing the firmness of the mattress. Abruptly he stood and moved without faltering straight to the double window, reached up and felt along the very top of the frame.

After a minute he brought his empty hand down, and Briony thought he seemed disappointed.

Giggling, she asked, "You didn't really expect the key to still be there, did you?"

He raised his eyebrows. "Did *you* find it?"

"No, Mom did, right after Steve moved out. We knew immediately that it must fit the trunk in the garage, the one full of 'Steve and Patrick's secret things,' the trunk I had been warned to stay away from all the time we were growing up." She couldn't help the mocking laughter in her voice. "You two guys! I couldn't believe the things you had saved. A stack of ancient *Playboy* magazines, a package of Lucky Strike cigarettes, and an empty bottle of Southern Comfort."

Patrick tried to look outraged but succeeded only in appearing shamefaced. "Hey, we thought we were pretty tough in those days, Briony."

"How long had you hidden those things there? Since you were nine?"

"Twelve. They made us the envy of every other guy in the neighborhood. I don't suppose," he added hopefully, "the stuff's still around someplace?"

"Don't tell me you want to see it for old times' sake?" she teased him. "I think Mom threw it out. She had no idea the illustrious Dr. Donahue would ever want to see it again. Can't you buy your own *Playboy* these days?"

"Very funny," he grumbled. "Show some respect for your elders, Bri."

"Yes, sir." She smothered her laughter, taking his arm again to resume their circuit through the house.

"I don't think we've moved much since you were here last," she observed as they ended up downstairs in the hall again.

"The grandfather clock used to be in the foyer," he corrected her, "and you have new furniture in the living room."

"Oh. Right. Okay, smartie, I didn't tell you about the paintings. What do we have over the living room fireplace?"

He smiled. "When I left you had a New England landscape hanging there, but now there's a portrait of you in your beauty queen days. You have on a long white dress, and you look like a moonbeam against a black velvet sky.''

Briony shook her head. ''Patrick Donahue, you never cease to amaze me. Dad told you, of course. He's daffy about that painting of me. He's also a little prejudiced.''

He didn't say anything to that, just stood waiting, his lazy eyes on her mouth, his hand on her arm.

''Shall we have Dad bring in your luggage now, or wait till we get back?'' she asked, suddenly nervous.

''He took care of that while you were changing.''

She was surprised. ''Funny, I didn't see the bags when we were up in Steve's old room.''

When Patrick shrugged without answering, she dismissed the puzzle, deciding her father must have stuck them in the closet so Patrick wouldn't stumble over them.

Briony was used to being stared at. For years people had gushed over her pale gold hair and large green eyes. She had heard so many comments on her fairy-tale-princess loveliness that any mention of it bored her, as did the flirting that she frequently encountered. Her defense was to shut her mind to it and ignore its existence.

Tonight she couldn't help seeing, as she had this afternoon, that Patrick drew his share of attention too. She thought it was not his blindness that people noticed, but something magnetically attractive about the man himself. On the elevator going up to CCU, a bubbly young student nurse tapped his shoulder from behind and informed him when he half turned that he looked familiar. ''Could I have seen you on television?'' she asked, batting her eyelashes up at him.

Patrick laughed heartily at the idea. ''I think not.''

''Oh.'' She looked disappointed. ''Then have we met

somewhere before? I have a terrible memory for faces."

"I'm not very good at faces, either," he admitted, "but I'm an expert when it comes to voices and scents, and I can assure you we've never met before. I wouldn't have forgotten if we had."

Pleased with the compliment, the woman gazed after Patrick as he got off the elevator with Briony. An old man with the weathered look of a farmer exited at the same time, chuckling to himself over the little vignette he had witnessed. He walked a step behind Briony and Patrick to the waiting room, watching the way Patrick held her elbow and overhearing her quiet directions. "The room's full again," Briony said, "so we'll stand here by this rubber plant. If you reach out your hand you can touch the wall." He stopped near enough to converse with them, a wrinkled man in a shiny old suit with a kind look about him.

"You kids are brother and sister, ain't you? You're a good-lookin' pair. I'll bet that happens to you all the time. That saucy little girl, flirtin' with you like that. How long since you lost your sight?"

Patrick turned to the man. "I've been blind since I was ten."

"That's a mighty long time. Guess you haven't seen your sister lately, then, have you?"

"No." His eyes lit up with devilry. "Could you tell me about her? How does she look now?"

Briony smothered a giggle and moved closer against Patrick's side, meaning to reprove him, but he put a brotherly arm around her shoulders and continued to fix his eyes on the man.

"Oh, she's a real beaut, I can tell you that," the gregarious old gentleman said enthusiastically and launched a description that was so flattering it made Briony blush.

"She's that pretty, huh?" Patrick reflected. "Perhaps I ought to try to talk her out of taking her final vows at the convent. What do you think, sir?"

"You gonna be one of them nuns?" The man eyed Briony with regret, while she tried not to choke. "That's a dadburn shame. No offense to the Church, ma'am, but seems to me that's a powerful waste."

"My thoughts exactly," Patrick murmured, his grin wicked.

A nurse appeared at the door of CCU just then to signal the start of the brief final visitation period of the day. Tonight Uncle John looked no better physically, but his eyes were bright as he lay gazing up at his son. He was able to grasp the younger hand, although not with any strength, and he seemed eager to talk to Patrick about the future.

Briony left them alone for ten minutes and waited outside the cubicle before returning to tell Patrick with a light tug at his sleeve that it was time to go. She was kissing the thin cheek when he rasped hoarsely, "You'll keep him at your house, won't you, Briony my dear?"

"I told you so earlier, Uncle John," she scolded. "You know I keep my word, so stop being a worry-wart." She walked Patrick to the door, only to leave him stranded there momentarily when she dashed back to the bed and bent close to the old man's ear. "I'll take good care of your precious Patrick, Uncle John. Let's both go to sleep tonight on the thought of how marvelous it is to have him home again."

As they went outside into the fresh night air, Patrick said without preamble, "He's decided to have the surgery." His grip was tighter than usual on her arm.

Briony didn't know whether to be glad or frightened. "Did you . . . ?"

"I didn't talk to him about it at all. He's evidently been thinking about it a lot. He knows he can't go on much longer the way he is now."

"When?" she asked simply.

"Dr. Hayes told him he'll schedule it as soon as Dad's stronger."

"You're not to worry about Uncle John," she insisted earnestly, wishing she could soothe the lines from Patrick's brow. "He's in the best possible hands."

Patrick only nodded and indicated by a change of subject that he didn't want to talk about it anymore.

Thinking he must be tired after the long and eventful day, Briony drove them straight home. When she came around the car and joined him on the driveway, they stood side by side for a moment, enjoying the cool evening air. Patrick's face was turned up to the sky as if he could actually see the stars and the silver half moon. On an impulse, Briony reached for his hand, twining her fingers through his, and he lowered his head abruptly. "Mind walking me home?"

She didn't hesitate. Of course he would want to pay a visit to his old house. After all, he had grown up there.

"I'll be glad to. From the cars parked along the street and the heads I can see through our front window, I'd say Mom and Dad are holding court again, and I don't mind missing that. Should I run in and get our key, though?"

He patted his pocket. "I have mine right here." At the door he insisted on finding the keyhole himself and opening up.

The first thing she saw in the big entry hall were Patrick's three suitcases in a neat row, out of the way against a wall.

"How in the world did your bags get here?" she asked in astonishment. Seeing his impassive face, she knew how. "Wait a minute. You had Dad bring them over, didn't you?"

He nodded. "I'm staying here, in my own room."

"But there's no one else here. The place is empty."

He shrugged as if that was of no consequence, and she remembered that he had lived alone for five years.

"Patrick, you haven't been here in ages. You'll break your fool neck trying to get around the place."

"It's my nose that's in danger, remember?" he asked dryly. "I was counting on you to be big-hearted enough to show me around."

"But—but I promised your father you'd stay at our house, and you agreed."

"I didn't agree. I never had any intention of staying at your place. There's no need for it. The only reason I didn't make that plain at the hospital was that I didn't want to upset Dad."

"But he'll kill me if anything happens to you."

"Dear little Briony, I accept full responsibility for staying here by myself. Shall I put that in writing?"

"Dammit, Patrick," she fumed in frustration, "you know I'm not really worried about Uncle John getting mad at me."

"No, you wouldn't be. I imagine you can handle angry men with ease, provided they can see you. Your beauty is as wasted on me as it would be in a convent."

"Don't joke about this. I'm entirely serious—"

"So am I," he cut in quietly. "I'm aware of the role you play around here."

"What role are you talking about?"

"Angel of mercy. Giver of comfort. I remember very well the eager little girl who ran errands for me tirelessly and sacrificed her play time to lead me around when I couldn't have gone anywhere by myself."

"It was no sacrifice."

"And I suppose you still enjoy being a guide dog to the blind? You do a splendid job of it, as you demonstrated today. Just as you do a good job of looking after my father. I appreciate it, Bri, but I'm not interested in being a millstone around your neck. I do not need to be taken care of."

"I *want* to."

"But I *don't* want it." He turned in his impatience and stalked a step or two before he realized that he was on unfamiliar ground and halted. He turned back. "All I need is to be reoriented to things, so I'll know if everything is in its old place."

Uncle John had always been fanatical in his insistence that every item of furniture remain exactly as it had been when Patrick left, so his son would feel right at home when he returned, but she didn't tell him that. Instead, she took him on a reluctant tour, unable to hide her pique, giving him short answers to his attempts at friendly conversation.

"You wouldn't have to worry about all this if you'd just be sensible and come home with me," she complained when he asked for a more extensive description of items on the kitchen cabinet.

"Who's worrying? I know how to make coffee. I just want to be reasonably sure I'm putting in sugar rather than salt. Have you ever tasted salty coffee?"

"No."

"Well, I have." His lips quirked. "It's one mistake I've got down pat from repetition. I've also seasoned my coffee with flour and sprinkled spoonfuls of cocoa over my cereal."

He meant for her to laugh at that, and she did, against her will. She laughed, then sighed. "I guess you've made up your mind about this?"

"Most definitely."

"Stubborn pigheaded male," she muttered, staring at him shamelessly since he would never know and there was no one else to see. He looked so much like the Patrick of her youth with his slightly curly dark blond hair, his lazy eyes, his tall granite-hard body, that she felt the stirring of a dangerous need in the very center of her. What would he do if she admitted that need to him? The idea intrigued her.

Hoping to sidetrack such thoughts, she moaned, "What am I going to do with you?"

"Love me just the way I am, I guess." Patrick grinned, leaning back against the sink and shoving his hands in the pockets of his pants. He had no idea how very attractive, how lazily inviting, he looked.

Instinctively Briony moved close to him. He had been teasing, but she couldn't help her reaction or her fervent words: "Oh, I do."

Patrick blinked as if she had startled him, and for a moment she saw hunger at war with caution in his expression. Unfortunately, caution won. He forced a neutral smile. "And I love you, Briony, as a dear little sister."

"But I'm not your sister," she pointed out softly.

Patrick stared at her breasts for a long moment as the smile faded. "Thank you for all your help today. As the saying goes, I couldn't have made it without you." He straightened up, lifting his chin. "I should be able to manage okay from here on."

Instead of leaving as he must have hoped she would, she held her ground. "Don't dismiss me, Patrick. I told you, I'm *not* your little sister."

Amusement flickered in the green depths of his eyes. "My apologies for seeming to dismiss you. Did I wound your dignity?"

Her indignation flared at his patronizing manner.

"Just exactly what will it take for you to regard me seriously?" she demanded. "I let you braille me at the airport, but that didn't seem to convince you of my maturity. How about this?" She grabbed his left wrist and pulled his hand up to place it on her breast. "You see? I'm not a kid, Patrick, I'm a woman. I'm clean, and soft where it counts, and some men find me sexy. Do you?"

His surprised resistance lasted all of ten seconds. After that, although still looking a little stunned, he quickly closed the few-inch gap between them, his left hand cupped her firm breast on its own, and his right found and stroked the curve of her hip. Slowly his hands slid around to her back, pressing her close against him. It was remarkable how well they molded together, she thought, and how wildly her senses were exploding, her whole body suddenly more alive and aware than it had ever been before.

What brought her to this state of full joyous life was the touch of his hands as they moved leisurely, with sensuous skill, learning her shape and texture. His expression intent, he translated his tactile impression of her into a mental picture that seemed to urge him to investigate further, and everywhere his magic fingers explored, her nerves begged for more. His lips were on her forehead, and then her eyes, and now her mouth, tasting, seeking. She kissed him in return and pushed her hands inside his coat, clasping them behind his back. Oh, God, he smelled good, and the hard warmth of his chest against her breasts was too sensual an experience to bear.

He must have agreed, because he drew his mouth away from hers and buried his face in her hair, giving a low groan. He seemed to be having difficulty breathing. "Oh, hell," Patrick muttered hoarsely against her temple. "What's the matter with me? Have I lost my mind?"

"There's not a thing wrong with you," Briony whispered, her arms tightening. She kissed his ear and felt him shiver.

"Don't do that," he said sharply.

"Why not? Don't you like it?"

He spoke shortly, with a hint of exasperation. "How I would love to—"

"What?" she asked immediately, thrusting her pelvis forward, to his apparent agony. He groaned again and lowered his head to consume her mouth in another kiss, savagely hungry this time, more exciting and warmly demanding than she had ever dreamed a kiss could be. Her mouth worked against his, their tongues teasing each other, until he pulled back his head abruptly.

"How I'd love to spank you," he finished his earlier statement, a real edge to his voice now. "But you've just shown me once and for all that you're not a little girl any longer. So what can I do with you?"

"You can love me just as I am," she suggested demurely.

"I may spank you yet," he growled.

She kissed his chin. "You won't."

"You tempt me."

"And *you* tempt *me*."

Briony nuzzled his neck, but he suddenly pushed her away from him, disengaging her arms from his chest, and turned to move away. Puzzled and hurt, she just stood and watched him, and when the width of the room was between them, he stopped. "You're going to marry Dennis," he said, his voice hard, "and I'm a damned fool. I think it would be a good idea for you to go home now."

"Patrick—"

"No." He shook his head. "I'm tired. I want to go to bed. *Alone*." He started from the room. "Thanks again for everything you did today for Dad and me."

Chapter Three

It was only right, what Patrick had done. It was the gentlemanly thing to do. After all, she *was* engaged, and she had been coming on to him like a trollop. What was he supposed to think, being barely aware of the existence of some faceless, formless person named Dennis Phillips whose ring graced Briony's finger?

Damn it all! she fumed as she slipped quietly in the back door of her house and went upstairs without interrupting her parents and their talkative colleagues. *What am I doing engaged to someone other than Patrick Donahue, anyway?*

The question shocked her into immobility. Half-undressed, she stood frozen before the mirror in her bedroom, staring at her delicate reflection in the oval glass. The girl who looked back at her at least appeared to be possessed of normal human feelings and the capacity for fairness. Briony had heard herself described as an exceptionally sweet-natured girl on occasion, although she acknowledged to herself that the description often didn't fit.

But now, for the first time, she was looking at something she had never dared to examine before: her relationship with Dennis. How had it started? What had motivated her to get involved with him in the first place? Was it really as wrong, as unfair to both of them, as she suddenly feared?

Sitting down at her dressing table, she rested her chin on one hand as she recalled the meeting that had occurred more than two years before.

Briony had been in the habit of running every evening with a group of friends whose favorite place to do so was the oval cinder track in Memorial Stadium. For a week straight, as she ran, she was aware of the compactly built, movie-star-handsome young man who was also out jogging. The first few times she noticed him, he was running with a pretty brunette, but after that he always seemed to be alone. Every time they passed, their greetings increased in frequency and length.

While his dark, even-featured perfection didn't appeal to her nearly as much as fair-haired, broken-nosed good looks, she nevertheless had to admire this guy's well-muscled athletic body. She suspected that he approved of her too, and he confirmed it the evening when he caught up with her from behind and slowed down his pace to stay abreast of her.

After their usual exchange of hellos, he introduced himself as Dennis Phillips.

"I'm Briony Hammond," she answered, smiling easily.

"Ah-ha." He pounced on her name with pleasure. "Miss Texas, right?"

Puzzled, she nodded. "Two years ago. How'd you know?"

"I thought you looked familiar. I asked a few questions of the right people." Dennis, she was to learn later, knew all the right people. "You know," he said with disarming sincerity, "you have to be one of the most beautiful women I've ever seen."

Her year as Miss Texas having prepared her for such direct statements, she merely smiled again and murmured, "Thank you." She couldn't help adding, "You're not so bad yourself," hoping to shake him up.

She *wasn't* prepared for his matter-of-fact response. "I know. Can you imagine what our kids would look like if we got married?"

Temporarily shocked into silence, she wondered if he was joking. His voice had been grave, but she thought maybe he had a dry sense of humor. Giving him the benefit of the doubt, she tried to laugh it off. "Are you proposing?"

He gave her another of those brilliant smiles. "Now that's not a bad idea, Briony Hammond. You and I owe it to the world to procreate and pass our good genes on down to the next generation."

His smile persuaded her he was kidding, and it wasn't until a long time later that she came to realize how serious he had been.

From their first date he wanted to marry her. When he learned she was also a teacher, he pointed out how much they had in common, and how smart their children would be. She couldn't deny any of what he said, nor did she try, since he said such nice things to her. He complimented her continually on the way she looked, which was enjoyable even if she would have liked him to comment on her thoughts once in a while.

Well, good grief, did she expect him to be a saint? She already knew he admired her brain. And he got along so well with her parents. For that matter, Dennis was polite to all of Briony's family and friends. Quite a charmer, as Esmé Hammond said. And his family thought Briony was just perfect for him and treated her

with gracious warmth when she went home with him
for a visit.

No, she didn't dispute his arguments when he told
her all the reasons why they should become engaged.
He was like a smooth-talking salesman once he got
started on that line, and she thought it must have been
the single most important project in his life from the
day they met until he finally convinced her to accept
his ring.

Oddly they had never spoken in terms of love. Besides telling her every chance he got how lovely she
was, Dennis called her "my best girl" and freely admitted how much he adored her. She, in return, kissed and
hugged him affectionately and shortened his name to
Denny when they were alone, but she had never
spoken the words of love, either, nor did he seem to
notice.

At the back of her mind she was never entirely free of
her memories of Patrick. She couldn't deny she loved
him. She thought of him when Dennis was pressing especially hard for her to accept his marriage proposal, acknowledging a fleeting wish that it were Patrick who
wanted to marry her.

But Patrick had been gone for so long, living way off
there in New Hampshire, and sometimes she thought
he was never coming back. His letters were so few and
far between, and he treated her so casually and wrote
so thoughtlessly of all the things he was doing—with
other women, of course—and the very idea that Patrick
should ever return her love became more and more
improbable.

One day, when his sales tactics had worn her down
unmercifully, Briony surprised herself and Dennis by
saying yes. So far, the engagement had been very pleas-
ant and undemanding. Other people seemed to think

she was old enough to be settling down, and Dennis was thrilled to have won her over. He spent a great deal of time showing her off to anyone who was even remotely interested. Lately his possessiveness had started to grate on her nerves a little, but that might have had something to do with Uncle John's recent news that Patrick was coming home for a visit. After hearing that, she had been too preoccupied with excited pleasure to pay much attention to Dennis, or anyone else for that matter.

She frowned at her image in the mirror, then rose to finish getting ready for bed. It appeared that for the past week she had been treating Dennis unfairly, and Patrick could hardly be blamed for wondering what in the world was wrong with her. Attractive as he was to the opposite sex, she doubted if he was accustomed to having to fight off other men's fiancées. Not being a home-wrecker type, he was only reacting normally when he told her to get lost. And he was absolutely right.

When she thought it out logically, she knew her love for Patrick was only a beautiful dream, left over from a childhood spent worshiping him. In the cold light of reason, she recognized that it would be a foolish mistake to risk her steady, safe relationship with Dennis for a fling in bed with Patrick.

So why did she feel so wretched?

Because Patrick had rejected her, when she couldn't possibly have brought herself to reject him, ever.

Because she had carried that dream around inside her for years, even when she thought it had gone on vacation and left her. If she would only admit it, she had fantasized endlessly about what it would be like when Patrick came home, when he discovered that she was grown up now and desirable. Always the fantasy had culminated in their lovemaking. Passionate, tender, perfect lovemaking.

Because, reason aside, she really did love him.

Oh, God, she thought as she lay in bed and waited for elusive sleep, *what must he think of me?* He came home expecting to find a slightly taller version of sweet little Briony, all innocence and sisterliness, and he was greeted instead by a brazen, liberated hussy.

Yep, she thought ruefully, *that's me. I know what I want and I go for it. What will he think of the new Briony? I wonder. . . .*

The next morning she was scheduled to teach an eight-o'clock class on sociological theory, which necessitated that she leave the house at seven thirty. Both her parents had gone by seven. At seven fifteen, after gulping down a cup of black coffee and half an English muffin, she tossed her notebook into the front seat of her T-Bird and crossed the dew-damp grass to the Donahue house, hugging her tan corduroy blazer to her against the nip in the air.

She found Uncle John's five-days-a-week housekeeper, Lizzie Bates, just coming out the front door to shake the throw rug from the entry hall.

"There you are, Briony my darling," the big heavy-set woman enthused in her hearty baritone. As usual, her frizzy red hair was wild and her tight white uniform had the remains of a purple stain on the hem. Briony could imagine Lizzie explaining, "Spilled my grape jelly at breakfast, but didn't it wash out well?"

"I was just thinking of popping over to your house to see about the dear boy." She began flapping the blue-and-cream Oriental rug with her wrestler's arms, completely oblivious of the fact that she was shaking dust and lint all over Briony.

Moving calmly out of range of the fallout, Briony

said, "That's why I've come over here. To see about Patrick. Isn't he up yet?"

Lizzie's arms stilled momentarily. "Is the dear boy *here*? I thought it was all set that he would stay at your place."

"The dear boy has a mind of his own," she replied dryly. "I suspect he feels better able to cope with things here in his own house."

"Sort of the home-court advantage, hmmm?" Lizzie mused. Her fourth husband had been a big basketball fan, and some of his favorite phrases had stayed with her after all these years. Her arms resumed their ungainly flapping with renewed vigor. "Bless his heart, then, let him stay if it comforts him. He must be asleep because I haven't heard a sound from upstairs."

"I think I'll go check."

When she walked in, Briony saw that the foyer was a mess. In her typical well-meaning but haphazard fashion, Lizzie had started three or four projects in the hallway and not finished any. The vacuum cleaner was plugged in, the mirror half cleaned, and the small table that usually sat beneath the mirror and held a vase of flowers now stood in the center of the floor with an assortment of cleaning supplies on it.

Briony shook her head and laughed to herself over Lizzie's eccentricities, glad Uncle John kept her on despite her maddening lack of organization. The huge old body housed an even larger heart that would gladly take on the burdens of the world if humanly possible.

"Briony? Is that you?"

The husky voice made her heart jump with pleasure. She looked up and watched Patrick confidently descending the stairs, dressed in a black turtleneck sweater and jeans. Probably no one but Briony, who knew most of his tricks, would have noticed the way he trailed his left thumb down the wall, a means of unobtrusively keeping track of his location.

"Present," she responded lightly. "Did you have a good night?"

"Fine, thanks."

With the next step his foot shot out from under him, and attempting to stop his fall, he flung himself at the banister and missed. The corner of the newel post struck his eye and grazed his cheek as he went down. He had turned in midair so that he landed heavily on his side, and his head made a dull thump on the bottom step.

Briony was at his side in an instant, kneeling over him where he lay stunned, one hand moving to his forehead and the other reaching for his wrist. She heard a soft moan and realized it came from her own throat. Patrick made no sound at all.

In that horrible moment of his absolute stillness, all her childhood nightmares came back to haunt her: Patrick walking unknowingly beneath the wheels of a gigantic truck as he crossed the street alone; or beset by criminals, beaten and left for dead in an alley somewhere; or, as he moved with apparent ease through his perpetual darkness, losing his way and wandering for days before he collapsed in hunger and exhaustion in some distant desert where no one would find him until it was too late.

Her moan threatened to become a sob. With tremendous effort she loosened her fingers on his arm and reminded herself that Patrick Donahue was a grown man now and that he wasn't likely to tolerate a display of hysterics.

Calm down, she ordered herself mutely, keeping her eyes on the lashes that lay long and thick against Patrick's cheekbones.

Behind her, Lizzie's footsteps hurried over the polished hardwood floor. "Oh, Lordy!" Lizzie wailed, dropping clumsily to her fat knees. "Oh, Lordy, I've killed him with my soap!"

Ignoring that, Briony moved her fingers over his wrist until she found the reassuringly steady beat of his pulse. Although she wanted to kiss him, she saw that his eyes were open now and that he was pushing against her hand, trying to sit up.

"Lie still, Patrick," she commanded him, but he sat up anyway, wincing a little.

"Lordy, Lordy," Lizzie cried again. In her distress she unconsciously gripped his shoulder until her big red hand was white with the strain, and Patrick looked bewildered by the unexpected punishment. "Lordy, Patrick, forgive me!"

"Lizzie, you idiot, I'll do anything you ask if you just turn loose of my shoulder."

"Oh, darling boy, of course I will!" She did so, only to turn right around and begin rubbing his shoulder and arm with anxious determination to atone for her mistake. "You'll forgive me, then?"

"Forgive you for what?"

"For leaving the bar of soap on the stairs."

Briony uttered a silent groan at the housekeeper's carelessness, but Patrick didn't seem upset. In fact, he tried to hide his amusement behind a scowl. "So that's what I stepped on," he said sternly, rubbing the back of his head with one hand. "Just as a matter of interest, why did you leave it there?"

Tuning out Lizzie's rambling answer, Briony gently ran her fingers through Patrick's thick gold hair and found a lump underneath. His cheek was raw and angry-looking, and it was likely that his eye would swell up too.

"—and you see, I didn't realize you were upstairs or I never would have done such a stupid thing," Lizzie concluded penitently.

"Sure you would, Lizzie Belle." He used his childhood nickname for her, grinning crookedly. "You've been known to forget me once or twice, haven't you?"

"Oh, but that's just because you were being such a good boy, so quiet and all, and I had a lot on my mind," she explained, "and I never forgot you for very long, either."

"That's true," he conceded. "So what is there to forgive?"

"Patrick," Briony interjected quietly, her fingers still laced through his hair, feathering over the swelling, "you have an enormous knot on your head, and your face is a sight."

"Isn't it always?" He touched the scrape that oozed tiny drops of blood. "At least this time my nose was spared. I would hate the thought of more rhinoplasty." He got slowly to his feet.

"You've had a nose job?" she asked in surprise, taking hold of one of his hands.

"Not out of any misplaced vanity, I assure you. It was a question of whether I wanted to breathe or not. The cartilage was messed up from my nose having been broken so many times."

Lizzie, wanting to be helpful, grabbed his free hand.

"Dizzy?" Briony asked.

When Patrick stood, the blood drained from his face and he seemed paler than usual. "I'm all right." He sounded irritable, arousing her suspicion that he had a blazing headache.

"I'm going to take you to see Dr. Travis," she decided.

"You're doing no such thing. I want some breakfast." He shook off their hands and, before either lady could stop him, turned to stride along the hall toward the kitchen. Almost immediately he bumped into the upright vacuum cleaner and almost fell, but managed to maintain his balance. His hand groped to investigate the obstacle. "What the hell's this doing out?" he snapped. "Lizzie, for God's sake, are you trying to do me in my first day home?"

Seeing the old lady's tears, Briony put a restraining hand on his arm. "If you'll slow down, Patrick, we'll all be better off. There's absolutely no need to impress us with your bad temper." In an aside to the housekeeper she murmured, "Go ahead and get this place straightened up, while I fix something for Patrick to eat."

He let her walk him to the sunny little breakfast nook, but as soon as he sat down, he asked coolly, "Isn't there somewhere else you should be right now?" He opened the crystal on his braille wristwatch and fingered the face. "Quarter to eight. Don't junior college instructors like you usually get stuck with all the early classes?"

Good Lord, she'd completely forgotten her class!

"Yes, Professor Smartass, we do. If I can curb your appetite for another few minutes, I'll call and make arrangements for someone to handle my theory students."

That was an overly optimistic statement, as Briony had halfway expected. When a hasty search by the campus telephone operator failed to produce a single faculty member not committed to an eight-o'clock class of his own, she resorted to an old habit of hers: going straight to the top.

"Hello, Daddy," she said when the operator put her through to the president's office.

"Morning, sweetheart." Dr. Hammond was much more cheerful then he had been at breakfast, numerous cups of coffee and another hour of daylight having done wonders for his outlook. "What's up?"

Briony explained about her lateness and her inability to find a replacement, conscious all the time that Patrick was fiddling idly with a spoon on the tabletop, his expression closed. Oh, he was listening, all right.

"Like me to take the class for you?" her father offered.

"Please!" she said, relieved.

"I had an appointment cancel out this morning, so you're in luck. Of course, I'm an economist, not a sociologist, but I believe I can manage. Will it deviate too far from your syllabus if we talk about Karl Marx?"

"Daddy dear, just this once you can talk about *Groucho* Marx if you like! I can't thank you enough."

"What time do you think you'll get here?"

"My next class is at ten. I'll make that one if I can."

"Will he let you take him to the doctor?"

She looked over at Patrick thoughtfully. "That remains to be seen." Hanging up the phone, she went to the refrigerator. "What do you want to eat? Bacon and eggs? Pancakes?"

"Nothing, thanks. You go on to work."

"Don't be silly. You just heard me on the telephone." Her voice was muffled as she poked around inside. "Here's some sausage. How about scrambled eggs and sausage?"

"No, thank you."

There was a no-nonsense quality about him that made her straighten to glance at him again. He sat erect, staring ahead at the blank wall. Letting the refrigerator door close slowly, she moved over to stand next to him. "Why don't you want to eat? You said you were hungry."

"I'll wait for Lizzie."

"Why are you being so stubborn? Lizzie will probably manage to set the kitchen on fire!"

"I'll take my chances," he answered evenly. "Would you please get the hell out of here now? Go on to Drey-Bart and at least finish up with your class. You don't seem to take your responsibility very seriously."

"Daddy will be having a ball with the kids. They don't need me."

"Neither do I." He smiled as he said it. It was hard to believe the clear green eyes couldn't see her, they met her eyes so steadily.

She wondered if he knew how much his words hurt. He discerned a lot, Patrick did, but when it came to Briony, he was strangely blind.

Or maybe he knew and was warning her off.

If so, the last thing she wanted was for him to guess that he had struck a nerve.

"Good for you," she said carelessly. "If you're not hungry enough to let me cook for you, you can certainly wait for breakfast until after Dr. Travis has checked you out." She went back to the telephone and picked it up to begin dialing.

Patrick rose swiftly and took two long steps to her side. He took the receiver from her and dropped it back on its cradle. "Don't you listen?" Putting both hands on her shoulders, he shook her a little. "I am not going to see Dr. Travis. Dr. Travis is not coming here to see me. You are not to try to arrange for *any* doctor to see me. I will decide for myself when and if I need medical attention."

"That bump on your head—"

"If I ran to a doctor every time I got a bump on my head, I'd never have time for anything else."

"But—"

"No buts, Briony."

"At least let me clean up the place on your cheek."

His fingers tightened. "For the last time, no. Lizzie can do it."

"Okay." Briony gave in abruptly, recognizing the futility of arguing with Patrick in his present independent mood. Evidently he had a big investment in avoiding her ministrations. "Angel of mercy," he had called her last night, implying scorn for the gentler traits of hers that came to the surface so seldom these days.

She could tell her acquiescence surprised him. He released her, his attitude wary, and her footsteps clicked across the room to the door. "See you," she said matter-of-factly and walked out.

His face, she noticed, was undecided. To speak or not to speak? He ended up not calling out to her, even though he had ample time to do so, and she experienced the unworthy hope that he might at least feel a little guilty for his curtness with her.

Briony arrived at her classroom just as her father dismissed the students. From their laughter and lively talk as they exited, and the cluster of four or five who had cornered the college president to ask questions, she knew he had gone over well, as always.

"Hello, Chad," she spoke to the only solemn-looking young person on the fringe of the group. He was a short but well-built boy of twenty, a loner who had confided the first time he talked with her after class that he lifted weights. Obviously he was quite proud of his physique.

"Miss Hammond!" he exclaimed, his usually expressionless face brightening. "I didn't expect to get to see you today."

His meaning was not lost on Briony, but she chose to ignore its implications. She supposed all teachers with a pretty face and decent figure must be prepared to deal with the occasional infatuated pupil.

"Something came up that made me late," she explained. "It looks as if you all made out okay without me, though."

"It wasn't like having you here." His closely spaced blue eyes appealed to her earnestly. "I need to talk to you in your office now, Miss Hammond."

"What about?" Abstracted, she kept one eye on her father, who was moving closer to the doorway, the students still holding his attention.

"Er, about our term paper. I can't decide whether to write on Comte or Weber."

"All right, Chad, run on to my office and wait for me. I need a word with Dr. Hammond."

"I'll wait and walk with you."

"No," she said firmly. "I need to talk to him privately." Briony was relieved when he finally trudged off.

As soon as she had thanked him again for handling her class, her father inquired about Patrick's injuries.

"I'm sure it's nothing serious," she answered, not sounding very certain. "But I'd feel a lot better if he had consented to an examination."

"Wouldn't go for that, would he?"

She shook her head. "I have this fear that Patrick's going to really get himself hurt trying to stay by himself."

"Don't forget he has lived independently for years."

"In an apartment, not a big house!"

"It's a house he knows like the back of his hand," Ryan Hammond reminded his daughter. "You said Lizzie had accidentally left some things out of place."

"And dear-but-scatterbrained Lizzie is going to be there daily, getting things out and forgetting to put them back. You know how she is."

Her father chuckled. "Yes, I do, bless her heart." His laughter died away. "Well, I see what you mean. It may pose a problem. He'll have to be more cautious—perhaps start depending more on his cane."

"Oh, Daddy!" she protested. "You know how he is about that. He doesn't always use his cane even when he's going out, much less in the house. He'll consider it a bother and end up killing himself."

"Surely not, sweetheart!"

"Then again, maybe he will," she brooded. "I couldn't live with myself if anything happened when I could have prevented it."

Ryan smiled down at her quizzically. "And just how do you propose to prevent Patrick Donahue from doing exactly what he wants to do? He's a very strong-minded young man."

"I'll think of something," she said evasively, an idea already taking shape in her head. "And I can be pretty strong-minded myself, you know."

Dr. Hammond gave a hearty laugh at that. "My darling child, you've just made the understatement of the year! I guess if you two clash, you'll be fairly evenly matched. It should be interesting to see who comes out on top."

Briony wished she could look at the problem as a mere game of wits between herself and Patrick, but she felt instinctively that too much was at stake for such a blasé attitude.

In her office she sat down with Chad Smith and went over with him for the second time the list of possible topics for his term paper in theory. He bent his dark head, watching intently as she made notes in the margins beside each subject. She hoped some little bit of information that she wrote would catch his eye and interest him in researching further.

Briony thought it was a near hopeless task, however, when she had finished writing and asked, "Well, Chad, what do you think?"

Lifting his head, he answered irrelevantly, "You have beautiful legs, Miss Hammond." And then, quickly, "I see you out running sometimes. Is that how you stay in such good shape?"

And while her face was registering confusion and at least mild shock, he added, "I run too but I really prefer working out with equipment. I've built my own gym in my apartment. Maybe you could come over and see it, try it out one of these days."

Before she could put her thoughts into words, he stood and picked up the marked-up list. "Thanks. See you tomorrow."

Briony sat back in her chair after he had gone, her heart pounding a little heavily from the odd exchange. What a strange boy! She had noticed the way he seemed to be able to blank his expression to hide whatever he might be thinking. Sometimes in class she saw him looking at another student with that blank stare, and it chilled her inexplicably, especially when it was accompanied by that tiny, superior smile of his. Anyway, she didn't feel comfortable with his suggestion that she come to his apartment, although at Drey-Bart teachers were encouraged to develop friendships with their students.

Without much effort she pushed Chad from her mind and got back to the business of considering what to do about Patrick Donahue. Or rather, she corrected herself, what to do about her love for Patrick Donahue, which implied the further problem of what to do about

Dennis Phillips. Remembering that they were supposed to have a date that evening, she debated whether to keep it or not. She knew what she wanted to do, and it certainly was *not* to go jogging with Dennis. She sighed over the dilemma.

It was a chore keeping her mind on the subject of sociology while she delivered her prepared lecture in the introductory course that she taught later that morning. At noon she ate in the college cafeteria, sharing a table with several other faculty members and a few students, but once again her thoughts were focused elsewhere. She had almost given in to the urge to drive over to the hospital instead of eating; however, her father had told her after theory class that he and Esmé intended to visit John Donahue for a few minutes at noon. If Briony went, Patrick would probably get the idea she was checking up on him. Restlessly she tried to evict him from her mind the rest of the afternoon.

Sometime before three o'clock she had enough foresight to cancel her running date with Dennis, knowing she would be less than good company anyway. By the time she usually left for home, Briony had convinced herself that she ought to go see Uncle John, that he would expect a visit from her. Cheered at the thought, a few minutes later she was walking briskly along the corridor to CCU, where she hesitated just inside the door of the waiting room. The big room buzzed with the quiet conversation that always seemed to spring up between those who were keeping a vigil over loved ones. Friendships were formed here, she knew—relationships that probably wouldn't extend beyond the span of one person's illness, but that nevertheless would bring a certain comfort while they lasted.

Patrick sat in one of the comfortable chrome-and-leather chairs next to the windows, one hand fingering his long thin metal cane with the plastic tip. He had been talking to the kindly old farmer-type from last night's visit, now seated next to him, but as she paused, he raised his head and seemed to look at her. His hand on the cane made a small movement, as if he started to get up and then stopped himself. Surely, she told herself incredulously, he couldn't have picked her footsteps out of all this chatter! But would that really have been any more amazing than his recognition of her footsteps and perfume in the airport lobby yesterday?

Briony continued across the room and stopped in front of his chair, giving the old man a quick smile. Close up, she could see the black and blue swelling on Patrick's right eyelid, the tender-looking patch of grated skin on his cheekbone. His mouth was tight as he got to his feet.

"Briony." He said her name calmly, without question. He knew very well who faced him.

She made herself respond cheerfully. "Hello, Patrick!" Moving closer, she planted a swift, ambiguous kiss on his unmarked cheek, trying to make it look like a sisterly gesture. He stiffened almost imperceptibly beneath the warmth of her lips. "What are you doing here?" There was no doubt about it, he was not pleased that she had turned up.

"I came to see someone I love very much." At his slight frown she added, "I'm referring to Uncle John, you conceited dolt. Not you."

His relief took the form of a subtle relaxing of his stance, but still he looked vaguely unhappy. A sudden fear hit her, causing her to disregard whatever sting she might have felt at his cool greeting. "How is he?" she demanded anxiously. "He's no worse, is he?"

Although he reassured her promptly about his father, Patrick's evasive manner led her to believe something was wrong. To get away from the other hospital visitors, who sat watching them curiously, she suggested that they step out into the corridor, an idea he quickly seconded. Briony studied his bruised countenance for the length of time it took them to walk across the room, suspecting she knew what was bothering him.

"How did he take your battle scars?" she asked softly.

From his defensive annoyance, she deduced that she had scored a hit. "He overreacted, just as you did. He thinks I've nearly killed myself." His voice was strained. "He's worrying himself sick."

Briony's heart plunged. "Oh, no! Poor old dear!" Almost to herself, she muttered, "And I guess he blames me."

"As a matter of fact, he blames himself," Patrick snapped, "which is just about as stupid as blaming you." He leaned back against the wall where she had positioned him, his half-closed green eyes brooding on her mouth. "No amount of assurance on my part seems to convince him I'm capable of surviving this sort of thing."

He wouldn't be convinced, of course, lying helpless in Cardiac Care, where he couldn't do a thing to protect his only offspring from the difficulties that Patrick seemed determined to shoulder alone.

Briony mulled it over for a moment before offering her opinion. "*You* know you'll make it by yourself, and *I* know you'll make it." She ignored his raised eyebrow which seemed to accuse her of exaggerating her faith in him. "Deep down inside, your father knows it too. But right now his illness has him so worked up that it's useless to try to reason with him."

"I recognize that," he said shortly. "So what are you suggesting? I'd be happy to avoid the issue, but he won't let me. Every time he takes a look at my face, he nearly goes into cardiac arrest. Dr. Hayes actually rushed in at noon to see what was causing the changes in his electrocardiogram."

"What I'm suggesting," she spoke evenly, "is that we humor him, go along with whatever he asks. Just to calm him down."

She was surprised to see that Patrick had blanched at that, his hand clamping tight over the end of the cane until his knuckles were white. "Is that so hard for you?" she asked with some impatience. "He's your father, Patrick! Can't you swallow your pride enough to let him die in peace?"

He raised his head, looking grim. "You don't know what he's asking."

"No, I don't." She waited and after a minute had passed in taut silence, decided to prompt him. "Do you plan to tell me, or should I guess?"

A muscle jerked along his jaw. "It doesn't bear consideration."

Mystified, she pressed him for an answer. "If Uncle John suggested it, I want to hear it."

"Well, get a grip on yourself," he said, an ironic smile twisting his mouth. "He wants us to get married."

She stared up at him, not quite believing what she had heard. "He wants you to get married?"

"Us," he corrected her. "He wants me to marry you."

For a split second all she felt was total shocked joy. When it dawned on her that it was this idea of Uncle John's that Patrick found so abominable, her elation fled, leaving her deflated. "I see."

"You *see*? Is that all you have to say about it?"

"What more can I say? Haven't you said it all? 'It doesn't bear consideration,'" she quoted.

"How can it? You're already engaged."

"And aren't you glad I am! I wonder what excuse you'd come up with if I weren't?"

"That's rather a moot question, don't you think? The point is, you're in love with Dennis Phillips."

"What do you know about whom I'm in love with?" she asked hotly. "The point as I see it is that your attitude is downright insulting. You may not find me attractive, but there are some men around who wouldn't be so quick to sneer at the prospect of marrying me."

He stood up straight, meeting her eyes with remarkable accuracy. "Not the least of whom is your genuine fiancé."

She almost said "To hell with him!" but caught herself in time. That would have been unforgivable.

He reached up to rub a hand tiredly over his eyes. "Oh, hell, Briony, why are we debating this ridiculous question? People don't get married to satisfy the whim of a parent, even if he is dying."

"People have married to please their parents for a lot more years than they haven't," she injected.

"Spoken like a true sociologist," he mocked her. "If it weren't so farfetched, I'd almost suspect you're arguing in favor of Dad's fantasy."

Uncle John's fantasy was so close to her own that it was scary. She wondered fleetingly if the old man might have been picking her mind during all those long talks about Patrick they had shared while he was away.

"Briony?" Patrick prompted her.

She glanced around nervously, not wanting to have to answer him, and at that moment saw the nurse throw wide open the double doors. "There's the signal for visiting time," Briony murmured, sounding a little breathless.

Patrick compressed his lips as he took her elbow.

Uncle John had been watching the doorway, and when he saw that Patrick was accompanied by Briony, he seemed excessively relieved. "Hi, kids," he said, his voice tremulous.

"Hello, Uncle John." She leaned down to kiss him. Giving him a brief but careful study, she saw that Patrick had been correct in thinking the old man was sick with worry. His eyes were watery with fever, and his skin seemed about to crack with the dry fragility of the very ill.

Speaking with forced lightness, Patrick told his father that he had spent the several hours between visiting periods in taking a taxi over to the archives at the state capitol building, where he met the archivist. They had discussed the proposed topic of Patrick's book, which concerned the role of a few special Texans in the Civil War. The man had impressed Patrick as being a knowledgeable resource and a willing pair of eyes to assist in his research. Tomorrow he planned to go to the U.T. library to find out what was available there and check into hiring a reader.

John Donahue listened with interest while his son talked but when the monologue ended and Patrick couldn't seem to come up with anything else to say, he changed the subject. "Son, have you given any more thought to calling Tom Clayton?"

Briony felt Patrick's grip on her arm tighten. "No, I haven't," he admitted.

"While you're out gallivanting tomorrow, you might drop by his office and surprise him."

"Some surprise!" he muttered under his breath.

"Dad," he protested in a nearly normal voice, "I don't have any idea where Tom's office is."

But John Donahue wasn't about to buy that excuse. "Any cab driver in Austin can take you to the police department, Patrick." Seeing his son's expression turn stubborn, he added on a pleading note, "Will you at least think about it, boy?"

Anything to get out of this discussion. "Sure, Dad, I'll think about it."

"Good." The old man breathed out noisily in relief. "Now I'd like you to wait outside for a few minutes while I have a word with Briony."

"Patrick"—she drew him over to the door—"why don't you sit right out here by the nurses' station while I try to appease Uncle John. I think I can put his mind at ease without committing us to each other for life," she said wryly. She left him sitting in a chair, holding his cane between his knees, his rugged features wary.

"Darling girl," Uncle John said affectionately as soon as she went back to his side, "I wonder if I've told you how much you have added to my life when you were younger but especially during these past few years?"

"I think you probably have. You're pretty free with your compliments," she teased.

"Good. I hope so, because you deserve to hear it at least every day."

She laughed. "I'll remember you said so when I'm feeling down in the dumps. It can warm me on a cold winter night."

She could have bitten out her tongue when he said, "You need more than words to do that, my dear. You need a husband."

"That's what Dennis keeps telling me," she said gently.

He was silent for a minute, frowning and breathing

unevenly. "I've sometimes thought you aren't as, er, taken with young Dennis as you try to act," he finally proposed. "You're always far too eager to neglect his wishes in order to take care of mine."

"That's because you're so very special to me."

He smiled at that, but shook his head. "It wouldn't matter how special I was, if he were the man you loved. You'd put him first. Now, take Patrick."

She clenched her fingers over the bedrail. "What about him?"

"I've always hoped—more than that, I've always *felt*—there was something between you two. Something... I don't know how to describe it without sounding like a mushy old man. I've sometimes thought you two were far closer to each other than you were to anyone else, despite the difference in your ages."

"We—we have been close, Uncle John. But I think you're talking about more than friendship, and Patrick has never seen me that way."

He watched her closely, starting to gasp a little. "But *you*—haven't you always put Patrick first? I remember how you used to drop everything whenever he called you, whether you were playing tennis with your friends or on your way out on a date or whatever you were doing. It didn't matter who had first claim to your time. When Patrick whistled, you came running. The prettiest little girl in the neighborhood, looking at him with those big eyes of yours just as if he could look right back at you."

Briony couldn't deny what he was saying, but she felt she must stop this talk before he completely wore himself out. "You've guessed my secret, then?" she asked softly. "You know how much I love him? It's true, Uncle John, but I hope you'll keep it to yourself. Your son would not appreciate hearing about it."

"You think not?"

"I *know* he wouldn't, darling. I've tried to tell him myself." She crossed her fingers as she prepared for the lie she was about to tell. "But you know something? I think with patience and a dose of my magic love potion, I'll be able to win his heart before his visit is over."

It was as if she had lit a candle in his tired eyes, they began to glow so brightly. "You mean...?"

"I certainly do! I mean if you give me a couple of months, I'll have that handsome son of yours at the altar. He'll be so smitten, he won't be able to resist me."

John's face relaxed and he seemed to breathe more easily. "Briony, you don't know how much good it does me to hear you say that. It's been my fondest dream." A remembered worry crept back into his eyes. "But in the meantime—"

"In the meantime," she threw in hastily, "I'm going to stay at your house, in the room just next to Patrick's. I'll take care of him, I promise on my honor. I won't let you down as I did last night."

"Oh"—he made a weak motion with his one free hand, the one without the I.V.—"Patrick explained... how he wouldn't listen to you...about staying at your house.... Stubborn boy...." His eyelids closed. "Sorry, but I'm so sleepy. Tell him good night for me?"

He appeared infinitely more content as she left him. At the door she met Patrick, who was making his way toward her with his cane, his expression grumpy, his dark blond hair rumpled by agitated fingers.

"What took you so long?" he muttered impatiently.

She didn't mince words. "We were discussing you."

"I gathered as much before I left the room. Well? Did you decide on the best course of action to handle the recalcitrant blind kid who thinks he's a man?"

"Sarcasm?" She clicked her tongue. "It ill becomes you." She held out her arm to him again. "Your father asked me to tell you good night. Our discussion exhausted him, and I'm sure he's asleep by now."

"I guess I'll have to take your word about that." His steps beside her were reluctant.

Briony stopped. "You don't believe me? Would you like to go back and check?"

"Oh, sure! I'll braille his face and wake him up, and the nurses will throw me out on my ear."

"If I lied to you and he's not really asleep, you can't very well wake him up, now can you? And you really ought to get the lowdown from him on what we decided about you. After all, I'll probably lie about that too."

Patrick's head turned slightly as he listened to the footsteps of people passing them in the corridor. His arm snaked around her slender waist, holding her in its ironlike grip. "Don't be an idiot," he warned her quietly, his mouth tantalizingly close to her ear. "I don't think you would lie to me—at least not without the best of intentions."

She stiffened with fury. "Your trust in me is awe-inspiring."

"That's exactly what I think of your trust in me," he drawled, not releasing her.

The hardness of their contact was starting to affect her, make her light-headed with pleasure. She felt the warmth of him searing her side where he pressed her to him. His fingers bit into her flesh punishingly, but she felt no pain, only an awakening of delighted feeling throughout her body.

The wicked look on his face spurred her to hiss at him, "Let me go! Do you realize we're in public?"

"No," he refused in a smooth undertone. "I'm blind, remember. I need you to guide me out of here."

"You got here by yourself. You can find your way out the same way!" She tried unsuccessfully to detach herself from his steely arm, conscious all the time that what she really wanted was to submit. It was the knowledge that Patrick wouldn't want her if she offered herself to him on a silver platter—it was that that infuriated her.

"Do you mean you'd desert me? Leave me here alone?" he taunted her.

"Yes, I would, and that's probably just what you want me to do!"

He laughed and let her go abruptly. "I like you when you're angry, Briony."

"Why?" she asked suspiciously, rubbing her waist where his fingers had dug in.

Shrugging, Patrick turned and started in the direction of the elevator, using his cane. After a moment's hesitation, she caught up with him and took his arm with the barest of pressure, and his sightless green eyes moved to her face.

"I think it's because I trust your anger more than anything else you feel for me," he said. "You say what you really mean when you're mad."

"And you think I don't otherwise?"

He shrugged again. "As I said, I'm sure you have pure intentions. It's the angel of mercy in you."

By now Briony was too angry to answer him. Unconsciously she stiffened her arm against the wool of his coat sleeve and all but pulled him along as her footsteps sped up. In her unthinking temper, she almost walked him into a cart of test tubes being pushed around a corner by a harried lab technician, and the near-hit frightened her.

Patrick ground to a halt and faced her, white lines of strain etching his mouth. "Wait a minute!" He was clearly annoyed. "Didn't you hear that coming?"

"No," she admitted, trembling at her carelessness. "I wasn't paying much attention."

"Then perhaps I ought to be leading you." His tone was grim. This time he put his arm around her, and without protest she let him take her to the elevator and push the button. He did so slowly but without apparent effort, without fumbling, and then led her off the elevator at the first floor. Walking with measured and silently counted paces, he escorted her to the exit.

Outside, there were eight steps leading down to the sidewalk. Patrick stopped at the top and inhaled deeply. "Someone has a fire going in a fireplace."

She smelled it too, now that he mentioned it, the delicious woodsy scent of cedar burning. "Mmmm... good idea!" The air was chilly, making her glad of her blazer.

"Is it dark yet?"

"Not quite, but the sun's been down for some time now. Everything is shaded a deep soft brown."

"For me, everything is always deep brown." He turned his face as if he were scanning the horizon visible from the hospital steps. "We're facing south, aren't we? Can you see the capitol?"

Briony could, and described for him how the pink granite dome in downtown Austin was bathed in white lights, while several miles closer to them the tall main tower of the University of Texas glowed orange.

He laced his fingers through hers and inclined his head, smiling a little. "Think you can take it from here, or would you like me to find your car?"

"Incurable showoff. I think I can manage." She hooked his arm with hers companionably as they walked the block and a half to her T-Bird, feeling relieved that the tension between them seemed to have dissipated.

Once in the car, a few well-phrased questions prompted him to talk about his research, but even as he spoke, Patrick seemed to be attending carefully to her driving. After an unexpected turn or two, he asked, "Where are we going?"

"Out to dinner." At her favorite restaurant, she didn't add, a small out-of-the-way cottage that offered continental fare and waiters much too well-trained to let their dinner be other than smooth and pleasurable.

He raised an expressive eyebrow at her. "What's the occasion?"

"It's just something I want to do for me. I treat myself regularly to something I really want."

"And you really want this?"

"Yes, I really do." She made no apologies, no explanations. He could read into it whatever he wanted.

"I see … Sounds like a good idea, pampering yourself," he commented thoughtfully.

It wasn't until after they had finished their escargots seasoned with tarragon and garlic, and their veal cordon bleu, that he brought up the subject he had allowed her to distract him from earlier. They sat so near to each other that it was no problem for him to find her hand and put his over it on the table. "Did you and Dad settle on a wedding date?" he inquired softly.

"What?" Briony blinked at him, unable to decipher much from his shuttered face in the candlelight.

"I'm wondering how you reassured Dad that there wouldn't be a repeat of this morning's fiasco." He drew Briony's hand up to press it to his injured cheek. "Did he persuade you that I'm a good marriage risk?"

"Your merit as a husband was never in question. We talked about other things."

"Such as?"

"Such as love."

Patrick grunted, his lazy eyes on her breasts, his hand still covering hers, playing idly with her engagement ring.

Her heart was doing funny things, as it usually did when he touched her, so that when she spoke again she sounded flustered. "I'm one of those oddities who believe...who believe two people should love each other before they get married, in spite of what I said before I went in to see Uncle John. So you see, you're off the hook."

His eyes lifted, as if searching for hers. "But I thought we agreed that I love you and you love me," he said ironically.

Don't mock me! she wanted to cry. *Don't you dare make fun of what I feel for you!*

"The kind of love I'm referring to is not the same kind you mean, Patrick," she murmured. *Not on my part, at least,* she added silently.

He looked grave. "So you convinced Dad we'd be a mismatched pair?"

"Uncle John won't mention the subject of our marriage again," she said evasively.

He released her hand and picked up his wineglass to take a drink. His face was faintly puzzled. "We both know he only suggested marriage because he thinks I need to be taken care of. Oh"—he raised a hand to stop her automatic protest—"I know he's proud as hell that I've lived alone for years, in New Hampshire of all places. That's why I went there. I didn't want people breathing down my neck, keeping me under constant surveillance and getting upset every time I stubbed my toe. People, of course, meaning my father and your family." He had a wry smile on his face. "It's hard to take at thirty, knowing Dad wants to marry me off to protect me from myself."

"Oh, Patrick—"

"So tell me," he interrupted, "what did you do to get him to drop that ridiculous idea?"

She swallowed. "I made him a promise. A promise I intend to keep, no matter how mad you get about it."

Chapter Four

Patrick hated the idea, as Briony had known he would. He refused even to consider it at first, until she pointed out that if Uncle John learned of Patrick's noncompliance, the old man would either suffer added emotional distress or come up with some other unacceptable alternative.

"Why don't you just relax and enjoy it?" she suggested after he had pondered it somberly for a while over his drink.

At that, his face darkened. "You sound pretty flippant about this. Have you thought about how your parents are going to react to the idea of our living together?"

"'Living together?' That terminology is a little extreme, don't you think? I wasn't proposing that sex be included in the deal, although"—her voice lowered and her eyes caressed his long supple form as he leaned back with unconscious grace in the chair next to her— "I think something can be worked out."

Watching him brood over that, Briony recognized fleeting traces of anger, and reluctant interest, and dismay, as they passed across his mobile features. "Is that what you meant by 'relax and enjoy it'?" he asked at last, his voice taut.

"What I meant was that you'll probably benefit from having me around. Ask Steven if it isn't nice to have a woman in the house, even if it's only his sister. I'm pretty handy at cooking and cleaning in a pinch. I'll keep your shirts clean and marked with color-coded tags, just the way you like them. I'll make sure Lizzie doesn't leave things out for you to trip over, or mix up your socks so you can't match them with your suits."

"You sound indispensable," Patrick observed dryly. "Do you mind telling me what you're supposed to get in return? A sense of altruism, of having helped someone who was less fortunate than yourself?"

"Damn your stupid, blind pride!" she exploded. "If you don't know by now that I don't feel sorry for you, then more than your sight is missing. I'd say you're not playing with a full deck, either!"

"I was just checking." He looked somewhat sheepish, but she suspected he was pleased as well. All of a sudden he seemed to become more aware of the restaurant around them, lifting his head and listening to the low murmur of conversation at nearby tables. He motioned with one hand. "Was all this wining and dining meant to soften me up, so I'd give in more quickly to your scheme?"

"Partly. Did it have the intended effect?"

"Mmmm...it's been very nice. What was the other part of your reasoning?"

"Honestly? I just wanted to come here with you. To act like a real couple out on a date. You've never asked me out, in all the twenty-six years I've known you."

"I've been remiss, haven't I?" His disturbingly attractive features softened with amusement, his cheeks creasing. "One of these days I'll have to make amends. Tell you what. Just as soon as Dad's doing better, you can take me out dancing, okay?"

"Okay," she agreed promptly. "I'm ging to hold you to that. In fact, let's try to speed up Uncle John's recovery. I think it's pretty clear that something else that would make him feel better would be for you to call this Tom Clayton that he keeps mentioning."

Looking suddenly uncomfortable, Patrick didn't say anything. After watching him finger the silverware for another moment or two, Briony put her hand on his sleeve. "Listen, I know you can't be too thrilled at the prospect of getting in touch with Tom, no matter how often you insist it was an accident, but if you could bring yourself to do it for your father—"

He shook off her hand impatiently and found his wineglass, sipped it, then set it back down with a violent clink, luckily in the correct spot because she thought his mind wasn't paying much attention to what his hands were doing. "You don't understand, Briony."

"I understand that you seem resistant to talking to the person who was responsible for blinding you," she said softly, sorry she had spoiled the good-humored rapport that had been starting to grow between them the last few minutes. "And I don't blame you."

"You don't understand!" There was repressed frustration in his tone. He stood up abruptly, bumping the table and rattling the dishes, but he didn't seem to notice. "Could we get out of here, please?"

"Of course." Briony got them out of the restaurant with good speed and into her car, where she turned to face him on the seat. "All right, Patrick." Her voice was low, calm. "Tell me what I don't understand."

"What you don't understand"—he glared at her throat—"is that I'd be glad to see Tom Clayton, but he doesn't want to talk to me. He doesn't want to see me! I think I must be some kind of nightmare he'd like to forget." His right hand groped out toward her and she placed her hand in his, only to have it squeezed by his tense fingers. "Every time I've tried to talk to him, it's been a disaster."

"You're saying you have tried?"

He nodded. "We were friends before the accident, and I knew it probably shook him up pretty badly, so I asked Steve to tell him I wanted to see him when I first came home from the hospital. He promised he'd come, but he never did. After I went away to school out of state, I called him a couple of times when I was home on vacation in the summer, and he always had some excuse why he couldn't come over. I got to thinking, well, you know, that he was one of those people who just can't stand to be around someone with a handicap."

Briony looked tenderly at Patrick's averted face. "And that hurt you?"

"Of course it hurt. I was just a kid. I didn't know how to handle that then. Later, when I started to junior high school here in town, I had algebra with Tom, and it was hell for both of us. Steve and I would come into the classroom, and Tom might be the only other person in the room, but he wouldn't say a word, not even if Steve spoke to him. It was like he thought I wouldn't know he was there if he didn't talk. After a while I got to where I could tell when Tom was in the room by what Steve didn't say, just by the vibrations.

"I guess the worst part was that everyone else was talking about us. I heard the whispers wherever I went, if Tom was around too: 'There's Tom Clayton. He's the kid who blinded Patrick Donahue.' It nearly drove me insane, and I can imagine what it did to Tom. One day before class I heard some guys dragging the story out again, all the gory details, and I started swinging my fists at them and yelling for them to shut up, to stop talking about it." He laughed shortly, bitterly. "The teacher thought I'd flipped out. He made Steve take me to see the school nurse and the counselor, and I guess they decided it was a case of a blind person getting paranoid, which isn't all that uncommon. They wanted me to see a psychiatrist, until Steve made them understand that I hadn't just imagined the whispers, that the talk was *real*."

Hearing the distress in his voice as he relived the past, Briony wished she hadn't ever brought up the subject of Tom Clayton. Patrick turned his face back to her now and fixed his eyes on her chin.

"I tried speaking to him when I knew he was somewhere nearby, in the hall or in class, and dammit, Briony, he never would answer me! He'd sneak out and I'd think he was still there and the next thing I'd know I was talking to myself. Quite a joke. At least the other kids must have gotten a laugh out of it. I got mad as hell and stopped trying to be nice and forgiving. I thought maybe the guy really was a son of a bitch, like some of my friends called him. Then good old Steve had to go and tell me how miserable Tom looked, hanging his head and slinking around like the weight of the world was on his shoulders, and I thought, oh, hell, he feels guilty, and I couldn't let it go.

"This time I wrote him a note, which wasn't easy. After all, he couldn't have read it if I'd used braille, so I hand-wrote it out on a sheet of notebook paper. 'Dear Tom, I'd like to see you after school. Meet me behind the gym at three thirty.' Something to that effect. It probably wasn't very neat, but I let Steve read it so I know it said what it was supposed to say. I passed the note to him in class and went to the meeting alone, because I figured it was just between me and Tom. Anyway, I was a little late getting there, and I waited for half an hour and he didn't come. I wandered all over the back side of the schoolyard looking for him, calling him, and by the time Steve finally came and got me, I didn't know whether to cry or cuss. I ended up cussing Tom, calling him every name I could think of.

"The next day he didn't come to school, and I heard a week or so later that his family had moved across town, that he had transferred to another school. And I was just so damned glad, Briony! So relieved to know I wouldn't run into him anymore, and I felt guilty about that. Guilty about his guilt, like it was my fault, if you can sort that out! But I was glad for him too that he wouldn't have to see me anymore and be reminded of the accident. I've always hoped he got over it."

Shaken and drained, Briony didn't know what to say. She looked at Patrick's half-closed eyes and instinctively reached out to him again. She stroked the back of his restless, long-fingered hand, running her index finger over his knuckles lightly, hoping to soothe him. "Oh, Lord, Patrick, what a mess! No wonder you've resisted your father's suggestion."

"Yes, well, Dad knows there's a problem. He just doesn't realize the extent of it. For years now he's talked as if Tom and I could be buddies again if I'd just give the guy a call. He thinks since I don't blame Tom for what happened, everything should be just peachy between us."

"How long has it been since you tried to talk to him?"

"Tom? That time in junior high when I wrote him the note."

"Maybe it's time you tried again," she offered quietly and felt him stiffen, his hand pulling back from hers. She caught his fingers and held on. "Now, listen, Patrick. You're both grown men now—"

"And I don't like being rejected any more now than I did when I was thirteen. No, thanks."

"What I'm saying is, maybe he won't reject you now."

"What *I'm* saying is, I'm not going to risk it again. I don't like sticking my neck out when I can't see what's about to cut my head off." He sounded firm and unmoving. "I'm afraid, Briony, that Dad's going to have to get well without this particular incentive."

"Oh, Patrick," she whispered, putting her left hand to his cheek, still clasping his other hand. "Oh, Patrick..."

"Oh, Briony." His voice mocked her, and he leaned a little toward her, brushing his mouth across her cheek and ear, almost as if by accident. Her breath caught in her throat at the gesture, and she wished he would follow it up with a genuine kiss. Instead, he freed himself from her gentle touch and settled back on the seat with a sigh.

Now just what was that sigh supposed to mean?

On the drive home, puzzling over that question, Briony said a silent prayer that she wouldn't see a policeman, drunk as she was not on wine but on the sexy scent of Patrick in the enclosed car, the impact of the story he had just told her of his youth, the awareness of him sitting lost in his thoughts within arm's reach of her, the knowledge that she was going to sleep in the room next to his tonight. Picturing him lying in bed, golden-skinned, virile, warm, and hardmuscled, brought a flush to her face. She rolled down her window to cool off, even as she held on to the picture, enjoying it.

She sobered up abruptly when she pulled into the Donahue drive. Dennis's red Mustang was parked in front of her house.

Oh, Lord! The fun part was coming—explaining to everyone that she was moving over to John Donahue's house, at least temporarily.

She glanced at Patrick as he got out of the car, trying very hard to be objective about him. In love with him or not, she couldn't deny that he looked the part of the sophisticated college professor that every freshman girl on campus got a crush on before the year was out. He wore his gray herringbone wool jacket casually over his blue button-down shirt and gray slacks. Straightening to his full six feet one, he snapped open his collapsible cane as she continued to study him.

What would Dennis think when he finally met the man Briony had raved about for the two years Dennis had known her? She suspected he had a totally errone-ous expectation of what Patrick would be like—some-one nice but mildly klutzy by virtue of his blindness, and definitely not a threat. No matter how often Briony bragged on Patrick's achievements, Dennis would give his ain't-that-a-shame headshake and tsk-tsk in sym-pathy. She felt sure that if she had informed him that Patrick had just won the Nobel prize, Dennis would invariably reply with his stock "Poor guy."

But Dennis wasn't totally obtuse. If he met Patrick tonight, he was finally going to get the picture that there was nothing pitiful about Patrick Donahue.

And when she told him she was going to move next door...?

No. He'd never go for that, not if he met Patrick first.

"Briony?" Patrick broke into her thoughts. "What are you waiting for?"

She hurried around to him from her side of the car. "We're in your driveway. Want to go inside? I'll come over as soon as I get some things together."

"After you tell your parents? I'd be interested in hearing what they have to say about this. I think I'll come with you."

"I would have thought you'd be tired. Why don't you stretch out in your living room with a drink? I can fix you a terrific whiskey sour or tequila sunrise—whatever you like—and you can start winding down."

"Winding down from what? I haven't exactly put in a hard day at the office."

Briony pushed on desperately. "No, but I know how uptight you can get, sitting at the hospital all day."

"I didn't sit there all day," he reminded her. His acute perception took over. "Briony, is there some reason you don't want me to come with you?"

"I just think I'll handle this better alone." That was at least a half truth.

"Maybe you would, but I think I have a right to know their arguments since this concerns me too."

Briony took a deep breath and looked up at him in the darkness. "Okay, but Dennis is there."

"Ahhh...." As she watched, his lean face with the night-shadowed eyes changed, becoming more determined than ever, the chin jutting. "That's all the more reason for me to be there. I'd like to meet the young man who won your heart." He sounded sardonic.

The three in the study looked up in unison when Briony and Patrick entered. Ryan and Esmé put aside their reading material with identical expressions of relief, and Dennis stopped his pacing. His smile was noticeably nervous, his brown eyes avoiding Patrick even as they clung to Briony.

"Hello!" she greeted them brightly. "This is a nice

surprise, Dennis." She walked over to give him a brief hug.

"We were *supposed* to run tonight," he said pointedly, looking properly athletic in his orange sweatsuit and track shoes.

"Didn't you get my message? I left word with the school secretary that I couldn't make it. You should have gone alone."

"I did," he complained. "It wasn't any fun without you."

He still hadn't looked fully at Patrick, who stood near the door, his broad shoulders squared, his eyes seeming to focus on Dennis.

As if he felt Patrick's gaze, Dennis reluctantly glanced over at him, then blinked and did a double take. Briony exchanged an amused wink with her father, knowing Dennis must be having a hard time adjusting to the idea that this man, who looked as if he could hold his own on a football field, was actually blind.

"Patrick," she spoke his name loudly enough to give him a base to home in on. "Come over and meet Dennis."

Coming into the house, he had refused Briony's offer of an arm, and used his cane instead, which had been mildly puzzling to her. Now he strolled over and shook hands with her bemused fiancé, giving him an easy smile and politely acknowledging the introductions.

Dennis's response seemed stiff and unnatural, to Briony at least, and she recalled what Patrick had said earlier about some people feeling uncomfortable around the handicapped. She hoped Patrick wouldn't notice the way Dennis drew back from his handshake as if contact with a blind man was distasteful to him, but from the tilt of Patrick's head, she suspected he had picked up on it.

"Sit down, everyone," Esmé invited them, ignoring the tension Briony suddenly detected in the air. "Sit on the couch, Patrick, and tell us how your father is tonight."

Patrick found the sofa without fumbling and sat down, turning to face Mrs. Hammond at her desk. "You'll have to ask Briony how Dad's looking, but he sounds pretty bad. He's short of breath, and he can't talk above a whisper. He gives out if he has to say more than three consecutive sentences."

Briony nodded, sitting down beside him. "I'm worried about his appearance, but Patrick said Dr. Hayes hasn't indicated that he's getting any worse."

As John Donahue's old friends discussed the precarious state of his health, Dennis Phillips stood in apparent indecision. After a while, a disgruntled expression on his handsome face, he sat in an armchair and all but glowered at Patrick.

He stayed so completely out of the conversation that a few minutes later, Patrick turned his head, listening, searching the room for a clue as to where Briony's boyfriend sat. With a sense of shock at Dennis's behavior, she saw that he knew what his silence was doing to Patrick and that he had no intention of helping him out.

Instinctively going to Patrick's aid at the first opportunity, she forced Dennis to reveal himself. "I haven't seen you in a couple of days, Dennis. What's been going on?"

"Not much," he muttered in rather sulky tones, and Patrick's gaze swung in his direction.

"I understand you teach math in high school, Dennis."

Dennis probably felt outnumbered by college faculty, Briony told herself. That might have put him on the defensive and accounted for his bad manners.

"I consider myself a coach first and math teacher second," he coolly informed Patrick. "I think athletics are often underrated, when they ought to be emphasized. As far as I'm concerned, physical fitness is of primary importance. How can you have a healthy mind without a healthy body?"

If he had thought to put Patrick down, he was sadly disappointed.

"For the most part, I agree," Patrick said. "It's only been a couple of days since I worked out, and I'm already feeling the need."

"Worked out? You?" Dennis gaped at him.

"Back in New Hampshire I ran every day."

"Ran?"

Patrick smiled a little grimly at the horror in the young man's voice.

"How did you manage that?" Ryan Hammond asked with interest.

"A friend ran with me, holding one end of a length of cord, while I held the other end. We ran on the college oval track. After a while I became so familiar with the track and our rhythm that I could judge the distance around the track pretty well. Sometimes we left off the cord and just ran." The expression on his face told them how much he enjoyed that freedom.

"You don't want to get out of shape," Briony cautioned him. "What you need to do is recruit a running partner." It was on the tip of her tongue to volunteer for the position, but she thought that might be pushing her luck a bit far.

Patrick must have known what she was thinking, but he made no comment.

"We can certainly ask around at Drey-Bart," Esmé suggested. "It wouldn't surprise me if we found someone right away who would run with you." Briony wondered if her mother had surmised, as Patrick had, that she wanted to run with him.

"Thanks, but I'll find someone," Patrick declined evenly.

"And until you do?" Briony asked.

"I'll manage. Didn't you tell me we passed a fitness club not far from here? I might join and work out there."

Dennis gave a short laugh. "Don't tell me you play racquetball!"

"No, I don't."

"Of course not. Some things are beyond belief."

Briony was determined to shatter Dennis's complacency. "He plays golf, though."

"Come on!"

"That's right," her father confirmed, grinning with pleasure. "When Steven and Patrick were still at home, I golfed with them nearly every Sunday one year. I'll never forget how excited we were the day Patrick broke a hundred."

Seeing the dubious frown Dennis wore, Briony explained, "For the long shots, Patrick followed verbal directions. For the putts, one of them called to him from the hole and he aimed for the voice."

"Oh, well, if they *helped* him...." The well-built young man dismissed the accomplishment with a shrug, and Briony was torn between anger and amusement at his stupidity. Her parents, she saw, were embarrassed by his rudeness, but Patrick's lips were twitching as if he were trying not to smile. Probably he recognized that Dennis was motivated by jealousy.

"I'd like to see you play golf blindfolded," she

snapped. "I doubt very much if all the voices in the world would help you get the ball in the hole."

Dennis looked stunned at her rebuke and had the grace to flush. Patrick, on the other hand, didn't appear especially pleased by her defense. He shut his mouth tight and stared straight ahead of him.

As if sensing that a change of subject was in order, Esmé said, "Before I forget, Briony, your father mentioned that he was concerned about one of your students in class this morning. Chad Smith."

"Really?" She looked to Dr. Hammond. "What about him?"

The college president considered it a moment. "You know, it's funny but I'm not sure what it is about him that bothers me. I think it was his expression—it was almost vacuous. I thought he wasn't listening in class, and I called on him to answer a question the others were having trouble with. He certainly looked out of it, but he gave the correct answer."

Briony nodded. "Chad surprises me sometimes like that. He bothers me too in a different way."

"What way?" her mother inquired.

Briony would have felt foolish admitting that his sidelong looks of admiration sometimes made her skin crawl, so she merely shrugged and muttered, "Who knows?"

Having evidently decided to stop pouting, Dennis joined the discussion at that point. "Wasn't that kid named Chad—the one you spoke to the other day over at the stadium when we were running?"

"Yes, that was Chad. For some reason he was just sitting in the empty bleachers, watching everyone run."

"You sure he didn't come to watch you specifically?" Patrick asked suddenly.

"I don't think so. He didn't even speak to me at first. I happened to recognize him and called out to him, and he just waved and said hello. He was still sitting there when we left."

Esmé looked over at her husband, frowning. "I'm going to check his records tomorrow. He's a transfer student, I think. I really don't like what I'm hearing, but it's nothing I can put my finger on." Dr. Hammond nodded his agreement.

"Well, I hope you're not concerned on my account, because I can take care of myself," Briony said emphatically. "Your little girl is all grown up now."

That declaration brought mixed reactions, although no one actually challenged her on it. Her parents looked fondly skeptical, Dennis put on his macho-protective face, and Patrick merely smiled to himself.

She decided she might as well make her announcement on that note and proceeded to do so.

Total silence ensued. Dr. and Mrs. Hammond became engaged in some kind of eye combat. Patrick's smile had twisted a little and he appeared to be studying the floor in the middle of the room. Dennis was glaring again, from Patrick to Briony this time, unsure just whom to blame for this unwelcome development.

Ryan Hammond was the apparent victor in the mute contest with his wife. He spoke calmly. "If you promised John, of course you have to keep your word. Your mother and I expect that, don't we, my dear?"

But Esmé didn't answer, just looked at Briony pleadingly. *Don't. Don't get hurt! He doesn't love you!*

"Well, personally I think it will look bad for you to be staying with a man," Dennis muttered, "even if he is—" He broke off but everyone in the room knew what he had been about to say.

Briony jumped up from the couch, flushed with fury, her arms rigid at her sides. "Personally I don't care how it looks," she said between clenched teeth, her green eyes flashing at the snobbish young man she had foolishly agreed to marry.

Moving swiftly, Patrick leaned forward and caught one of her stiff arms, pulling her back down beside him. "Don't be so rash," he admonished her, his voice quiet. "That was a pretty irresponsible thing for you to say. I'm not sure your parents would agree with you. In fact"—he turned to look straight into her mother's distressed eyes—"I'd like to hear what you have to say about this, Esmé."

The slender fair-haired woman glaced at each of the others before answering, wanting to say more than was her right to say and knowing she couldn't possibly say enough. "I think," she sighed at last, "Briony knows her own mind. It doesn't matter what I think, she's going to make her own decisions. I only hope she's willing to accept the consequences." And her gaze clashed spiritedly with her daughter's.

"Mother, you know I am," Briony responded, her voice firm, her heart soaring. They weren't going to try to talk her out of it! She stood up again, shooting a glance at Patrick, whose face was unreadable. "I'm going to pack some things."

Dennis followed her out of the room. "I want to talk to you about this."

She stopped at the foot of the stairs and faced him coolly. "Well? What do you have to say?"

"Briony, I don't know what's come over you." He sounded bewildered, running a hand through his curly black hair and shaking his head. "Ever since you found out this guy was coming home, you've been in another world. You don't talk about anything else. You make all kinds of plans for things you can do with him, places you can take him. You cancel all our plans and ignore me for days. And now you tell me you're going to be staying at his house with him...alone! What am I supposed to think?''

She wondered how close he had come to the truth. ''What *do* you think?''

He looked uncertain, a most unusual mien for the opinionated, self-assured Dennis Phillips. ''That you... well, I guess that you feel sorry for him. I know it's rough being blind, not being able to get around much by yourself or do anything exciting. Always needing to have people offer to take you places. I guess that's what you're doing...just being nice to a blind guy. You probably don't even enjoy it.''

Briony stared at him for a long moment, both relieved that he didn't realize the depth of her feeling for Patrick and exasperated at his conceit. As she thought back on it, it seemed to her that he had always cut her off when she tried to talk to him about her childhood hero. He probably hadn't heard her say that Patrick always traveled alone, that he lived alone, that he was independence personified. It would most likely never occur to Dennis that his little speech analyzing her feelings for Patrick was so much rot, full of stereotyped garbage about the blind. He hadn't heard because he had never wanted to hear how she really felt. His mind had been too full of the things that were important to him: his job, his sports, his looks, the status he and Briony would achieve together.

Appalled, she asked herself what she had ever seen in this shallow man. Had she ever really thought he could take Patrick's place in her heart? There was no substance to him, nothing beneath the handsome exterior that was worth getting to know. Certainly nothing that would help them hold a marriage together over the rough spots. If an accident should ever shatter Dennis's safe, smug world, how well would he adjust?

Briony knew in her heart there could be no comparison between the two men. Patrick was worth ten of Dennis, and she had made an awful mistake by overlooking that fact for the past two years. Somehow, somehow she had to extricate herself from this relationship that was suddenly so disgusting to her.

It was time to start preparing Dennis that Patrick was here to stay in her life. That he was more important to her than Dennis could ever dream of being. That her future had no room in it for Dennis.

"I'm sorry," she managed to say, struggling for words to explain. "It's only natural that I consider Patrick special. Our friendship goes back a long, long way. Try to understand. . . ."

Dennis latched on to that at once. "I know. You're friends. That's okay with me, Briony. I mean, I don't begrudge the poor guy your friendship. God knows he probably gets little enough pleasure out of life."

She groaned inwardly. He had it all wrong. As she searched about mentally, wondering how to break it to him, a sudden small noise in the hallway behind Dennis caught her attention.

Patrick stood there, his cane in his hand, his eyes uncannily meeting hers.

"Don't let me interrupt," he drawled.

How long had he been listening? Had he heard Dennis's condescending statements? Was that what caused him to look so—so alien?

Briony's face reddened as she started up the stairs. "I'll hurry and pack, Patrick. I won't be a minute."

"Take as long as you like," he said indifferently. "I'm going home now. It doesn't matter to me when you come, or *if* you come. I'm sure you'll be all right, whatever you do. After all, you're all grown up, aren't you, old friend?"

He turned and tapped his way to the front door and let himself out into the evening.

So he had heard some of what they said. Briony sighed. She looked down at Dennis, who wore a totally confused expression. "I think we'd better finish this another time," she mumbled.

"Tomorrow night?"

"I don't know."

"I'd like to take you out to dinner. We can talk then privately."

Reluctantly she agreed, resenting whatever time she would be away from Patrick. She made the date for late, however, so she could pick Patrick up at the hospital after the final visiting period ended and bring him home. She refused to consider the possibility that Patrick might actually prefer to take a taxi.

If was a half hour later before she escaped next door with her overnight bag and a hanger bearing her burgundy pullover sweater and pleated wool skirt to wear tomorrow. She had kissed her parents good night without receiving a lecture, and her spirits were lifting as she opened the front door of the Donahue house.

Despite his disclaimer about not caring if she came or not, Patrick had left a lamp on in the foyer in her honor. Briony grinned a little as she walked up the staircase and deposited her things in the walnut-furnished guest bedroom next door to his. Soft music drifted to her through the wall, and she listened for a moment, trying to place it. Ah, yes. Beethoven's Fifth Symphony. One of the best-worn of Patrick's classical collection. Her smile became tender with memories as she went back into the hall and tapped on his door.

The door opened almost immediately. The room was dark, of course, but light from the hall struck Patrick full on the face as he stood there in his slacks and long-sleeved shirt with the sleeves turned back to the elbows. His clothes looked slightly wrinkled, as if he had been lying down. "Yes?" he said curtly.

"I'm here."

"Good for you."

"What kind of greeting is that?"

"I just spent the evening with you. What kind of greeting do you expect."

She laughed softly. "Would you really like to know?"

He scowled. "No, I wouldn't, and don't get forward, my girl, or you can pack up and go back home."

"Am I really your girl?" she dared to ask, and saw his face darken. "Okay, okay!" Laughing again, she held up a hand as if to ward him off. "But I was only using your words."

"Briony, do you have something to say?" he asked with taut impatience. "Because if you do, say it, and if you don't, go on to your room and give me some peace and quiet. I don't care much for your adolescent flirting."

"And I don't really care for your high-handedness. 'Go to your room,'" she mimicked him. "You can't order me around like that. I'm going to take a shower now, for your information, and when I get out of the bathroom, I may run stark naked through the entire house. I may go down to the kitchen dressed in my birthday suit and have a cup of tea. What do you think about that?"

He shrugged. "Feel free, if that turns you on. It's not likely to get *me* all stirred up." Turning abruptly, he shut the door in her face.

The fury caused by his rude gesture carried her through her nightly ritual, but by the time she had blown dry her golden mane, she had cooled off considerably. Dusting herself generously with her cologne-scented talcum power and slipping into her favorite maize silk pajamas, she decided that a cup of spiced tea didn't sound half bad.

Barefooted, she padded down to the kitchen and brewed two cups of the fragrant liquid, arranged them on a pewter tray and carried them back upstairs. In the hall she stopped and listened briefly. The music was playing, softer than before, and she could hear Patrick speaking quietly, evenly. What was he doing? She took the tray on to her room, removed one cup, and brought it back to his door.

She knocked. "Patrick? I have a peace offering."

There was a click and a moment later the door opened again in a wide sweep, showing her a wary-looking Patrick, still fully dressed in shirt and slacks. "What now?" His voice was long-suffering.

"Hot spiced tea," she informed him, brushing past him into the room and flipping on the light switch as she went. When she put the cup down on his desk, she saw that his cassette recorder was set up there. "Recording something?" she asked curiously, looking back at him where he stood holding the doorknob, glaring at her chest.

He nodded shortly. "A letter. What makes you think I want a cup of tea?"

"Don't you?"

"Not especially."

"All right. I'll take it back. I can drink two cups myself."

"Oh, leave it. I'll drink it." He added grudgingly, "Thanks."

She moved back toward the door. "Who are you recording a letter to?"

"A friend. No one you know."

"He must be a special friend for you to stay up late in order to write."

His smile was deliberately mysterious, she thought, but he didn't answer.

"Male or female?" Briony asked after a minute.

"What do you think?"

"Male?" she ventured, and he just continued to smile. "Okay, female, dammit!

"Don't swear, Briony," he murmured. "I'm sure Dennis wouldn't approve."

"To hell with Dennis!"

There, she'd said it. She grinned when she realized God hadn't stricken her instantly dead for her disloyalty. Even God, she thought, would be disgusted with Dennis after tonight.

Patrick clicked his tongue and shook his head sardonically. "Is that any way for a young woman to talk about her intended?"

"I think it is if he's a jerk. I never before noticed what a jerk Dennis can be."

Patrick's teasing mood vanished in a flash. "I'd better finish up that tape now. Thanks for the tea."

Briony moved closer to him, stood six inches from his chest and gazed up into his unfocused eyes. "You're trying to dismiss me again."

Everything about him suddenly seemed tight, as if he were a spring about to come unsprung. His jaw was clenched, his mouth shut in a thin line, his wide shoulders straining against the blue of his oxford cloth shirt, his hands knotted, one at his side, the other over the doorknob. He looked as if he wanted to pull back from her. Although they weren't actually touching, his nostrils twitched from the merciless assault of her perfume.

"Go away!" He ground out the words.

"Why? Do you think I'm naked?"

"I know you're not."

"How do you know?"

He twisted his head. "I just know. When you came in, I heard the sound of silk against silk."

She touched his scraped cheek and he jerked away. "Patrick, what are you afraid of?" she whispered, her hand making him turn his head back toward her again.

With a violent thrust of one arm, he shoved her away from him and turned so quickly that he bumped into the door with a sharp whack. He clapped a hand to his nose, but not before Briony glimpsed blood spurting freely.

Muttering a pained oath, he groped for something to steady himself and she took his arm with both her hands. "Come on, sit down," she urged him, contrite at her part in this. He let her lead him to the bed, where she released him just long enough to dash into his private bath and grab several towels. Spreading one across the pillow, she pressed another to his face. "Here, move your hand." Somehow she managed to wipe his bloody fingers without uncovering his nose, and eased him back against the pillow. "You need to hold your head back and apply pressure...here...to cut off the blood supply. I'm going to get you an ice pack." She stopped at the door. "Don't you dare move."

Patrick was still where she had left him when she came back with the small clear plastic bag full of ice cubes—the best ice pack she could improvise on the spur of the moment. She wrapped it in a facecloth and held it to the bridge of his nose, gently working with the other hand to clean up the blood that still flowed sluggishly.

His eyes were almost closed, his face pale, and she wondered what thoughts his expression hid. Briony sat on the edge of the bed next to him, neither of them speaking, listening to a Schumann record on the stereo.

Perhaps ten minutes later she removed the ice bag and found that the bleeding had stopped. She got a fresh facecloth and used warm water to wash all traces of blood from his face, neck, and hand. "It probably would be a good idea for you to lie quietly for another few minutes," she told him as she dried his hand on a towel. She put the dirty linens in the bathroom clothes hamper and came back to look down at him. "Can I help you get ready for bed so you don't have to get up again?"

His eyes shut for a second, and then opened to show her a black fury she hadn't known he was capable of feeling. His face screamed of rage, a flushing, gut-wrenching anger that scared her. His whole body shook with it.

He sat up and swung his legs over the edge of the bed. "No, Little Mary Sunshine," he snarled, "you can't get me ready for bed!"

"Patrick," she began, "calm down—"

"Like hell!" He stood up. "Thanks to you I've got a black eye and I damn near broke my nose again."

"Thanks to me!"

"You've got me so damned confused I don't know which end is up!" An artery pounded in his temple and another pulsed along his neck, making her think he was about to have a stroke, but he caught himself and continued in a rigidly controlled voice. "I take pride in the fact that I can get around by myself with very few problems. Maybe my pride is excessive, but that's the way I am. I don't know if you deliberately set out to sabotage me, but what else can I think? In the five years I lived in New Hampshire I never had a day as awful as today! I just don't run into doors and fall down stairs!"

"Patrick, believe me—"

Shaking his head, he reached out, found her silk-clad shoulder, and began pushing her toward the door. "Maybe you do it to prove how much I need someone like you around, or to show everyone how self-sacrificing you can be. Maybe you just want to charm the pants off your big brother's best friend. Honest to God, I've been trying to figure you out and I can't. Whatever it is, it's driving me crazy, and I've taken all I'm going to take. I want you out of here. Now!" He released her and pointed.

Briony looked back at him, blinking rapidly to keep the tears at bay. That little-girl helplessness worked on her father and Dennis. It had even worked a time or two on Steven. But it was lost on Patrick, who didn't see her wide green eyes, the light caught in her silvery-gold hair, or her quivering, full rose-petal mouth.

Oh, he sniffed her expensive cologne to the point of distraction...he heard the silky swish of her walk...he sensed the same thing she felt between them—a bond that demanded contact and sensitive exploration. But all the physical stimulation did was confuse him.

Briony could certainly understand that, because she had never been so confused in her life. Nor so sure she loved him.

"Good night, Patrick," she said meekly. "I'll see you tomorrow."

He looked grim. "I'm afraid you're probably right."

Chapter Five

I need to give Patrick time, Briony thought. *Time and space. I've been crowding him, because I've known for so long how I feel about him. If I don't want to scare him away permanently, I'd better back off.*

Besides, there was still the little problem of her engagement to Dennis. Her first impulse was to remove the ring and return it to him that night when she went out to dinner with him, but she thought he deserved better than that. When she took off the ring, it would be in his presence, and she would tell him why. Even so, there was a part of her that looked forward to opening his eyes and ears. She would make him listen once and for all while she told him just how much she loved Patrick. She would finally make him understand that Patrick's worth as a man was in no way related to how far he could see.

She didn't linger in the morning, although she did follow Lizzie around for a while, picking up after her and reminding her that Patrick was home. The redhead took the reminders good-naturedly and promised to make sure she kept things out from under his feet. Briony told her about the bloody towels that needed laundering, perforce explaining how they had come to be bloodied in the first place. At that, Lizzie reversed their roles and lectured her on the inadvisability of leaving doors ajar where Patrick might walk into them.

As soon as she heard him stirring upstairs, she left for Dreyfuss-Bartholemew, even though her earliest class didn't start until ten thirty today.

Briony had decided that busy involvement with her work might help take her mind off of Patrick and what he was doing. When at the end of her sociological research class, half the students were still deeply embroiled in a discussion about what kind of class research project to undertake, she suggested that they finish the debate over lunch.

In the cafeteria Chad Smith brought over his tray and asked if he could sit at her table. "It's not *my* table, Chad!" she pointed out, gesturing at the empty chair just down from her. "Go ahead."

"Seriously, Miss Hammond," one of the basketball players in her class, a boy named Andy, appealed to her. "I'm curious to know if there's a correlation between a guy's brand of after-shave lotion and his athletic ability as determined by, say, participation on a school team."

"Who cares?" Connie, who was a more studious young lady, asked, bringing loud guffaws from the others. "That sounds as bad as some of those ridiculous research projects people have actually received government grants to carry out. Like studying the courtship of crickets. A total waste of taxpayers' dollars, not to mention the researchers' time."

"I second that," a thin, bookish-looking young man named Tim threw in. "I want to research something that really carries some social significance. For instance, your father was talking in theory class yesterday about the loss to our economy because some of our best potential employees—the handicapped—are on welfare instead of working. I'd like to do a survey and find out about local attitudes toward hiring the handicapped."

Seeing the heads nod along the table, Briony agreed. "That sounds fine to me. It should be interesting to see what you find. One would hope the prevailing attitude in Austin would be favorable, since the central headquarters of our state vocational rehabilitation program is located here. It's their job to promote the hiring of the handicapped."

"Your father was telling us about a good example of someone a lot of people might consider unemployable—some blind dude he knows," Andy said. "I mean, I guess it might be easy to get to thinking you couldn't do much if you couldn't see. But he said this guy got his Ph.D., and teaches at some exclusive college in the East, and writes books that get reviewed on *The Today Show*."

So much for not thinking about Patrick.

"Not only that, but he plays golf, rides horses, runs, swims, and waterskis," Briony added.

"No kidding!"

She couldn't resist the chance to brag on his achievements, and the students lapped it up with fascination. All but Chad, who never took his eyes off her but who, she thought, was not really listening to what she said about Patrick. At Briony's mention that the "blind dude" was visiting in Austin right now, someone asked if it might be possible for him to speak to the class one day. She liked the idea but was reluctant to offer a guess as to whether or not he would grant the request.

"Aw, Miss Hammond," Andy quipped, "I'll bet *you* can persuade him!"

She laughed along with the others, until she noticed Chad's gaze had shifted to the grinning athlete who had made that suggestive comment, and then her laughter faded at the malice she read in his eyes. Shivering, she turned the discussion back to a more serious vein.

While the kids were leaving the cafeteria, Briony hung back to watch Chad and see if he struck up a conversation with anyone else. She wasn't really surprised to learn that he didn't, that he was gathering up his books and walking out alone, a lonely-looking figure in the crowd of college students crossing the sunny campus.

Her heart reluctantly touched by the strange young man, Briony caught up with him. Greeting him cheerfully, she asked, "Tell me, Chad, have you decided on a topic yet?"

He shook his head. "I'm still looking over your notes. I don't have to tell you right now, do I?"

"Of course not."

"Good." He stopped suddenly. "Miss Hammond, I have something to show you in my car."

Briony had stopped too, and now she looked at him in surprise. "You do? What?"

"Come with me and you'll see."

"Well, I don't know." She glanced at her watch. "I have a conference with the department head in fifteen minutes."

"This won't take long," he assured her, his expression eager, and she nodded agreement, recalling how this boy was always alone.

Luckily his car was parked nearby, so it took just a few minutes to reach it. As they walked, she questioned Chad about his other classes and found that the only courses he professed to enjoy were sociology and physical education. He shrugged off any mention of his family, refusing to be drawn into a discussion of anything more personal than school.

She noticed that he seemed unfriendly and totally disinterested in the other students whom they passed on their way to the car, even though at least a couple spoke to him. Since Drey-Bart was small enough for students and faculty to know each other fairly well, nearly everyone greeted Briony by name, and she smiled and spoke in return.

Chad stopped at a small black M.G. of classic vintage and opened the trunk to remove a book of some kind. It turned out that he had brought a scrapbook full of photographs of himself and clippings about weight-lifting and boxing events he had won in high school. From the looks of the clippings, he had lived in a small town in Mississippi then, and the local sports editor had evidently thought Chad had great potential.

In the photographs he posed in the usual exaggerated stances, limbs flexed and muscles bulging, wearing only brief shorts. Although Chad couldn't have been called handsome with his shaggy dark hair and too-close-together eyes, Briony had to admit that he had muscles. Very apparent muscles. She thought, though, that in the pictures he looked as if he were trying too hard to be sexy, and the strongest emotion she felt was embarrassment for him because he had failed.

"Who took these pictures?" Briony asked lightly, trying to think of something complimentary to say.

"My sister," Chad said. "Do you like them?"

"They're very... nice," she lied, unwilling to risk hurting his feelings with the truth.

"I have some trophies at home I could show you," he offered. "You can see them when you come over to see my gym equipment."

"Mmmm," she murmured noncommittally. "I'd better go if I don't want to be late. Thanks a lot for showing me these things, Chad."

Feeling relieved, she hurried away to spend the afternoon in one meeting after another.

It was after four o'clock and Briony was in the middle of a conference with a senior sociology major when Dr. Hammond rang her on the telephone. 'I'm sorry to interrupt you,'' he said, ''but something has come up that I need to see you about.''

From his voice she knew it was important, but she asked anyway. ''Can it wait half an hour?''

''No, dear. Please come over now. Oh, and lock up your office for the day. I doubt if you'll get back to it.''

Briony apologized to her student and hurried across the campus to the picturesque, ivy-covered administration building. In the president's elegant outer reception area her father's secretary told her to go right in. As soon as she walked in to the plush ash-paneled office and found both her parents standing as if waiting for her, their faces sober, she knew something was terribly wrong.

''What's up?'' she asked, going cold with dread. ''What's the matter?''

Both their heads turned instinctively to look at the man sitting in the big leather chair facing her father's desk.

''Patrick!'' she exclaimed, surprised not just at seeing him here but at the odd lack of expression on his tanned features. He merely nodded in response, not turning his head, his eyes staring at the watercolor of Drey-Bart that hung over the desk.

Esmé Hammond moved closer to Briony and laid a hand on her shoulder. ''Darling, I'm afraid we've got some bad news for you. Your Uncle John died just after noon today.''

''He had another heart attack,'' Dr. Hammond added gently. ''He just...didn't make it.''

"Oh, no!" Briony whispered the words, her eyes brimming with tears, looking with compassion at John Donahue's son, who didn't move. "I'm so sorry! So very sorry!"

"Patrick took care of everything before he came here to tell us," Esmé said quietly, gripping Briony's shoulder with enough pressure to tell her to pay close attention because this was important. "He's handled the details marvelously, but he needs to rest. Your dad and I are going to the funeral home to be sure Patrick's instructions are being carried out. I think it would be wise for you to take Patrick home now so he can relax. Don't let anyone bother him tonight, dear. We all need the opportunity to let out our grief in private."

Briony understood that her parents were worried at the way Patrick was taking his father's death, and that they expected her to work some kind of miracle on him, to get him to release the emotions he was holding so tightly in check. It was an overwhelming assignment, but staring at Patrick's set profile, she knew she would not relinquish the task to anyone in the world.

She nodded, wiping away her tears and giving her parents a tremulous smile.

Patrick went with her without protest. Walking beside him to her car, she felt the rigidity of his strong arm, the taut fingers gripping hers, the tension that permeated his whole body and kept him silent. On the drive home she glanced at his stony face a couple of times and started to say something, but bit off her words, not knowing what to say and hating to be one of those people who talk from sheer nervousness.

In the front hallway of the Donahue house they both stopped. Briony eyed him uncertainly. "Would you like to sit in the living room for a while and let me fix you a drink?"

"That would be nice, thank you."

He sounded so polite, so distant! She walked him to the couch and left him with the suggestion that he lie down there, but when she returned a few minutes later with a Bloody Mary in a crystal tumbler, he still sat stiff and upright, his eyes wide and staring.

She put the drink in his hand and went to turn on an FM radio station on the big built-in stereo system. As quiet violins filled the room with Massenet's Meditation, he held up the glass. "How much vodka did you put in this."

"Not much," she lied. The alcohol might do him good. He had never been very big on drinking, maintaining that in order to get around safely, he needed to be sober, but this once she thought it might be just what he needed to loosen him up.

Accepting her word without comment, Patrick took another sip and then another, while Briony sat in a nearby chair and watched him.

What was he thinking? Was he, like Briony, remembering the basic gentleness of the old man with the sometimes gruff exterior?

John Donahue had loved passionately. The premature death of his wife had been a bitter blow that he could never bring himself to talk about, not even to Patrick and Briony, whom he loved more than anyone else left on earth. Even when he pushed himself to work the killing hours that had aged him before his time, Briony knew his thoughts were always with his favorite youngsters. Perhaps it was because he felt so strongly what Patrick was going through that John couldn't let himself spend as much time with his son as other fathers. She recalled from years past having seen Uncle John standing just out of sight, watching Patrick as he played with Steve and Briony; she remembered the times when his eyes would fill with tears and he would have to hurry away to cry in privacy. Perhaps the pain of Patrick's blindness had never completely left the old man, although she thought he had seemed resigned the last few years. John had told her once that the hardest thing he'd ever had to accept was that the doctors couldn't use his eyes to make Patrick's better. He had offered, he confessed, and been told in a very kindly way that for both his and his child's sake he'd better stop hoping for the impossible.

Briony studied Patrick as he sat and drank, watching the slant of his head and the way his throat muscles worked. Gradually his face became more shadowed, and she got up and switched on a lamp, but he didn't seem to notice her movement. It was as if he were all alone in the world, and she wanted to cry out at the thought: *Take me, Patrick! I've always been yours. You'll never be alone if you let me stay with you!* She wanted very badly to wrap her love around him and protect him from the hurt he was experiencing tonight.

Two hours and three drinks later, he declined her offer to cook dinner and insisted on going upstairs alone to lie down. There was nothing unsteady about his gait as he left the room, and she doubted if the vodka had affected him at all.

She called Dennis to cancel their date, and was shocked when his initial disappointment turned rather quickly into annoyance with her, as if she had spoiled his evening on purpose. "This is kind of short notice, don't you think? I was just leaving to come get you."

"I know, and I'm sorry," she apologized. In other circumstances she would have been glad to keep the date, if only because it would mark the end of her engagement.

"I think you might have called earlier to let me know."

"This is the first chance I've had. I didn't want to call in front of Patrick."

"You've been with him all evening?"

"Yes, I have. He shouldn't be alone at a time like this. I'm worried about him."

Dennis thought that over, his silence stern. "Well, get someone else to baby-sit," he finally suggested arrogantly, "and go out to eat with me. We won't be gone more than a couple of hours."

Briony was starting to steam herself. "Dennis, I don't think you understand what I've told you. Uncle John is dead. It's unthinkable for me to go out to dinner. We were like his family. Besides Patrick, we were the only family he had." *And now we're the only family Patrick has*, she added silently.

"I still don't see that it would hurt anything," Dennis argued. "You have to eat, don't you!"

"Look, we don't seem to be communicating very well for some reason. I'm trying to tell you I can't leave Patrick alone, and I'm not about to go off and leave him with someone else."

"Oh, no!" he muttered sarcastically. "Of course not. Never mind me—I'm only your fiancé."

"Your father didn't die today, Dennis! For heaven's sake, grow up. You're acting like a spoiled child," she said coldly.

"I think I'm acting pretty normal for a guy who's getting the shaft. What's the deal with you and him, anyway? Doesn't it matter to you that for all he knows you may be cross-eyed and buck-toothed? I can see you, Briony! I know how beautiful you are, and I love you accordingly. Would you rather I was blind like him?"

"Shut up!" Briony hissed, her stomach churning at his words. "I won't talk to you when you're like this. I'm not sure I ever want to talk to you again, in fact. I think"—she shuddered—"I think I made a mistake when I said I'd marry you. In a few days I'll return your ring to you." There. It was out in the open. Not exactly the way she would have chosen to tell him, but at least she had said it.

"Briony—"

"I said I don't want to talk to you now!" And she hung up, shaking and relieved at the same time.

Upstairs she heard the sound of footsteps—pacing, restless footsteps. After an hour the noise began grating on her nerves, driving her into the kitchen where she whipped up a fluffy cheese omelet. When she knocked on his door and told him firmly what she had prepared for him, Patrick thanked her and accompanied her downstairs to eat. She saw that he ate every bite on his plate, but when she asked if he cared for seconds, he refused. "I think I'll have a shower and go to bed," he said, his voice flat.

Briony got ready for bed too, although it wasn't yet nine o'clock. She hadn't had a chance to get clean lingerie next door, so she decided to sleep in the raw. She donned her maize silk robe and tied the sash, too preoccupied with grief and concern to enjoy the seductive feel of the silk on her skin.

Instead of returning to the guest bedroom, she stopped in front of Patrick's closed door. There was no sound inside. She knocked, but he didn't answer. Opening the door, she walked in on quiet feet and found him lying on his back on the bed, covered with the bedclothes from the chest down, bare from there up, his eyes half closed in the dim room.

"Patrick." Her voice was husky and hesitant. "You're not sleeping yet?"

"I can't sleep." He stirred restlessly. "Briony, if you're not too tired, could you stay with me for a few minutes?"

She went to his side immediately and sat on the edge of the bed, taking hold of his hand where it lay on top of the cover. "Do you want to talk about it?"

Shaking his head, Patrick gripped her hand fiercely. "No, no talk. I just want to have you here. I don't want to be alone right now. I don't know if you understand."

It was just what she had been thinking about him earlier. "I do understand," she nodded. "I know just what you mean, because I don't want to be alone, either. Death seems so much worse, somehow, if you're alone."

"Death!" he rasped. "Don't talk, Briony! Would you—do you suppose you could lie here beside me?" He edged over in the bed and made room for her, and she stretched out next to him.

The only thing separating them now was a light blanket and the sheet. Her arm barely touched his, but that touch created a burning sensation that she couldn't lose consciousness of. This close to him, she could breathe deeply and smell his just-showered scent and the musk after-shave he favored.

A primitive need for him began eating at her, making it impossible for her to lie still, although she made a valiant effort. Stifling a groan, she moved uneasily and her hip nudged his. Instantly, all the desire she had ever felt for him was right at the front of her mind and she could think of nothing else. But then, in all honesty, she had to admit the desire for Patrick had never left her. She had ignored it at times, but it was always there, at the core of her being.

Without a word, Briony slipped off the bed, raised the sheet, and got beneath. He was naked, just as she had known he would be. Her toes brushed his long muscled legs, sensing the taut sinewy strength and the crisp hairs that would shine gold in the sunlight. She slid close to him, resting her hip against his.

She didn't know what he was thinking, but he turned to her just then, sighing aloud and taking her in his arms. His hands moved down her back, pressing her close to him. Her cheek rested on his. Crushed against his bare chest, her robe came open, allowing her breasts to experience the smooth warmth of his skin over the hard chest muscle. She felt his heartbeat against her own as he held her, and she realized vaguely that he was murmuring something into her silky hair.

"What is it, Patrick? Do you want something?"

He held her tighter. "I want *you*. I need you tonight, Briony. Love me."

Her response was immediate. "I do love you, and I always will."

Sighing again, he nodded and lifted his head to kiss her forehead, and then moved his mouth down her face lightly until he found her lips.

As they kissed, there was that same tightly coiled tension in him that she had felt last night. His mouth was demanding as it played against hers, his tongue insistent and probing, hungry for what she had to offer. After a moment he sat up and reached for the belt of her robe, untying it silently and then moving his hands up to slide the robe off her shoulders and guide her arms out of the sleeves. Tossing the silk aside, he pushed her back down onto the pillow and covered her small, firm breasts with his hands.

His fingers, which so often served as his eyes, traced patterns over her supple skin, stroking her with heavenly eloquence until her nipples hardened under his sensitive touch. Slowly he caressed the peak of one breast, catching it between his thumb and forefinger, putting a flame to the delicate tinder of Briony's passion and setting loose a wildfire. Moaning, she arched her back, raising her body up toward him. In response, he lowered his head until his searching mouth contacted her breast and closed over the tip of it.

"Oh, God!" Briony gasped at the unexpectedness of the pleasure.

Her whispered cry must have sounded to him like a protest, because he took his mouth away at once and moved it to the hollow of her neck.

"No!" she said urgently, reaching for his head and pulling it back down, locking her hands behind his neck. "It's okay. Oh, God, Patrick I need you too!"

The fair hair beneath her fingers was thick and damp as she raked it, deliriously happy to be sharing this intimacy with him, even if it were only a product of his grief. Patrick greedily devoured first one breast and then the other, and then nibbled an enticing path all the way back up to her mouth, tasting the sweetness of her as he went.

Wanting to arouse him as he was arousing her, Briony kissed his earlobe and his chin and throat, and rubbed her small straight nose back and forth along his collarbone. As she kissed one of his nipples, she eased a hand between them and placed it against his flat stomach.

"Ah!" he groaned, his stomach muscles jumping at her touch. With his magic fingers he studied her, learned her outline, the fine texture of her skin, and the secret places no man had known before.

Trusting him totally, Briony delighted in the feelings he gave her. When at last he settled down between her legs and entered her, she was ready for him, and the pain was nothing compared to the state of elation that he brought her to. He moved against her with exquisite

ease and skill, and she forgave all the women he had
had before her because they had contributed to making
him the Patrick she adored.

He let the lovely tension mount, stretched into a tantalizing limbo that blocked everything else from her
mind. When she thought she could hold no more pleasure, he made one final thrust that sent them together
over the brink of ecstasy, to drift and drift on the reced-
ing waves, back to sanity, back to the realization that
they were wrapped tightly in each other's arms in his
big comfortable bed, and that he was crooning in her
ear, "I'm sorry, Briony. I didn't mean to hurt you."

"Oh, Patrick," she laughed softly. "You didn't hurt
me! You've made me feel so beautiful. So very special.
I always hoped it would be like this."

Patrick raised his head over her a minute, as if he
were scrutinizing her, and then he lay back down on
the pillow and drew in a ragged, shuddering breath.
Although he held her loosely, without the rigid control that had gripped him all evening, there was no
doubt that he wanted her to stay right where she was.

Some time later she became aware that his cheeks
were wet. Alarmed, she wiped a hand across the damp-
ness and saw in the dark that he was crying. His
shoulders began shaking in silent sobs, as if he had
been trying to hold them back until now. She snuggled
down against him and embraced him, kissing his closed
eyelids and stroking the back of his head, her fingers
lost in the thickness of his almost curly hair.

"Cry, darling," she soothed him, her own tears for
Uncle John returning. "I know you're sad. So am I. It's
all right to cry."

Patrick didn't answer, just held on to her as to a life-
line, while the healing tears cleansed his eyes and his
heart. Tasting the salty moisture when she kissed his

clenched jaw, she whispered, "You won't be alone, Patrick. I promise you that. I'm here. You don't ever have to be alone again."

At her words of comfort he started to relax. Gradually the tears slowed and after a while stopped altogether. The last of the tension seemed to have drained out of him when he fell asleep, exhausted, in her arms.

Briony slept later in the morning than usual. It was daylight when she stirred and stretched and looked at the rumpled covers on Patrick's side of the bed, wondering where he was. Feeling too comfortable to move, she was still lying there when the door opened and Patrick came in from the hall, carrying a steaming cup of what she hoped was coffee. He was dressed in a white button-down shirt and brown tweed trousers.

With a tender little smile she watched him walk straight to the desk and put down the cup carefully, then turn toward the bed. "Good morning."

"How did you know I was awake?" she asked curiously, sitting up and drawing the sheet up under her arms to hide her nakedness. The realization of what she had just done broadened her grin.

"Your breathing is quicker, more uneven, when you're awake. Want some coffee?"

"Mmm-hmm! Are you going to bring it to me."

"But of course." He felt around cautiously for the cup, then delivered it accurately to her. After handing it over, he made a sweeping bow. *"Voilà!"*

"Merci, monsieur."

"How would I be as a stand-in for a maître d'?" He sat on the foot of the bed, wearing a quizzical look and waiting for her answer.

"Interesting," she conceded. "I'll bet things would really pop around your restaurant."

Laughing, Patrick found her toe and pinched it, almost causing her to spill the hot coffee.

"This is good!" she declared gratefully. "Did you make it?"

"Uh-uh. Lizzie's the cook around here."

Briony jumped. "Lizzie's here?"

He put a hand on her foot and patted it. "Relax. I sent her on some errands. She doesn't have to know where you slept."

"And where did you sleep?" she inquired, trying to sound off-hand.

"Where do you think?" He looked surprised at her question. "Right here. I told you once before, being blind doesn't necessarily mean I'm stupid as well."

"What do you mean?"

He shrugged his wide shoulders. "I gather that if I could see, I'd have to be certifiably crazy to leave your bed."

"I'm glad you didn't. Leave my bed, I mean."

He moved his head and looked right at her breasts. "Yes...well...about that.... Good Lord, I'm acting like an adolescent! I want you to know I wasn't quite myself last night."

"I know that, Patrick," she said softly.

"What I mean is, it didn't occur to me until it was too late that it might be your first time."

Ouch! She guessed her behavior warranted that. "You think I'm in the habit of going to bed with other men?"

"Briony, I wasn't thinking at all last night! I apologize. No, I didn't think you sleep around. But for it to be your first time...I'm really sorry."

"Don't be," she said coolly. "I told you then it was all I ever wanted it to be."

Patrick was quiet for a moment, weighing her sincerity. "I hope you mean that. Obviously I was thinking only of myself last night. That's inexcusable."

She finished her coffee and put the empty cup on the bedside table. "Ordinarily I would agree with you, but I think you can be forgiven for what you did last night. You'd had a blow. And let's don't forget that I was a willing partner in the whole thing."

"You're very generous," he said dryly.

"Not at all. I'm just very happy that my first time happened to be with you. No doubt I have your experience to thank for the fact that it was a thoroughly beautiful moment in my life. Matter of fact, it could be addictive."

"Yes, it does tend to be that. I don't imagine Dennis would appreciate my role in it, however."

"How did Dennis get into this conversation?" Briony asked with some annoyance.

"It just occurred to me that he's someone else I wasn't thinking of last night."

"Why on earth should you be expected to? You've only met him once and he hardly made a good impression that one time."

Patrick sat in thoughtful silence for a minute. "Why are you defending me?"

"I might ask why you're so determined to be the bad guy. You didn't rape me last night, you know. I'm old enough to say no if I don't want to do something."

"But you're engaged."

She twisted the ring on her finger, wishing she had been wise enough to give it back when she first heard Patrick was coming home. It would have solved so many problems. "This has nothing to do with Dennis."

He raised an eyebrow at her. "If you say so. Well,

look, I think I ought to apologize for what happened afterward too. God knows I didn't intend to unload on you."

Briony leaned forward, stretching out her arm to finger the soft gold hair over his left ear. "I'm glad you did. I'm glad I was here for you to unload on. No apologies are needed."

Patrick caught her hand and pressed the palm of it to his lips for a whimsical kiss. "No wonder Dad was so crazy about you. Would you accept my thanks, then?"

"Of course."

Nodding, he released her hand and rose. "I think I hear Lizzie's car. If you hurry, you can get dressed and still have time to mess up your bed before she comes up here to clean." He was grinning faintly as he left the room.

Chapter Six

Briony hardly strayed from Patrick's side all day. He seemed to like having her there where he could touch her arm and be sure he wasn't about to take a step into open space. When John Donahue's friends came to pay their last respects, she cued him in with a quiet word as to who had just arrived so he didn't have to fumble for names or worry over vaguely remembered voices. The callers all went away murmuring among themselves at how amazing was Patrick's recall, not to mention the confident way he moved beside the lovely Hammond girl.

Patrick heard their whispers and shared an amused triumph with Briony, which was all the reward she could ever want.

What with all the coming and going at the Donahue house, and with the funeral set for Saturday, Lizzie insisted on working over the weekend to help. She wore her black uniform with its frilly starched white cap and apron, and she nearly drove Patrick mad by pouncing on him at the most unexpected and inopportune moments to cry all over his collar and hug him. "Comforting him," she called it, although everyone secretly knew it was old Lizzie who wanted comforting.

"She's taking it hard, bless her heart," Briony sympathized, watching Patrick change shirts for the second time on Friday afternoon, Lizzie having just smeared mascara and rouge all over the front of the one he had been wearing.

He nodded. "I guess she's bound to be wondering how much longer she'll have a job now that her boss has died."

Briony had been wondering that herself, anxious to know whether Patrick would cut short his stay in Austin, but it was an untimely subject for discussion now. "It's more than just that," she protested. "Lizzie's really fond of you Donahues. How long has she worked for your dad?"

Patrick stood at the open door of his closet, feeling the little metal color-coded tags sewn out of sight under the collars of his shirt. He found another white shirt and took it down from its hanger. Briony enjoyed the sight of his bare tanned back, the muscles flexing beneath his skin as he pulled the shirt on and turned. "Lizzie Belle was the third housekeeper Dad hired after my mother died. The first two didn't work out for some reason or another. Lizzie was a disaster in her own way, but once she had found us, she never let go for a second. Dad couldn't have fired her if he had wanted to." He laughed quietly. "And I don't think he ever really considered it."

"Although he threatened," Briony remembered, smiling too.

"Oh, yes, he threatened, and she pretended to worry that he meant it. It was all an act, I think, to entertain me. I never took it seriously."

"I can't imagine life around here without Lizzie," she mused. "She's been here since you were four?"

"Four or five. Around the time you were born. She knew me when."

When he could see, he meant. There were only a handful of people left in his life who had known him when, and they were most of them here now. Ryan and Esmé and Lizzie were all downstairs with the visitors.

"Steve will be here tonight," she told him, watching him tuck his shirttail into his pants, and he nodded, already knowing that. "Steve and Carol and little Carly," she added. "They didn't have Carly when they drove to New Hampshire on vacation to see you, did they? She's only two."

"Uh-uh. Their trip was three years ago."

"I really like Carol," Briony remarked.

"So do I." He picked up a brush from the top of the chest of drawers and used it on his neat, slightly curly hair. "She sent me a picture of Carly, did you know that? I guess in her motherly pride, she got carried away and forgot I couldn't see it. She included it with a letter she and Steve had taped for me, and I wasn't sure what it was until I asked a neighbor to look at it."

Briony didn't know whether to laugh or cry at her sister-in-law's gaffe, so she merely asked, "Did you send it back?"

"Good Lord, no! Do I seem that tactless? I carry it in my wallet, in a place of honor, as a matter of fact. No one else has given me a picture in twenty years." He was smiling a little as he said that, but unaccountably she found it a sad confession.

Abruptly Patrick replaced the hairbrush and turned to face her squarely. "How's that? Am I clean, all zipped up, and presentable? Does anything clash?"

She pretended to inspect him, although she had watched every step of his slow but thorough grooming process and knew he hadn't neglected a detail. "Hmmm... not bad," she pondered aloud. "I could go for you myself."

He raised one hand to his cheek. "What about this? Does it still look awful?"

"Actually, no. Your eye is still a little discolored, but the swelling is down and you have to get pretty close to notice it. From a distance you seem your usual devastatingly attractive self."

Making a successful grab for her hand, he pulled her close to him and grinned in her direction. "Watch the sarcasm, my child, or—"

"Or what?"

He didn't finish the threat because at that moment Esmé Hammond tapped on the closed door. "Patrick? There's a Patty Shafer on the telephone for you. And do you know where Briony is?"

Patrick made as if to release her, but Briony linked arms with him and moved over to the door to open it. "Here, Mom. Need me for something?"

She met her mother's eyes bravely. *You see, I'm really and truly all grown up. I go in men's bedrooms and close the door. No, not just men's rooms, but Patrick's. And, yes, I know you disapprove, but since I'm twenty-six there's not a whole lot you can do about it, except make a scene, and you're definitely not the screaming shrew type. Not my gentle well-bred mother.*

She wondered, though, at the way Patrick had stiffened slightly, and the uncomfortable look on his face.

"Lizzie thought you might help her mix up some of that lime punch for the non-coffee drinkers in the crowd," Esmé said calmly, her gaze not wavering from Briony's.

"Oh." Briony didn't move.

"She's in the kitchen, waiting for you."

"All right." Still she hesitated, wondering what Patrick would say to Patty Shafer—whoever Patty Shafer was. Briony suspected it was the gorgeous airline stewardess from his flight into Austin. "Tell Liz I'll just deliver Patrick to the telephone first and then I'll be right there."

Patrick tried once more to pull away from her, but she refused to relinquish him. "I can find the phone myself," he said, annoyed.

"Of course." Esmé reached out and took his arm from her daughter firmly. "But I can walk a handsome young man to the telephone as well as she can, and I'll enjoy it more, since I don't get the chance that often. Come along, dear. Patty sounded lovely, and quite anxious to talk to you..."

By the time Briony finished helping Lizzie mix the punch, Patrick was off the telephone, and of course she couldn't ask him who had called or what he had said to his caller. But she was equally certain he wouldn't have made a date to see her today. Sighing with relief, she resumed her place by his side.

A few minutes later one particularly long-winded army buddy of Uncle John's cornered Patrick for the purpose of retelling old war stories. The man seemed to think that because Patrick couldn't see his graphic gestures, the accompanying sound effects should be that much more thunderous.

Briony carefully watched Patrick, whose ears must have been sensitive to loud and unexpected noises anyway. When it became apparent to her that he was trying not to flinch at the man's descriptive version of artillery shells and hand-grenade explosions, she decided she'd better rescue him before he himself exploded.

"Patrick"—she tugged at his arm the next time the man paused for breath, her voice urgent—"it's time for your medicine!"

Patrick turned a blank stare toward her. "My medicine?"

"Your *medicine*!" she repeated. "You know how important that is. You know what happens if you forget to take it. Come along with me now." She touched the older man on the arm and whispered confidingly, "You'll excuse us, won't you? Patrick can't skip his medicine, you know."

"Of course, of course," the man murmured, wondering doubtfully what kind of medicine the healthy-looking Patrick had to take. Was it something for his eyes?

Briony clutched Patrick's hand and pulled him with her out of the room, down the hall, and into the kitchen. There, she broke into giggles at the expression on his face, while he leaned back against the counter and crossed his arms on his chest.

"Medicine?" he queried, his voice shaded with an odd mixture of disapproval and amusement.

"Don't complain," she managed to gasp when her laughter finally died away. "It got you out of there, didn't it?"

"Yes, it did," he conceded. "I guess I should be grateful for that and stop worrying about what you did to my image."

She stepped directly in front of him and placed her hands on his arms. "I'll take your gratitude like this." And she leaned forward just enough to kiss him on the lips.

Her heart soared with joy as his firm mouth welcomed her soft one and began to seduce it. For once in her life Patrick was returning her kisses with whole-hearted enthusiasm—and here it was broad daylight!

Sliding her hands up the front of his shirt and over his shoulders, Briony clasped them behind his head. This way she could hold his hard warmth close to her from breast to thigh. She recognized that the burning in her loins was desire, pure and simple, and that there was only one way to satisfy it. *This kiss*, she thought desperately, *isn't making it any easier!*

Reluctantly she pulled her mouth away from his and rested her head on his shoulder, her eyes closed. "I think"—she sounded breathless—"I'm getting carried away. I think I'd better calm down."

"Me too." His voice was low and husky. He continued to lean against the cabinet, cradling her in his arms with her head under his chin.

She loved it there. It was such a comfortable, comforting place to be. After a few minutes her erratic heartbeat slowed down and she opened her eyes and gazed happily out the window that was visible beyond Patrick's shoulder.

She saw the man then, a man of medium height and build with reddish brown hair and wearing a conservative gray business suit. He stood alone between several cars in the crowded driveway, studying the concrete at his feet, his hands shoved in his pockets. At first she thought nothing about it. All day long there had been so many people stopping by that what was one more strange face?

But none of the others had stayed alone like that, outside, looking almost...guilty. And this man seemed somehow familiar in a way that nagged at her. Oddly familiar. The red hair....

"Tom Clayton," she said aloud, barely a whisper.

"What?"

"I think," Briony ventured, "Tom Clayton is outside."

Straightening up, Patrick released her. "Here? Tom Clayton?" He frowned. "Are you sure?"

"No, I'm not." Now she peered out the window at the man who had half turned so his profile was all that was visible to her. "I haven't seen Tom Clayton since your accident, I guess, so I'm not sure at all, but he looks a little like I remember. Tom *did* have red hair, didn't he?"

Patrick nodded. "And freckles. What's he doing?" Briony told him, and he made a small movement of what she thought was resignation, almost a slight squaring of his shoulders. "All right. Let's go outside."

"You're going to talk to him?"

"Yes, Briony," he said dryly. "I'm going to talk to him."

"What are you going to say?"

"Well, let's see. First I'll probably say, 'Hi, there. I'm Patrick Donahue. Do I know you?' And then, depending on who he turns out to be—"

"Okay, okay, smartass. Let's go."

At the door he halted and said, "Maybe I should use my cane."

"Where is it?"

"I'm pretty sure I left it in my bedroom. He may leave while I go look for it. Oh, hell!" he swore, then sighed. "You'll have to do."

"Thanks a lot," she hissed as he took her elbow, and he sent her an absentminded smile.

When she shut the kitchen door behind them, the man turned quickly, looking startled. He watched the two of them approach, his sharp brown eyes skimming over Briony and then focusing on the tall blond man who strolled along beside her, seeming to hold her arm for no reason except that he wanted to.

Patrick spoke as soon as Briony stopped. "Hello?"

Briony added a bright "Hi!" to let him know he was on the right track.

Still eyeing Patrick, the man didn't seem to know what to say. He had a square, blunt-featured face with a few freckles on his nose—probably a mere fraction of those he had sported as a youngster—and Briony thought he looked like he would be a nice person to know, but for that dark look of repressed pain in his eyes.

When the silence stretched, Patrick's gaze shifted toward Briony, his face uncertain. She wished she could tell him *Chin up, darling. It's Tom. I know it's Tom.*

As if he'd gotten her unspoken message, Patrick's clear green eyes moved back in search of the other presence that he sensed was nearby, and he ended up staring at the man's chest. "Tom Clayton?" he said, determined to get an answer this time.

The man's face whitened, confirming for Briony that it was indeed the one who had accidentally blinded Patrick so long ago. "Yes," he finally mumbled, his voice hoarse. "Hello, Patrick."

At the greeting Patrick lifted his eyes higher and turned loose of Briony to extend his right hand. After a brief hesitation Tom shook it.

"It's good to see you Tom," Patrick said with quiet sincerity. He must have felt Tom's tremor of shock, because he quickly added, "That's just a figure of speech."

"Oh." Tom sounded faint, and Briony saw that he was still very pale. She thought with a twinge of sympathy that this meeting must be difficult for him.

Patrick released Tom's hand and waved his own in a gesture that encompassed the driveway. "What are you doing waiting around out here? Why didn't you come inside?"

"I guess...I was trying to work up my nerve," the other man admitted, giving Briony cause to admire his honesty.

Patrick merely nodded.

"I'm not sure I'd ever have decided on my own to come, but I saw in the paper about your father, and my—my wife said...well, she said I should have come a long time ago, but that if I wanted to keep living with myself I'd better come now." Tom swallowed, watching Patrick's unfocused eyes. His forehead beneath the reddish hair was beaded with perspiration and that expression of pain darkened his whole face now. "I want you to know how sorry I am...about your father... and...about *everything*."

For a tense moment Briony felt the anguished words hang in the air between the men, and then Patrick accepted the apology with another small nod and a simple "Thank you, Tom." Raising his head, he reached for Briony's arm. "Let's go inside and have a cup of coffee. We've got a few years to catch up on. Did you say you were married?"

Once back inside, Patrick gently pushed Briony in the direction of the dining room, where the coffee urn was set up. "Two cups of coffee, please, waitress, and make mine black." While the red-haired man looked on, impressed, Patrick found a chair at the kitchen table on his own, sat down, and motioned to another nearby chair. "Have a seat, Tom. How would you like your coffee?"

"Black will be fine, thanks," Tom murmured as he took the seat indicated.

Briony brought their coffee and slipped out of the room again, noting with a rueful smile that neither man knew when she left. For half an hour she guarded the kitchen to keep out any possible interlopers, and then Patrick appeared in the doorway, calling her name. "Briony? Where are you?"

She moved over at once and took the hand he held out. "Need more coffee?"

"No. Tom reminded me I didn't introduce you two. Come on back and meet him before he goes."

The change in the other man was dramatic. He was standing up straighter, and he no longer had that almost furtive look about him. He smiled at Briony and even laughed, although obviously still a little awed, when Patrick said, "You remember Steve's sister, don't you, Tom? Briony's a whole lot prettier than a guide dog, wouldn't you say?"

"She sure is," he agreed, but he was looking at Patrick as he said it, and Briony knew he wanted to believe Patrick was as well-adjusted as he seemed.

"Tom's been telling me about his work," Patrick informed her. "He invited me down to the police department for a tour, and you can come along if you're interested."

"Oh, I am!" she exclaimed at once. "I'm probably going to teach a criminology course next semester, and I'll need all the inside help I can get."

"Feel free to call on me any time," he offered. They talked for a few minutes more before Tom glanced at his watch with regret and said that he really had to get back to work. "I'll stop by next week to see when would be the best time for you to come down to headquarters."

"Great. I'll see you then."

The policeman couldn't help giving Patrick one more close look at that, but there was no sarcasm in his tone, nor bitterness in his manner. It really was just a figure of speech as far as Patrick was concerned, and it didn't bother him in the least to use it.

"Okay," Tom said. "See you then."

Just then Lizzie came in to insist that Patrick return to the living room and speak to several guests who hadn't yet seen him. Briony walked Tom part of the

way to his car, despite his protest that it wasn't necessary.

"I wanted to tell you how glad I am you came," she
said warmly.

"So am I!" he replied fervently. "You don't know
how close I came to staying away. I didn't think I could
ever face him again. Thank God I did, though. He's
terrific, Briony! Seeing him like this makes it possible
for me to forgive myself at last."

"There's nothing to forgive. Patrick has never blamed
you. He says it was an accident."

"So he told me just now." Tom looked as if he
couldn't really believe it. "All these years I've felt like
such a fool, not only for hitting him in the first place,
but for not being able to go to him afterward and apologize. I see now that he wanted to tell me not to feel bad
about it, but back then I was positive he planned to tell
me just what he thought of me for ruining his life." His
voice turned anxious. "You know him better than most
people, I guess. His life isn't ruined, is it?"

"Patrick's?" she asked in astonishment. "Good
heavens, no! Oh, I'm not saying it's easy being blind.
No one could ever think that. But he didn't put on an
act for you today. That was Patrick, the genuine article.
He does very well, and"—she smiled unconsciously—
"he's the most fantastic man in the world."

Tom nodded. "You'll get no argument from me
about that. I only hope someday I have a chance to do
something for him. Not because I feel guilty," he has-
tened to add, "but because I just want to."

The whole episode left Briony feeling very good, and
very proud of Patrick for the way he'd taken that load
of devastating guilt away from Tom.

Steve and his family arrived an hour later, having
driven down from Dallas, where he worked as a re-

search chemist for a major oil company. "Sorry about our delay in getting here," her unemotional brother muttered as he clasped Patrick's hand and then embraced him in a hug. Embarrassed, he pulled back almost immediately.

"Steven worked most of the night and until noon today, finishing up a project so he can take off next week," Carol explained in her soft contralto drawl.

"Do you mean to say you're going to stay a whole week?" Briony asked in delight, holding the squirming cuddly toddler who was the image of both her dark-haired, brown-eyed mommy and daddy.

"If the Hammonds can put us up," Steve confirmed.

"If they can't, there's plenty of room at the Donahue house," Patrick offered, and everyone laughed at the idea of Ryan and Esmé letting their only grandchild sleep anywhere but under their own roof.

A moment later Briony watched Steve lead Patrick aside, out of the general crush of people. "I'm sorry about Uncle John," she heard him say with difficulty. "Really sorry. I'd give a lot for him to be here to enjoy our reunion."

And Patrick answered, speaking too low for Briony to understand his words, but Steve agreed with whatever he said.

She compared them as they moved even farther apart from the rest. Patrick was tall, muscularly lean, and golden-haired; Steven, several inches shorter and a little stockier, had straight Indian-black hair that was forever falling onto his forehead, to his consternation. Their heads were close together in discussion of something, perhaps trivial or perhaps near and dear to their hearts—their faces didn't reveal which. She had a notion to move closer and eavesdrop, but it was just a fleeting thought that she tabled without much consideration, respecting their right to privacy for this long-overdue visit.

Dear Steven! Her heart swelled with pride as she saw once again how her brother acted around his best friend. There was no shrinking from him, no condescension or pity, no overloud talk as if he were not just blind but deaf as well. Probably more than any of the rest of them, Steve knew Patrick's limitations, by virtue of having spent so much time with him when they were kids. Whenever necessary, Steve offered to help. When Patrick could do something himself, Steve let him do it, no matter how difficult it appeared to everyone else. Unlike Briony, Steve didn't sometimes take Patrick's arm just for the sake of touching him. Reluctantly she acknowledged to herself that it would be good for Patrick to have Steve home for a while, even if it meant she had to share him.

It was Steve who drove Patrick to the funeral home that evening for his final, unobserved farewell to his father. After a late supper, when all the superfluous guests had departed, the two of them disappeared again out into the brisk fall night for a long walk.

Esmé and Carol had long since retired next door to put Carly to bed, so Briony and Dr. Hammond were alone in the Donahue kitchen, drinking hot chocolate, when the two younger men came in the back door.

"I thought the class seemed awfully reticent about asking questions after my lecture," Patrick was saying with a grin, "especially since their regular professor had assured them he would arrive in time to give them a quiz on the material I covered. I don't know how long I might have continued trying to get them interested in Shiloh, if their honest-to-goodness prof hadn't finally found the nerve to stand up and make his presence known to me and tell me I was in the wrong class. A

Spanish class, at that," he put in for Briony and Ryan's benefit, shaking his head and laughing over it. "The poor guy was so apologetic, he almost had me convinced it was his fault."

"What did you do?" Steve queried, chuckling along with the others.

"What *could* I do? I gathered up my notes and tried to make a dignified retreat. By that time I was sure the students would have gone from the class where I was supposed to be filling in. But as soon as I stepped out into the corridor, they found me. They'd evidently figured out that I was probably lost, and had scouts out all over the place looking for me. So I repeated my lecture, or an abbreviated version of it, and talked their prof into forgoing the quiz. There wasn't time for it, anyway. Needless to say, Princeton has never asked me back."

"That's their loss," Briony commented indignantly.

"Do you think so?" Patrick asked with interest.

"Yes, I do, and I'll bet the kids in that class where you lectured would agree with me. That reminds me, I've been delegated by the students in my sociological research class to invite you to come to class on Tuesday. They'd like to meet you."

"Why?" He looked suddenly suspicious. "How did they happen to hear of me?"

"Oh"—she grinned over at her father—"you can thank the president of Drey-Bart for that. It seems that when he was boasting about your exploits to my theory class the other day, he really fired their imaginations. I think they want to see your bag of tricks, to decide for themselves if you're really the eighth wonder of the world."

Patrick grunted, and she added quickly, "No, what they really want is to talk to you about the hurdles you overcame on your road to success."

He made a face. "That sounds like the story line on a bad soap opera."

"Don't forget," Ryan Hammond threw in philosophically, "not everyone is as familiar as you are with what people with disabilities can do. You may be tired of hearing your own success story, Patrick, but it can have a positive influence on others."

"Who knows how many lives you may change by sharing your experiences," Steve said dryly.

"Yes, well, let's not get carried away with our expectations," Patrick muttered, moving over to stand behind Briony's chair at the table, putting his hands on her shoulders to rub gently. "Was the invitation for real?" She nodded, knowing he could feel the movement beneath his hands. "Well, I'll certainly consider it." He stopped stroking her to check his braille watch. "Shouldn't you be in bed, Bri? It's past your bedtime—nearly midnight."

"Better go home or you'll turn into a pumpkin," Steve urged her.

"Ho, ho. I can outlast the best of you. You're not getting rid of me so you can talk man-talk and keep Patrick up all night. Besides, Steven, I'm staying upstairs. Here—not next door."

"Why? We're not putting you out of your room, are we?"

"Not at all. I...we—we just, er, decided it would be better all around if I stayed here a while," she stammered, noting her father's quiet watchfulness, Patrick's listening attitude and Steve's puzzled frown.

"Who's 'we'?"

"Oh...Uncle John and I. He was worried because, er, well, you see— Did you notice Patrick's black eye?"

Patrick turned his head a little, but Steve only gave it

a glance. "Yes. So what? I can't remember seeing Patrick too many times that he didn't sport a black eye or some other trophy of a battle with a stationary object."

"Right, but sick as Uncle John was, we thought it best to reassure him that Patrick would be okay. That I would be here in case he needed me."

"Oh, I see." Steve didn't sound as if he saw at all. "So you've been staying over here at night?"

"Right."

Steve's frown cleared up. "Well, I tell you what. *I'll* stay here instead."

"Oh, no," Briony started to protest, but her brother insisted.

"Sure, no problem. Carol gets me all year. She'll probably be glad to give me up for a few days. It'll give us a chance to do more catching up, Patrick."

"I told you, Patrick should go on to bed. We all should. It's been a long day, and tomorrow won't be easy," she argued. "Carol said you were up all night working, Steve. You just get yourself on home. Dad, take him home." She rose and pulled her father to his feet, pushing him toward his son.

When Ryan hesitated, eyeing both his children to see which one was going to win the skirmish, Patrick spoke up quietly with the deciding vote. "Don't be offended, old buddy, if I prefer Briony this time."

"But—"

"It takes a special person to be as comforting as your sister has been lately. If she hadn't been here last night, I don't know what shape I'd be in today."

Briony watched Steve reluctantly accept Patrick's choice, still not looking pleased about it. A moment later the Hammond men had said good night and gone, and Briony locked the door after them.

It wasn't until they were upstairs, lingering outside

his bedroom, that she wondered aloud, "Did you mean what you said about me?"

"That I couldn't have made it last night without you? Yes. Your parents remarked earlier today how much better I looked. More relaxed. Not so fragmented. That's how I feel too."

She smiled to herself. "And do you suppose they're too naive to know just how I wrought such a miracle on your behalf?"

"I think they trust you." He sounded stern.

"And you." She laughed softly and threw her arms around his neck, startling him. "You're priceless, Patrick Donahue! I do believe you're about to go all protective of my morals and refuse to let me share your bed again."

His expression sheepish, his lazy eyes stared down at her nose. "Does that seem so ridiculous? Your father and brother have just left us alone. I'll feel like a heel if I betray their confidence in me."

"What if I didn't have a father or brother?"

"I don't know. Maybe I'd have to come up with some inner strength of my own."

She pressed closer to him, determined to get him to acknowledge some of the wildfire she was feeling for him right now, the electric charges running up and down her limbs, the aching need that stirred her to the very center of her being.

Instead, he removed her arms from his neck and stepped back.

"Darn it, Patrick!" she sighed. "I'd say you have more than your share of inner strength, and it's frustrating the hell out of me just now."

"I told you it was addictive, didn't I? One of us has to be strong."

"Why? And don't say it's because I'm engaged."

"Because you could get pregnant. If last night was your first time, I don't suppose you've been on the pill, have you?"

"No, but couldn't you—"

"I could, except that I'm not prepared. I was coming home to visit my old dear friends, the Hammonds, with their sweet little girl Briony. Charming child. No one told me I'd need a supply of contraceptives to make it through the first week."

When she gasped, he reached for her quickly, wrapping her tightly in his arms. "I'm sorry! I didn't mean that the way it sounded. I was trying to be funny, because I'm having a hard time convincing myself to keep this safe." He kissed her eyes. "You're so sweet and giving, Briony! I could take what you have so easily and leave you with nothing."

"If you loved me just a little," she whispered shakily, "I would have all I want."

He groaned. "Don't say things like that! Don't you know what you're doing to all my inner strength?"

"I hope I'm destroying it."

"Bit by bit." He nodded. "Shred by shred, it's leaving me." He buried his face in her hair and shuddered. When he raised his head his face looked at peace. "Do you want to stay with me again?"

"Yes, I do," she said honestly. "Now here's one for you: Do you want me to stay with you again?"

"What a question! Of course I want you to stay! I'm tired of the dark, Briony. Oh, yes, I want you."

She left the light on, partly because she wanted to enjoy the sight of him in bed, naked and beautiful, partly because he had said, "I'm tired of the dark." Of course the soft glow from the bedside lamp didn't help Patrick, but it symbolized Briony's intent to dispel his darkness in every way she could.

Tonight they undressed each other with tantalizing slowness, and to Briony it was a ritual of love, unbuttoning his shirt, reaching inside to caress his smooth golden chest, moving down to his pants and undoing the belt buckle, then the zipper; seeing him harden and grow demanding before her very eyes; watching his persuasive hands remove each item of her clothing and pause in between to entice her with feathered strokes and kisses that inflamed every inch of her slender body.

By the time they faced each other in a completely natural state, their mutual awareness was like an electrical field humming between them. Staring at his blatant masculinity, Briony thought she would cry out with the sharp pain of desire if he touched her, yet when he did—when he took her hand and drew her with him to lie down upon the bed—she could only sigh her pleasure and smile against his throat. He gathered her into his arms and molded her soft form to his strong hard one, making them a single entity again, a merging that was as inevitable as every sunrise.

Tonight their communion climaxed in an explosion of sensational feeling that left Briony clinging to Patrick in happy exhaustion. Neither seemed capable of speaking, nor was there anything that needed to be said. She wanted only to touch him, and later, to move back just a little so she could lie there and study his long-limbed perfection. She knew it was a sight she would never tire of gazing upon....

"Bri?" he asked quietly, shifting his head in her direction. An hour had slipped away during which both had lain in mellow languour with their bodies touching lightly at shoulders and hips. "What are you doing? Not sleeping?"

"No, watching you. My favorite pastime."

"Can you see me?" He raised his eyebrows. "Is the light on?"

"Yep. I left it on just for this purpose, so I could see you, all of you."

"Oh." He smiled slightly. "Well, be my guest. I hope you enjoy it."

"Thank you, sir. I intend to."

"Tell me something, Briony?" His voice had become suddenly grave.

"Anything, Dr. Donahue," she returned.

"Seriously, Bri. This isn't something I can ask just anyone." He seemed uncomfortable, and she tilted her head so she could see him better. In the dim light she recognized a sober face he seldom showed the rest of the world. "I remember how I looked as a ten-year-old, but I've often wondered what I look like now."

As she stared at him in shocked silence, her heart lurched with sadness and tears brimmed her eyes. *Oh, Patrick! Oh, darling, of course you'd want to know. How could I—how could all of us—never have guessed at your very natural curiosity?*

Too choked up to speak, Briony had no choice but to remain silent another minute, and Patrick's expression grew increasingly embarrassed. His eyes slanted down on her shoulder, he muttered, "I didn't want to ask Dad, after all." Still she couldn't find her voice, and he finally gave a short laugh. "It's that bad, huh? You're scared to tell me?"

She slid over and turned to put her arms around his neck, pulling his face close to hers. Kissing each lazy eye, she said huskily, "Patrick, you know damned well you're the handsomest man in town."

Although he didn't withdraw from her, he didn't exactly respond to her embrace, either. His chest was warm and vital, rising and falling deeply against her bare breasts. "I don't want flattery, Briony. I want to know what I look like."

Settled against his hard length, she scrutinized the rugged contours of his beloved face. The blond hair, golden tanned skin, unforgettable green eyes, oft-broken nose, firm mouth, and strong jawline, all combined to make him an incredibly sexy-looking man. Feeling her recently sated need come to life again deep inside her, she confessed, "You, my darling Patrick, are the best of Ryan O'Neal and Burt Reynolds and Robert Redford all rolled into one gorgeous man."

"Damn it all," he sighed with mild frustration. "I don't have any idea what Ryan O'Neal and Burt Reynolds and Robert Redford look like. I've never *seen* them."

"Oh!" She thought for a moment. "Well, then, what if I said you were better looking than Rock Hudson and Cary Grant and Clark Gable? Is that any help? And you are, by the way."

In spite of himself, he laughed with wry good humor. "Come on, Briony. You're trying to snow me. I know I have a crooked nose. What about the rest? Do I have any scars I'm not aware of?"

"Listen, buster"—she kissed his nose—"don't slander this. As far as I'm concerned, it's your best feature."

"That doesn't say much for the rest of me, does it?" But he was still smiling. "So what about scars?"

"No scars."

"No?" He raised one hand to his face and ran his fingers over it with quick, sure movements, as if searching intently. "You may be telling me the truth, at least about my not having any scars, but I can't help wondering what I look like as a man."

She pushed his hand aside and replaced it with both

her own. Gently, caressingly she traced his forehead, eyebrows and cheeks, and excitement traveled from her fingertips all the way to her toes, inch by shocking inch. Leaning forward, she brushed her soft lips down his nose and over his mouth, then across his obstinate chin to his jaw.

"Patrick," she murmured when her mouth reached his ear, "take my word for it, you're beautiful."

"Mmmm..." he responded in a low growl, twisting against her and holding her to his virile warmth. "I guess I'll have to take your word for it, since I don't seem to have much choice." He began to nibble at her hungrily, thrilling both of them with the silk of his lips against her satiny body. "And you are delicious," he informed her hoarsely, moving over on top of her to partake once more of the ultimate communion between them, a communion that would last all night long.

"It's funny," Partick observed later, sounding a little sleepy, a little dreamy, his voice vibrating softly on her cheek and in her ear.

"What's funny?"

"How you make me forget the darkness when I hold you like this. You brighten things up for me, like my very own source of light."

Her breath caught in her throat. "That's all I want to be. Your light."

"Just don't ever go out, hmm?" His arms tightened. "You're so much better than the dark."

It took her a while to get up the courage, but finally she asked, "Is your darkness very black? Is it that awful, scary black that nightmares are made of?"

Patrick roused himself in surprise. "I thought I told you... it's not really black at all. It's brown." She made a small sound, and he moved one hand enough to touch her damp face. "Briony, don't!" he protested at once. "Don't cry. There's something almost soothing about a world of soft velvet brown." He was smiling at her, his face very close, his eyes so beautiful she felt herself drowning in them.

"Anyway," he went on in a low voice, "sometimes I make it red or blue or yellow... any color that I decide I want to surround myself with. It's just a matter of using my imagination, after all."

She sniffed, blinking away the tears. "You remember colors pretty well, I guess?"

He nodded his head against her. "I remember all the brightest colors... the most breathtaking sunsets and fields of wild flowers and night skies full of stars so brilliant, so close, you can almost reach out and touch them."

"Is it all beautiful, all that you remember?" she asked with tender curiosity.

"Sure. That's one nice thing about being blind: You can make the world as beautiful as you like. Sometimes I remember the whole world as a rainbow"—his hand sliced a long arc in the air over them—"after a spring shower. And then I thank God I had my vision for ten years. Ten years of rainbows, sunshine, and people, Briony. I'm damned lucky."

Not for the first time tonight Briony was too moved to speak. Without a word she turned into his arms, pressing her mouth over his and letting her kisses tell him of her love for him. By the time they finally drifted off to sleep, she knew he had gotten her message.

The funeral was over. The first-day-of-November afternoon had been unseasonably warm and sunny as they stood by the grave, bidding a respectful good-bye to a fine old gentleman.

In spite of all those watchful eyes Patrick had neither stumbled nor groped. He had taken it well, as they said to each other in awe. The young man would make it all right, and there had been some who doubted if he would.

Of course the girl at his side must have had something to do with it. His hand remained clasped in hers, except when he held her arm just above the elbow as they walked. They made a remarkably good-looking couple, his blindness obviously meaning nothing to her. Rumor was, she had loved him for years. He couldn't see the adoration on her face, but women did have ways of letting men know. Another rumor was that the girl had been seen coming out of the Donahue house very early one morning since Patrick got home, that she had been spending the night there every night, with her own home and parents right next door.

"I heard talk today," Steven said in an undertone, dropping down into a chair at the table in the Hammond kitchen as Briony scrubbed potatoes to boil for dinner. "It wasn't intended for my ears, but I heard it."

"What kind of talk?" she asked, her curiosity piqued at his unhappy look.

"Talk about you and Patrick. Speculation as to just what's going on between you. It seems word is out that you've been staying next door."

She shut off the water and leaned back against the sink. "Neighborhood gossips are at it, huh?"

Shrugging, he met her eyes levelly. "I'm not surprised. Are you? That kind of thing would be frowned on here."

"*What* kind of thing?"

He compressed his lips. "Living together. A casual affair."

She smiled in spite of herself. "Do you think Patrick and I are having a casual affair?"

"I don't know.... There's something different about you two this time."

"There's nothing different about *me*. And what I feel for him is not at all casual."

"That's what I was afraid of." Steve stood up abruptly and paced around the room a time or two, then sat back down to scowl at her. "Times like this, I'd like nothing better than to paddle you, baby sister."

"Dear Lord"—she rolled her eyes heavenward—"how many more people am I going to have to remind that I'm not a child any longer? I ... am ... a ... woman!" She spoke the words slowly for emphasis. "I don't need protecting."

His brown eyes raked over her grown-up figure assessingly, and then scanned her face again. "You look it, but I don't think you're acting the part. I used to hope you'd outgrow this adolescent thing you have for Patrick, but I see you haven't yet."

Briony stiffened. "I hoped you'd approve of the way I feel about him."

"Approve!" he all but shouted, then quickly lowered his voice. "You've got to be kidding!"

Briony's green eyes widened at him. How could she have been so wrong about Steve? Her own brother, whom she loved dearly and admired to no end, had the same prejudices she had observed so often in others! His were just better hidden and only surfaced with provocation.

Shock and disappointment gave her delicate features a vulnerability as her eyes filled with tears. "Oh, Steven!" she breathed, appalled. "You of all people!"

"Me of all people?" he repeated. He rose deliberately and walked over to her, gazing down into her face, his dark eyes puzzled. "Why are you looking at me like that?"

"I thought you were his friend! I never suspected you would hold his blindness against him."

"His blindness?" He gaped at her. "What the hell does his blindness have to do with any of this?" Understanding dawned suddenly, and with it came outrage. "You think I don't approve because he's blind?" His brow lowered dangerously. "You think *that*?"

"Isn't that it?"

Steve put his hands on her shoulders and shook her. "I'm worried about you, because you're playing way out of your league. You're very likely to get hurt."

"Is that all?" Relief flooded through her, leaving her weak. She clung to the cabinet on either side of her for support. "I know what I'm doing."

"Do you? I doubt it. You've always been so open to being hurt, by Patrick anyway, and he's never really known it. I sometimes used to think he didn't want to know how he held your heart in his hands, because if he knew, he'd have to be responsible for it."

This, from Steven? Briony stared.

He went on quietly. "Patrick's the closest thing to a brother I've ever had, and if he loved you the way you love him, no one would be happier than me. I would give anything, except Carol and Carly, if you two could find the kind of happiness together that we have. But you being you, and Patrick being Patrick, I'm afraid you're in for some bad times."

She didn't want to hear this, but she had to. "Why? Why is it so hard for you to imagine him loving me?"

"Oh, honey"—he touched her cheek—"he may love you, but that won't stop him from loving others too. Remember, we went through quite a few romances together back in high school and college and I had plenty of opportunity to watch him at work. Patrick's a born charmer. I say that with admitted envy. Part of his charm is his blindness. He jokes about it, he's very brave, and sometimes he can seem helpless. That's a pretty potent combination. I can't name all the girls it knocked for a loop. At one point in my life I actually considered impersonating him, carrying a white cane."

She didn't laugh. "But you're talking about years ago. He's too mature for that now."

"He doesn't use it consciously. He never did. I told you, he's just got something the rest of us don't have—an extra helping of charm. When Carol and I visited him three years ago, it hadn't changed. The women are still there, calling him, coming by, offering to drive him to Timbuktu and back. And he's not any closer to settling down than he ever was."

No! Her heart protested. *Don't tell me that! I've been so sure I could make him love me…that he's already started loving me! I thought that's what the last two nights were all about.*

"Little sister," Steve went on, pulling her into an awkward hug, "can I give you one piece of advice? If you're thinking of throwing Dennis over just because Patrick's here, don't. You may not feel for Dennis what you feel for Patrick, but he's less likely to break your heart. Patrick—well, Patrick won't do it on purpose, but it will still have the same result. I'm sorry."

Chapter Seven

Steve meant well. Briony knew that, and loved him in spite of the way he had jerked the rug out from under her and made her look at Patrick with new eyes.

Watching Patrick closely at dinner, she saw how Carol and even her own mother were captivated by the story he told of getting lost in New York City when he was on his way to a conference of college history teachers at Columbia University. He had everyone except Briony roaring with laughter by the time he got to the part about having to ask his female taxi driver to escort him to the nearest men's room.

Right after dinner she came upon another scene that disturbed her. He was reclining in Ryan Hammond's favorite chair in the study when little Carly wobbled over to him, clutching a children's book, and climbed up on his lap. "Wead me," she demanded, pushing the book into his chest.

As the rest of the family were in the living room playing bridge, Patrick thought he had the room to himself. Briony had paused quietly in the hallway to watch, and he wasn't aware of her standing there outside the door.

"Read to you, hmm?" he asked, using both hands to shift Carly into a more comfortable position on one thigh, her head leaning back against him. "Okay, but first you tell me what's in the pictures."

As he turned the pages, Carly named the characters. "Pig, kitty, dog, moo-cow, horsie, chickie." The second time he went through the book, he told her a simple story about a sad little pig that envied all the other farm animals and dreamed about changing places with them. He tried being a cat, a dog, a cow, a horse, and a chicken, but he soon found something about each of those experiences that he didn't enjoy, and in the end, he returned to his pigpen a very contented pig.

It was the effortless way he delighted Carly that made Briony accept what her brother had been saying. He didn't really have to work at it. The soft plump little girl crowed with baby laughter and then cuddled sleepily against him when he finished. Patrick looked pretty content himself, his chin resting on top of Carly's curly head, his eyes closed.

He has a compulsion to charm every female in the place, and I'm just one of the available ones. The thought came to Briony as she stared at him, and it was followed swiftly by a shaft of cold anger.

With sudden businesslike movements she marched into the room and took the startled child from his arms. "I'm putting her to bed."

"No, no, no, Briney!" Carly protested, but Briony ignored the whimpers and hurried upstairs with her, where she spent half an hour soothing her back to sleep.

In her own bedroom Briony changed into her navy blue warm-up suit with white piping. Although she came down the stairs on tiptoes, she saw Patrick step out of the study and come toward her as if he had been listening for her.

"Briony?" He reached out to find her hand, and for

once she didn't help him. He moved closer to her, his expression becoming somewhat confused. "Briony?" he said again.

"Yes."

His face relaxed. "For a minute there I wondered if my ears were playing tricks on me." He did catch her hand then and laced his fingers through her stiff ones. "I guess it's too early for us to consider going to bed yet?"

Was that all he thought about? Was that all she had become for him now—someone to sleep with? "Yes, it is!" she snapped.

He looked surprised at her short answer. "Are you okay?"

"I'm fine." She added belatedly, "Thanks."

"I thought you seemed not quite yourself this evening. Are you sure you feel all right?"

"Quite sure." She tugged at her hand, trying to free it. "If you'll excuse me, I'm going out to run a couple of miles."

Holding her hand more firmly, Patrick gave her an appealing smile. "Great idea! Would you give me a few minutes to change clothes and let me come with you?"

She drew a deep breath. This was what she wanted, wasn't it? Two days ago she had been eager for such an invitation. Now....

"I don't know," she stalled. "I didn't plan to run on a track. I was just going to stay on the streets."

"There's not much traffic out now, is there?"

"Probably not a whole lot."

"I can manage, then. Wait for me, or do you want to come with me while I change?"

"I'll wait outside," she said coolly, reluctantly.

It was while she was walking briskly up and down the driveway, trying to keep warm, that she saw a dark form separate itself from the shadow of an elm tree and approach her. Before she had a chance to be afraid, she recognized the muscular young man.

"Chad!" she exclaimed in surprise. "What are you doing here?"

"Hi, Miss Hammond. I've been waiting to see if you'd come outside so I could talk to you. You weren't in class again yesterday." He made it sound like an accusation.

She explained briefly about the death of her long-time friend. "What did you need to talk to me about?"

"I've decided to write my paper about Max Weber, and I can't find anything about him in our library."

"I see. Well, several other students in class chose Weber as a topic, too, and it would seem that they've already checked out the books at Drey-Bart. It may be that you'll have to go over to the U.T. library, or perhaps the public library, to find anything. I have a list of titles in my office that may help you." She didn't point out that if Chad had been quicker in deciding on a topic, he wouldn't have run into this snag.

"Can you give it to me tonight?" he asked, surprising her with his eagerness.

"As I said, it's at school."

"I'll drive you there. While we're at it, I can show you my apartment—"

"No, Chad. I'm afraid not," she interrupted him. "I'm busy right now. Surely it can wait until Monday, can't it? The list of books, that is."

"I guess so," he agreed, still lingering and looking at her oddly in the darkness.

"I'm sorry you came all the way over here for nothing."

"I'm glad I came," he insisted. "I like this neighborhood. I like to come here."

As he glanced around at the other quiet houses, she felt a nagging little qualm. How had he known where she lived? Had he been here before?

"Well, the next time you want to talk to me, call. Don't just come over. You'll save both of us some inconvenience." She was pleased at the firmness of her tone. First thing tomorrow she needed to ask her mother what, if anything, Chad's records had shown, because suddenly he worried her.

"Are you going to jog?" he inquired.

"Yes. With a friend."

"Your fiancé?"

She shook her head. "No, another friend."

At that moment Patrick's front door opened and closed, and with relief she saw him standing on the step. "There he is now," she told Chad. "I'll see you in class Monday."

Turning her back on the student, she called out, "Here I am," and went to meet him in the middle of the yard. Chad, she saw, disappeared back into the dark shadows near the street.

Patrick's warm-up suit was plain gray, like his track shoes. Eyeing him in the glow from the streetlight, she had to acknowledge to herself that he looked splendidly masculine, a tall lithe athlete standing there with his hands on his lean hips, his head cocked to one side as if he were watching her approach.

"Did I hear you talking to someone?" he asked. "I didn't recognize the voice."

"It was just someone out for a walk," Briony evaded, not wanting to get into another discussion of Chad and his idiosyncrasies.

"Oh, okay." Patrick seemed willing to let the subject go. He handed her one end of a thick smooth cord. "The knot will keep this from slipping out of your hand," he said. "Don't wrap it around your wrist like one of my friends did."

"Why?" Her question was sulky.

"Because I fell, and pulled her down with me. If you'll just hold the cord, you can turn loose if you feel me start to go down."

"Why on earth would you think you're going to fall? Don't you expect me to look where we're going?" she asked impatiently, thinking that his "friend" must have had her head in a cloud. But was that so strange, around a man like Patrick?

"It's dark, isn't it?"

"Yes, but I'll keep us on well-lit streets. Good grief, if you have no faith in my ability to lead you, why run with me?"

He lifted his head, but she couldn't see his expression. "I get the feeling you'd rather not have me along, Briony. If it will bother you, the fact that I'll slow you down, just say so. Steve offered to run with me tomorrow."

"It won't bother me."

"The idea of running with a blind man puts off some people. You don't have to be ashamed to admit it if that's how you feel." There was an odd note in his voice, something she couldn't place. He added dryly, "I don't expect you to be the perfect seeing eye, after all."

"I said it won't bother me and I meant it," she muttered crossly.

Briony started out slowly, holding back out of some grudging concern for Patrick, but before they had gone far she discovered that if he looked in good shape, it was because he was in good shape. Excellent shape, in fact. With that knowledge, she opened up to full speed and ran lightly, while he stayed carefully a step behind her. From his smile and the way he held his head, she knew he was enjoying the cool wind blowing across his face.

Something tightened painfully in her stomach. Briony didn't want to feel the things she felt when she looked sideways at him. Admiration, desire, love.... *Damn it all, Patrick, do you have to be so lovable? Couldn't you have something that would make me sneer? Something besides an extra helping of charm, as Steve put it? I don't want to be just another in a long string of your conquests.*

"Did you ever finish taping that letter to your friend the other night?" she asked suddenly as they ran.

For a second he looked blank. "Oh, that. No."

"How come?"

"You interrupted me. By the time you left me alone, my nose was hurting too badly for me to think of anything else." He shot an ironic grin in her direction. "Why do you ask?"

"I just wondered." She was silent for another half a mile, but her busy mind wouldn't rest until she found out. "Well," she said brightly, "when will you be seeing Patty?"

"Patty?"

"Don't play dumb, Patrick!" She ground out the words. "Your stewardess friend. Didn't she call you yesterday?"

"Mmmm...was her name Patty?"

"You know very well it was. When do you have a date with her?"

He inclined his head toward her. "Would it bother you if I had a date with Patty?"

"Bother me?" Her laughter was forced. "Don't be silly! Why should I care who you go out with?"

Patrick hesitated before he answered. "I'm glad

you're not the possessive type," he said after a moment, his voice even. "I'll probably see her the next time she's in town."

"Great!"

He seemed to be frowning a little to himself, perplexed at her brittle gaiety, but neither of them talked anymore.

Back on their own block, they went first to the Hammond house to say good night to Briony's family.

"You wouldn't be interested in a game of gin rummy, would you?" Carol invited them. "No one here wants to play."

"That's because you beat us at bridge," Steve grumbled affectionately.

"Not me, thanks," Briony declined. "I think I'll go to bed." Let Patrick stay and do a number on his best friend's wife, if he needed feminine admiration.

But Patrick was shaking his head. "I'm tired. Briony said she was going to run a couple of miles, but we must have done five."

"Hey, you're just out of shape, old man!" Steve kidded him, patting his own flat stomach. "Now, me, I'll show you what good conditioning is when we run tomorrow."

Patrick groaned good-naturedly and took Briony's arm to leave.

"Oh, darling," Esmé called as they started out the door. "Dennis came by to see you while you were out. He asked that you call him tonight."

"All right," she agreed. "I need to see Dennis."

"You have been neglecting him a little, dear," her mother admonished her.

Later, as soon as she heard Patrick's shower running, Briony called Dennis and asked if he could drop by to see her. In his eagerness to please, he arrived ten minutes later, and Briony slipped out the front door, still wearing her running clothes.

He started to get out of his Mustang as she ran across the grass, but she motioned him back inside and climbed in to sit next to him. He put his hand to the ignition. "Can I take you out to eat?"

"Thanks, no."

"Please?" he asked, smiling very winningly at her. "I'm hungry. I waited to eat, hoping when you called we could have dinner together." Seeing the refusal on her lips, he hurried on, "Darling, you can't imagine how sorry I am for our misunderstanding the other day. It's all my fault. I'm just so darned jealous, I'm sure I acted unreasonable. Please let me make it up to you."

Briony shook her head. "I really can't go out with you tonight. And I want you to know you don't deserve all the blame for what happened. You had every right to be angry with me."

She could see that her announcement startled him. "I did? But I really shouldn't mind your being nice to Patrick. I've been telling myself that—"

"It was more than that, Dennis," she insisted. "In the first place, Patrick is a very attractive male, and he has an exceptional way of charming females. Every female he meets, in fact. Any male with good sense should keep an eye on him." There was an edge of bitterness to her voice that wasn't intended for Dennis. "In the second place, I haven't been fair with you. You were right: I was treating you shabbily. I would like to think that if I had loved you, I never would have neglected you like that." Her voice was softer now.

His eyes widening, he echoed, "If you had loved me? What are you trying to say, Briony?"

Despite the times she had rehearsed this mentally, it was still difficult. "I'm saying that . . . I don't love you,

Dennis, and...I'm very sorry." As she spoke, she removed her engagement ring and held it out to him.

Instead of taking it, Dennis just stared at her open palm in disbelief. "But—but *why*? We have so much going for us!"

"Individually, perhaps. Together, no. I'm afraid we don't have much in common at all."

"How can you say that? You're so beautiful, Briony! Everyone says we make such a great-looking couple. I don't understand...."

The sad thing was, he really didn't understand, she thought. "I guess," she began, struggling for tact, "I want to be more than just half of·a great-looking couple."

"But our goals—"

"No, Dennis, *your* goals. Your goals were all we ever talked about, and they're not the same as mine. I'm really very sorry." Now she picked up his rigid hand and put the ring in it, forcing his resistant fingers to close into a fist around it.

Bewildered, he stared down at their joined hands. "Briony, I don't want this ring." He sounded pained. "Please keep it. Think it over. You may change your mind. Don't do this to me now!"

"I won't be changing my mind."

For a minute he couldn't seem to say anything, and then he raised his head and his dark eyes met hers. As Briony watched, his expression grew sullen, his mouth twisting with scorn. "You're doing this because of Patrick Donahue, aren't you?"

"No, I'm not. I'm not breaking up with you in order to rush into Patrick's arms," she said in all honesty.

"Don't try to deny that you love him!" he snapped.

She only wished she could deny that. "All right, I won't. But I will tell you that what I'm doing now won't make a bit of difference in my friendship with Patrick. In fact, I don't even plan to tell him I'm no longer engaged."

"Well, I guess I should thank heaven for small favors," he sneered.

"What's that supposed to mean?"

By now all traces of his desire to please her had vanished. "Just that I'd hate to think what my friends would say if they knew you left me for a blind man." He made it sound like a dirty word. "It's going to be hard enough to explain without that crowning insult."

Her mouth dropped open at his crass bigotry, and she knew a strong impulse to scratch his eyes out.

"Oh, really?" she asked with deceptive sweetness as she opened the car door and got out. "Well, just tell them you dumped me when you discovered my one unforgivable deficiency."

"And what deficiency is that?" he inquired nastily.

"I didn't admire you one tenth as much as you admired yourself," she responded, her voice like ice. "Come to think of it, if you ever hope to find a girl who does, you'd better start looking right away. I have a feeling it may take a while."

Slamming the door with satisfying finality, she walked calmly back to the house.

After she showered and dried her hair, Briony went straight to bed in the guest bedroom, not saying good night to Patrick even though he had left a light on in his room, an obvious statement that he expected her. She could hear his favorite classical music through the wall between them, and the sweet sadness of the Chopin étude tugged at her heart. How could she take pleasure in having cleared her life of one major problem tonight, when another, bigger problem remained unsolved?

After a few minutes she heard Patrick's door open and then he turned her doorknob and appeared in the doorway of her room wearing a dark belted robe. Fingering the light switch, he found that it was in the "off" position and left it that way.

"Briony?"

"What?"

He walked directly to her voice until his knees hit the edge of the mattress, then stood over her in the shadowy room, lit only by a light in the hallway. "Why are you in bed?"

"You heard me tell the others I was going to bed. You said you were tired."

"But not *that* tired. I thought you were coming to bed with me."

"You presume too much." Somehow she kept her voice calm.

"I see." He thought a moment, everything about him slightly puzzled. "I apologize, then, by all means." He turned and walked as far as the door before he stopped again. "Did you go out a few minutes ago?"

"Yes."

"To see Dennis?"

"Yes."

"And how is he?"

With a terrible desperation she wanted to tell him, to see if it would make a difference to Patrick. If he knew she was no longer engaged, would he be more willing to accept the love she had offered so freely in the past?

But remembering Patty and all the others like her, Briony knew she had to use Dennis to balance the scales.

"Dennis is just fine, thank you."

"Good. Well, good night, Briony."

"Good night."

Perhaps if she hadn't had so much trouble falling asleep that night, she might not have slept so late on Sunday morning. By the time she awoke, it was nearly noon, and Lizzie had just about put the house back in order after all the commotion of the past few days.

As soon as she had dressed in jeans and a long-sleeved shirt, Briony looked around the house for Patrick, trying to appear as if she weren't really too interested in finding him. When her search proved futile, she headed for the kitchen door. "I think I'll go next door and visit with Carol," she called over her shoulder to Lizzie, who was putting away the good silver.

"Oh, she's not there," Lizzie informed her cheerfully. "She went with your brother and Patrick."

Briony halted and turned. "Where'd they go? Out running already?"

The housekeeper's frizzy red curls shook vigorously. "New Braunfels. The whatchamacallit."

"The *Wurstfest*?" Briony gasped, not quite believing the others would really have been so cruel as to go off and leave her when they were going to such an event.

"Uh-huh. *Wurstfest*. Now why can't I ever remember that name?" Lizzie mumbled to herself.

"When—when did they decide to go?"

"Well, darlin', at breakfast, I believe. Steven suggested it, and Carol was all for it, only she said they ought to wake you up so you could go too. But Patrick didn't think they should bother you. He said he heard you tossing and turning till late, and he thought you needed your sleep. So thoughtful, the dear boy is."

Briony's lips compressed. The dear thoughtful boy!

"Carol gave him a good argument about it, but then that friend of his called to say she was in town and had the day off and could she drive him somewhere. He ended up inviting her to go along."

"What friend?" But the pain in her stomach told her she already knew what the answer to that would be.

"Patty." Lizzie looked pleased. "She's a knockout, honey. Have you ever noticed how the prettiest girls seem to go for the dear boy? I recall how his daddy used to worry that the accident had ruined his life for good, but lookin' at him now, you'd never guess, would you?"

Briony ran upstairs without answering, fighting to hold back her tears.

So Patrick—and Steve and Carol, the traitors—had gone off to spend this glorious autumn day in New Braunfels, with Patty of all people! Briony felt betrayed, because Steve and Patrick at least were well aware that the *Wurstfest*, the Sausage Festival, was Briony's all-time favorite event. Better than a county fair, it was a noisy, exciting celebration that went on for ten days each November in the small German-settled town between Austin and San Antonio, a salute to the "best of the wurst."

There were plentiful helpings of homemade sausages of all kinds, as well as breads and pastries, but Briony loved most the traditional German bands, dancing groups, and folk singers in colorful costumes who performed for the crowds of visitors. Each time she had gone she had spent most of the time wishing she were there with Patrick, sharing it with the one person she cared about most in the world.

Once, a long time ago, he had half promised to take her to the *Wurstfest* "when you grow up." He and Steve had been about to leave for the festival with their dates, and the preteen-age Briony had begged to be allowed to go along. "One day, Bri," Patrick had soothed her.

And this is how he keeps his promises, she thought bitterly, staring at her tear-damaged face in the mirror.

Well, my girl, you claim to be grown up, so you'd better face it. The Patrick you fantasized about doesn't exist. He's just a charming shell, with no compulsion to be true to himself or anyone else. For your own sanity, give up your dreams!

Feeling subdued, as well as mildly tragic, Briony wandered next door and plopped down onto the couch in her parents' study. Ryan glanced up from the book he was reading to say hello, and Esmé smiled at her from the floor, where she was building a tower out of blocks with Carly.

"Morning, darling," her mother said. "Catch up on your rest?"

She nodded. "You two got stuck baby-sitting, huh?" she asked moodily.

Esmé laughed. "No, we didn't get 'stuck.' I volunteered for the job." She bent over and brushed her lips across the top of Carly's head, then looked straight at Briony. "Honey, are you upset at missing out on the trip to New Braunfels?"

"What do you think?" Darn her voice, it wouldn't stop shaking.

Esmé got to her feet and abandoned Carly to sit beside her only daughter and hug her. "Oh, Bri, believe me when I say I hate to see you hurt, but I think it's good that you're not with the others today. You've been spending so much time with Patrick since he came home, you're bound to let your hopes run away with you."

"Mom," she whispered, "you don't have to tell me I've been a prize fool for hoping." She shut her eyes against the humiliating tears.

"Not a fool, darling. A dear, loving, warm person. A young woman who has made me very proud to be her mother."

When Briony opened her eyes, she saw that her father was looking at her too, his handsome face lined with compassion. "Sweetheart," he said in his quiet voice, "you have all the qualities Patrick will need in a wife. I'm sorry for his sake if he doesn't know what he's looking for, or how close he has come to attaining it. Some men just never marry, you know. Please don't let that embitter you against men in general."

Her mother lifted Briony's left hand. "You've broken up with Dennis, haven't you?" she asked softly, and Briony nodded. Esmé squeezed her hand. "Well, perhaps that's for the best. It wasn't only because of Patrick that you gave him back his ring, was it?"

"No, it was... I guess it was seeing the way he acted around Patrick that made it crystal clear I couldn't love a man as shallow as Dennis. I tried awfully hard to convince myself I'd fall in love with him, but I couldn't. And I couldn't marry him, not loving him."

"Of course you couldn't," Esmé agreed.

"Do you think this will change anything as far as Patrick is concerned?" Ryan asked after a while, and Briony knew he hoped it would, that he would be pleased to have Patrick officially in the family.

Briony gave them both a small, tight smile. "I'll tell you what I told Dennis: I don't even want Patrick to know I've returned the ring."

As she watched, her parents exchanged a worried look. "Do you think that's fair to Patrick, honey?" Esmé spoke anxiously.

Was it fair that Briony had been given the lifelong burden of loving a man who was incapable of fidelity? Was it fair that he was off that very minute with another woman, just two days after Briony had delivered herself over to him, body and soul?

"I don't know what's fair," she answered unsteadily.

"I only know I'm not ready for him to know. I can't handle it yet. You don't have to lie about it, only please, *please,* don't bring the subject up."

"All right, dear," her mother murmured, and her father nodded.

Over lunch Briony broached the subject of Chad Smith. She learned that the dean of students had only been able to determine from the records that Chad had transferred to Drey-Bart in September and that he had dropped out of a college in Louisiana last spring, receiving grades of withdraw-passing in all his classes. His grades prior to that time had been average.

"That's strange," her father mused. "Why would a student drop eighteen hours when he was passing all the courses?"

"Oh, darling, it happens all the time," Esmé reminded him.

"Yes, but not without a reason. I wonder what happened in his case? Shortage of funds? Family trouble at home? Illness?"

Briony added her own suggestion silently: emotional disturbance. The loner was starting to bother her, subtly. But when her mother offered to call the school in Louisiana and find out specifically what the trouble had been, Briony asked her not to bother. "The semester's halfway over. I think we can make it okay."

She was debating how best to spend the day when an instructor at the School for the Blind called and asked if she would like to take advantage of an extra ticket to a philharmonic concert at the civic center that evening. "You won't even have to drive this time," the lady bribed her. "We've got enough cars."

Briony worked on notes for class for a couple of hours that afternoon before getting ready for the concert, determinedly keeping her mind off the foursome at the *Wurstfest*. At six thirty a car full of high school seniors picked her up, driven by the pert, thirtyish Kate Peters.

As always with the students, Briony had a good time. Their alert listening expressions during the orchestral performance reminded her just how important their hearing was to the blind, not just for survival and safety but for enjoyment of life. She shut her eyes as the music soared and throbbed throughout the huge auditorium, and when she opened her eyes at the end, she saw that Kate was watching her with mild concern.

In the car after the concert Kate took the students back to school first and then suggested that she and Briony go out somewhere for pizza and beer. "Shakey's okay?" Kate asked.

It was fine with Briony. She didn't really relish the idea of going home yet. They ate at the pizza parlor near the University of Texas, a dark restaurant that jumped with college students and loud honky-tonk piano music.

"Back there at the concert," Kate shouted over the noise, "what were you doing with your eyes closed? Having the blind experience?"

"No." Briony had tried that often enough in past years to know she would never really comprehend what blindness was like for Patrick, who couldn't just remove a blindfold and see again. "I was simply listening. Concerts sound much fuller in the dark."

"Do they? I'll have to try it sometime." Kate was thoughtfully silent for a while before asking, "Briony, is something wrong? You've been unusually quiet tonight."

Here's the test, Briony thought. *Can I stop being the tragic heroine for an evening at least? Must I inflict my broken heart on everyone else?*

"Oh, Kate, I'm sorry if I seem out of it," she apologized. "I've been awfully worried about one of my students...."

They talked for a couple of hours, and she allowed Kate to give her advice and cheer her up.

The beer helped too, she admitted as she stumbled while getting out of the car and called a noisy good night, then slammed the car door. She weaved a little on her way across the lawn, and then remembered that she should be going to the Donahue house instead. Changing course, she found the front door and tried to insert her key, only to discover that it didn't fit.

"Stupid key," she muttered aloud, searching around in her purse for another key and coming up with the right one this time.

Just as she started to try again, the door opened and Patrick faced her, still dressed although it was past midnight.

"Well, hello!" she said gaily. "I hope you didn't think you had to wait up for me! My key didn't work in your stupid door."

"The door was unlocked." His face looked stern and disapproving. "Would you come inside before you wake the whole neighborhood?"

"Certainly!" But she tripped as she crossed the threshold, stumbling against him, clutching at his arms for support.

In response, he grasped her tightly and used a foot to kick the door shut. His nose twitched. "You're drunk."

"Brilliant observation! What else can your remarkable insight tell you? Does it tell you how much fun I had getting drunk? Do you know how many pitchers of beer it took to get me potted like this? Oh, and tell me, dear old Patrick, did *you* have fun today? Did you and

Patty get drunk on German beer at the *Wurstfest*? Is she as funny when she's drunk as I am?''

His fingers bit into her arm so painfully that she broke off her words on a whimper. ''Come with me,'' he snapped, shoving her ahead of him through the foyer and up the stairs, then into his bedroom.

Briony was too stunned, and still too much under the influence of alcohol, to stop him when he began unzipping her dress and sliding it down over her shoulders. He knelt and took the shoes off her slender feet, tossing them aside carelessly. He pulled the clingy slip up over her head, and then removed her bra and pantyhose, all without saying another word.

Briony stood naked before him, staring with vague fear at his grim face. ''What did you do that for?'' she whispered.

''I'm going to sober you up.''

He led her into his dark bathroom, reached into the shower to turn it on, and then pushed her in under the cool spray.

She yelped from the shock of it, but after a minute the water warmed up and she began to enjoy the feel of the stinging drops on her numb face and shoulders. Although there was something rather disturbing about taking a shower in the dark, she reminded herself that Patrick did it. Every day, in fact.

An instant later she went rigid when a large, obviously masculine and obviously naked form squeezed her aside and entered the shower stall with her.

''Patrick!'' she gasped. ''What—''

''Be quiet.'' He had a washcloth in his hand, and he reached for the soap bar and got the cloth all sudsy. With their bodies only inches apart, he proceeded to scrub her all over, starting with her face and working down.

Briony was sobering up fast. Her head told her she ought to get out of this situation as quickly as possible, but it was too sensuous an experience to deny herself, even if Patrick would have let her escape.

His fingers were working their magic on her again, enticing, tempting, awakening her erotic senses to undreamed-of pleasures. He stroked every inch of her bare soft skin, soaping gently, tantalizingly, sending tiny currents of electric excitement through her limbs. When she was covered with a silky sheen of lather, he began rinsing her, holding the portable shower nozzle in his hand and massaging her with the strong, vibrant stream of warm water from her head to her toes.

Briony bit her lip, enjoying the riot of turbulent sensations that made her shiver. As the soap slithered off her slim body and disappeared down the drain, she literally ached to reach out for the man who stood so close to her that her nerves sang with joy at his nearness.

The proximity must have affected him too because she heard the low, almost animal sound that he emitted from deep in his throat as he touched her. It took all her self-control to remain motionless beneath his seductive hands, and all too soon his movements stilled.

"Now." His voice was husky. "It's my turn." He handed over the nozzle and washcloth and she took them obediently.

Briony enjoyed this part as much as she had the first, because it afforded her the chance to study his solid perfect body the same way he did hers: with fingertips, in the dark. Sudsing him up, caressing his broad back, running her hands down his rib cage to his lean waist and muscled buttocks, she formed a mental picture of the way she knew he looked in the light. In that moment the conviction struck her anew that her attraction to Patrick Donahue went far deeper than his external handsomeness; it included his warm magnetism, his clean sexy smell, the way he walked and held his head, his occasional blind uncertainty about his surroundings, the feel of his firm flesh against hers, his intelligence and integrity and sense of humor and boy-next-door good nature, and so much more.

"You're beautiful," she whispered against her will, one hand tracing down his hip and thigh and then circling up to knead the small of his back. Leaning forward a fraction of an inch, she brushed her lips across his chest and sucked in her breath sharply at her overwhelming need of him. It gave her sheer delight to know she was pleasing him, her delicate fingers grazing him, arousing his already urgent desire.

He let out another animallike groan and wordlessly took the shower nozzle from her. Clipping it back in place, he pulled her into his arms, the length of him burning against her softer, more vulnerable body. The water beat down on both of them as he kissed her with a seeking, hungry mouth.

Now Briony knew what it was to be helplessly pliant in a man's grasp, to be at his mercy. Melting against him under the warm pulsing spray, she strained to make contact with him wherever possible, desperate for the sensual fires his wet-hot skin ignited on hers.

When he reached out abruptly and turned off the water, she moaned. Ignoring the sound, he moved away from her to take a huge towel from the nearest rack and wrap it around her, rubbing her dry in its thick folds. He tousled her hair roughly, soaking up all the excess moisture, and then grabbed another towel and dried himself impatiently. Still confined with him in the small area of the bathroom, Briony sensed rather than saw his hard throbbing strength, and knew his need could not be put off any longer.

Tingling with anticipation, and with the stimulation of his brisk toweling, she gave herself up readily into his arms when he picked her up and carried her through the dark to his bed. He placed her on top of the covers and lay down at once, fitting his body over hers and beginning to take from her all that she had to offer him. Their still slightly damp limbs entwined, they joined together with a kind of primitive insistence, a raw passion that demanded everything of them and left them gasping.

Patrick's need was almost savage tonight, his hands and mouth plundering her; and the warm friction of flesh on flesh, the impelling movement between them, the receptive awareness of him that sensitized every nerve in her body, all combined to stir Briony to a similar wild response and carry her beyond the limits of her expectations. Out of breath, she clung to him and he to her.

She sighed, trembling weakly in his arms when it was over, and listened to his breathing gradually slow down. Unlike the other times when she had been able to help him relax so completely, there was still a tension in him tonight. His arms were stiff, his shoulder a rigid pillow for her head. She raised up and studied his face in the darkness and saw that his eyes were wide open, unblinking. Even in the dark she could see that he was unhappy.

Lowering her head again, Briony had to steel herself not to start crying. She had just given him all she had to give, all of herself, and he looked like that—miserably discontented, as if he were barely tolerating her presence next to him.

The sudden memory of how he had spent the day

washed over her, filling her with bitterness. Maybe he
was wishing right now that she were Patty. Maybe he
had fantasized when he made love to her, pretended
she were someone else.

Repelled by the very idea, Briony jerked away from
him and sat up, wanting to lash out at him and hurt
him. "Thanks," she said sweetly.

She felt him shift his head on the pillow. "For
what?" Patrick asked, his tone cautious.

"For the experience. Dennis thought I was very
good."

After a tense moment he asked, "You were with
Dennis tonight?"

"Yes." She hated the lie even as she told it. "I imagine you were right when you said he wouldn't thank
you for initiating me into the pleasures of sex. Luckily
he didn't even suspect he wasn't the first with me."

"He must be a fool," Patrick said under his breath,
sitting up abruptly so their bare shoulders touched.

At the unexpected contact Briony scrambled off the
bed. "Well, not all of us are sexperts like you," she
muttered. "Can you tell me exactly how many lovers
Patty had before you?"

He swung his legs off the bed and stood next to her.
"I'll ask her the next time I see her. Go on to bed,
Briony. I need another shower. A cold one this time."

"After tonight you need a cold shower?" she asked
with disbelief.

"It's like this," Patrick drawled, his eyes half closed
in the dim room, apparently fixed on her mouth.
"You're still something of an infant at this game. It
takes more than your meager experience to satisfy
me."

"You bastard!" she cried, drawing back her hand
and slapping him before she thought. The instant she

heard the thwack of palm against flesh, she realized she had struck his injured cheek and regretted having done it, but she didn't apologize. "Bastard!" she repeated. "I hate you!"

He raised his hand to his face for a moment, the only indication he gave that she might have hurt him. "Good. Take whatever it is you feel for me—if you have any idea what that is—and go to bed."

"You bet I will!" She nodded vigorously. "And you—you just keep your hands off me in the future."

"Now isn't *that* a switch?" he asked softly. "You evidently turn your emotions on and off like a water faucet. It can't have been more than two days ago that you assured me you would love me forever."

"So I made a mistake."

"Yes, I think you did. A rather big one too."

"Well, it's nothing that can't be corrected, and please rest assured, I won't make the same mistake again."

"That's just fine. I don't remember asking for your love in the first place."

"No, but you took it willingly enough."

"I took your body. There's a difference. I'd have been a fool not to take what you were throwing at me."

Briony shivered. The house was getting cold, and her heart felt like a chunk of ice. She turned her back on his taut face and walked to the door.

"Go to hell," she whispered, and left him alone in the dark.

Chapter Eight

Hadn't they all tried to warn her? Hadn't Patrick himself predicted he would take what she had and leave her with nothing? And wasn't that exactly what he had done?

When will you learn to pay attention to the signs, my girl? Briony chided herself, gulping down a cup of Lizzie's coffee the next morning, too ashamed of her haggard face to risk eating breakfast next door. She looked as if she'd spent a miserable night, as indeed she had! Steve, Esmé, Carol—they'd all take one look at her and know something disastrous had happened between her and Patrick.

She thought it qualified as disastrous—the complete destruction of her friendship with Patrick, the most precious thing in her life. No doubt facing him in the future would be impossibly awkward. She imagined he would avoid her, to make it easier for both of them.

It was a relief to escape from the refined dignity of the Donahue house, where her world had fallen apart, and surround herself with her noisy, irreverent, carefree students at Drey-Bart.

Make that *usually* carefree students, she amended as Andy hobbled into theory class on crutches, his forehead bandaged conspicuously.

"Good heavens, Andy, what happened to you?" she demanded with concern.

"You look like an advertisement for a trauma center," one student hooted.

"Some season our basketball team's gonna have if you're the best we've got," another teased him.

Andy lowered himself into the first empty desk he came to with a sigh, by all evidence in great pain. Briony was further convinced of that by the way he didn't respond to the joking of his fellow students.

"I had a slight...accident" was all he would say, and he looked pretty grim when he said it.

Quickly taking the hint, Briony got the class discussion under way, keeping it on track whenever anyone attempted to change the subject to Andy's injuries. When the bell rang at the end of the hour, she stepped over to his desk and asked him quietly to wait and have a word with her when the others had gone.

"Miss Hammond?" It was Chad Smith, at her elbow. "Can you get that list of books for me now?"

"I have it right here," she answered, sorting through some of the papers on the teacher's desk and handing it to him. "Here's a book of my own I'll loan you too if you like. It's a very good biography of Max Weber."

Chad looked pleased, although Briony suspected it was because she had done him a favor rather than because of any real interest in reading about a giant in the field of sociology. "Thanks a lot, Miss Hammond. Uh, I have something I want to talk to you about." He slanted a look over his shoulder at Andy. "Privately."

By this time Briony was learning that this was merely Chad's way of manipulating to get some time alone with her, and today she wasn't buying the line. "Sorry, but I can't make it right now, Chad. I've asked Andy to stay and talk to me."

Now Chad shot a quick, blank glance at the basketball player, who was slumped in his seat as if he wasn't sure he could get up again. Chad's thin lips twisted into a smirk that looked . . . well, *satisfied* was the only word Briony could think of to describe it. The look sent chills up and down her spine. "If you come in at ten o'clock tomorrow morning, I'll see you for half an hour before my research class," she said reluctantly.

The room was all but deserted now, and she walked Chad to the door and closed it behind him, glad to be rid of him. "Now," she said firmly, turning back to Andy, "what's this about an accident?"

He tried to laugh, but ended up flinching. "Ouch. I'm just quoting the police. That's what they called it. I was hit by a car last night."

"You mean, your car was hit by another car?" she asked, for clarification.

"No, I mean *I* was hit by a car. One of those hit-and-run jobbies like you see on the cop shows on TV."

Appalled, she sank down into the desk just across the aisle from his. "How badly are you hurt?"

"Oh, I'll live," he assured her quickly, seeing how pale she had become. "My right leg is pretty bruised up and the knee is twisted, but I don't think it'll keep me out of uniform long. It shouldn't affect the team's chances—"

"To hell with the team's chances!" she said in a low, intense voice. "You might have been killed! What about your head?"

He touched the bandage gingerly. "The impact threw me onto some gravel and I got cut up a little. Not too bad, honest. I'm really very lucky, at least according to the doctor."

"Hmph!" she exclaimed. "You don't *look* lucky. How do you feel?"

"Like one big ache."

"I can imagine. Tell me how it happened."

Andy told her that he had been studying at the library until it closed at eleven last night and was walking across the parking lot toward the men's dorm where he lived when a car had suddenly roared to life nearby, turned on its blinding headlights, and raced at him, knocking him fifteen feet across the pavement and then screeching away without slowing down.

Briony's face registered her horror. "Andy, the way you describe it, the driver must have intended to hit you!"

"I think he intended to *kill* me, Miss Hammond," he said soberly. "If it hadn't been such a little car, he might have done a better job of it."

"What kind of car was it?"

"Some kind of small foreign sports car. An older model, I think, and dark. Maybe navy blue. Maybe black or brown. It was so dark and things happened so fast, I'm not really sure about the details.

"Anyhow," he went on, "the police took down my description, and they're going to see what they can do. They asked if I had any enemies—you know, if I'd stolen anybody's girl lately"—he forced a smile—"and I couldn't think of anyone who'd want to hurt me. Not even for my place on the team," he added wryly.

The whole thing was too villainous to imagine happening right here on campus at Dreyfuss-Bartholemew. Briony shuddered. "Well, listen, Andy, if you need any help getting around while you're on crutches, or persuading your profs to go easy on you for a little while, I'm available."

"Thanks, Miss Hammond," he replied, "but your mother has already offered. She's even volunteered to drive me to my doctor's appointment on Friday. You come from a terrific family, you know that?"

She smiled at him. "Oh, I'm sure any dean of students would do as much." She watched him get to his feet and get settled onto the crutches awkwardly. "Be careful, will you, Andy? It would seem that you had a close call this time."

"Don't worry! I won't be crossing any more dark parking lots alone for quite a while. I've started traveling in a pack with my teammates for protection."

Briony sat in concentrated thought after Andy had gone, remembering the basketball player's words: "I couldn't think of anyone who'd want to hurt me...."

Suddenly she recalled the smirk on Chad's face as he stared at Andy, and the look of hatred he'd given the basketball player in the cafeteria last week. And Chad, she knew, drove a black M.G. Mere coincidence? She hoped so. Oh, God, to think of one of her students doing a thing like that.... She felt sick inside.

One good thing about Andy's injuries was that they occupied Briony's mind so she forgot all about Patrick. She forgot him so completely, in fact, that when she glanced up at the doorway of her intro classroom at a quarter to eleven and saw Steve and Patrick in the hall outside, she did a double take, scarcely believing it. He had actually had the nerve to come here! After what he had done to her last night, he had the gall to flaunt his blond good looks right in her face, and in front of her students yet! To stand there like that—coolly unaware of her shocked expression, his Ivy League shirt and slacks only enhancing the tall muscled beauty of his powerful body.

The distraction broke her train of thought and left her stammering, unable to remember what she had been about to tell her audience. Steve grinned at her, not in the least contrite about the way they had just thrown her for a loop.

Feeling her face redden, Briony immediately dismissed the class and gathered up her notes as the students left the room. She hugged the papers to the tuck-front of her green silk shirtwaist dress, her high heels clicking across the tile floor as she walked down the hall toward her office.

As she passed them, she greeted Steve and Patrick with a cool hello, and out of the corner of her eye, saw the surprise on her brother's face. "What's with Miss Texas?" he muttered, giving Patrick his arm and following her.

They caught up with her as she unlocked the door. "Don't act so thrilled to see us," Steve drawled, stopping in the doorway with Patrick, a step behind him, staring at the opposite wall. "Are you ticked off that we left you behind yesterday?"

She dumped her materials on her cluttered desk. "Did you intend for me to be ticked off?" she countered, her eyes clashing with Steve's.

He gave her a stern look that she interpreted to mean "I did what I had to do for your own good, brat!" but he merely said, "Of course not. If you hadn't been so tired...."

"Forget it." She brushed aside his explanation abruptly and glanced at Patrick's formidably shuttered expression, very much aware that he had not yet spoken to her. There was something so undeniably sexy about him, and he was so casually unconcerned with it, that she wanted to reach out and shake him. Instead she asked, "To what do I owe the honor of this visit?"

"We're just returning to our old stomping grounds," Steve answered. "Recalling the days of our youth."

"How exciting for you!" she exclaimed sarcastically. "Remembering all the virgins you deflowered, Patrick?"

"Briony!" her brother hissed. "Watch your mouth!"

"Oh, don't be a prude, Steven! You don't imagine I have any illusions about your best friend, do you?"

"You act as if college were one big orgy for him."

"Not just college. *Life!*" she said emphatically.

"Looks like she's on to my secret." Patrick, damn him, sounded amused! "Don't bother defending me, Steve. She won't believe you."

"Exactly right. I'm past all that."

"Briony!"

"No, it's okay, Steve." Patrick's clear green eyes rested on her chin for a thoughtful second before he released the other man's elbow and turned. "I think I'll go outside for some fresh air." Using his cane, he tapped his way toward the staircase and out of sight. Even in retreat, his sins as good as openly admitted, he was the most appealing man she had ever known. It took all her willpower not to call out to him to stop, to come back.

Steve watched him go in silence too, then turned to glower at her. "Don't you think you were a little hard on him?"

She didn't think she had even begun to be as hard on him as he deserved her to be. "Let's don't forget who it was that pointed out to me his weakness for women."

"Well, then, maybe I came on too strong. I never expected you to go for the jugular."

"You think I wounded him? Ho, ho! He's probably already found some lovely young coed out there who will manage to comfort him quite nicely for my cruelty." She spoke with sudden dead seriousness. "I want to thank you for opening my eyes. I had never seen Patrick as he really is."

He looked alarmed. "Exactly what do you mean by that? What sort of person do you think Patrick is?"

"A charming, attractive, intelligent, and totally faithless man. A playboy."

Groaning, her brother shook his head. "Oh, Lord, Briony, I obviously didn't handle this very well. I didn't mean for you to hate the guy. Can't you remember how long we've been friends? Doesn't it mean anything to you—all the three of us have been through together?"

What had all that meant to Patrick? Nothing! He had taken all he wanted and then turned on her.

"It's too late for friendship," she said quietly. "I'll never go back to being friends with him again."

When he found himself arguing until he was blue in the face, Steve gave up trying to revise Briony's opinion. "Look," he sighed. "This whole thing has gotten blown out of proportion. Let's just drop it for now, okay?"

She wondered what Steve would say if he knew she could now join the ranks of Patrick's discarded lovers.

"What we actually came up here for was to take you to lunch with us," he continued.

"I don't really think that's a good idea."

"If you're talking about Patrick's suddenly intolerable presence, let me assure you you won't have to sit next to him. Carol and Carly are here too, and we're meeting Mom and Dad at the cafeteria. It'll be practically a mob scene."

"Great! Sounds like a real blast," she muttered. "To be perfectly honest, I'm not sure I can be civil to him."

"No one will notice," Steve insisted. "I'll sit on one side of you, and Dad can sit on the other, so you won't have to be anywhere near him."

Terrific. That would leave Patrick to be flanked by Esmé and Carol, no doubt with Carly on his knee. Right in the middle of three females, just the way he liked it!

"Come on, honey. How will I explain if you don't come to lunch with us?"

She suspected Steve would stick with her until he got the answer he wanted, so she gave in grudgingly. "Oh, all right. But don't expect me to be nice."

"I wouldn't dream of it." He grinned, pleased with his victory.

But when they walked down the front steps of the class building, Briony's heart took a sickening plunge at the unexpected sight of Patrick and Carol strolling arm-in-arm over the grass, little Carly chortling playfully from her perch high atop Patrick's shoulders.

She didn't realize her fingernails were digging into Steve's arm until he winced and pulled free of her. "Briony, don't," he whispered in a gruff voice, hugging her when he saw her tears. "You don't need to be jealous of Carol."

"Jealous!" She spat the word. "You're crazy! And if you think for one minute that I'm going to eat lunch with that—that Lothario, you can think again. I'd sooner starve!"

And with that, she took off across campus in the opposite direction from Patrick, ignoring Steve's shouts for her to stop.

Briony hurried blindly at first, unable to see clearly for her tears, and finally she stopped running and ducked into the alcove shielding the side doorway of the science building, hoping no one would want to use that door. She pressed her face to her hands, squeezing shut her eyes and trying to stop the overflow. It was a wretched helpless feeling, to know she had no more control over her emotions than this. To think she could get so distraught over a little thing like seeing Patrick with his hand on Carol's arm, letting her lead him.

"Briony."

The voice was husky and male, and it came from just behind her. Stiffening, she tried for a moment to place it, and when she did, she groaned inwardly. Oh, no! Not him again! She wiped her tears away quickly before she turned.

"What do you want, Chad?" She sounded firm, authoritative, her voice giving no evidence of her dismay.

The muscular young man moved until he was very near to her. "I want to see you. I noticed your hand in class this morning, Briony. You're not wearing your ring."

Oh, dear heaven. All she needed right now was a romantically inclined schoolboy! "You should call me Miss Hammond, you know," she said sternly.

He merely smiled at her, his expression hungry.

"Please leave me alone. I need some time by myself."

Reaching for her arm, he murmured, "You've been crying! I can comfort you, Briony, if your fiancé broke up with you. I can make you forget about him. He's not the only man in the world, you know. I'll make you feel good again."

Briony was repelled by his suggestion. "Chad, thank you, but I don't need comforting."

He put his arms around her now and kissed her wetly before she could push him away. "Let me take you someplace nice for lunch today," he said hoarsely. "I know a place where we can talk. Later—"

Although she found the situation to be almost frightening, she stood still until her head cleared. "Let me go," she ordered him. "I'm not going anywhere with you."

Surprised, Chad released her and gave her a searching look.

"Yes, I'm serious," she nodded, calm now. She moved away from him. "I'm going to forget this happened, but please see that it doesn't ever happen again or I'll have to report it to the administration. You have to remember that I'm your teacher. Oh, and while we're at it," she added, "I'd like to know what you were doing at eleven o'clock last night?"

Caution dropped down over his narrow features like a veil, blanking the amorous expression. "Eleven o'clock?" he echoed. "Let me see.... I was at home studying."

"Your roommate can vouch for you, can't he?"

"I don't have a roommate." He smiled and raised an eyebrow. "Why are you asking these questions? Has something happened? Have I been accused of doing something?"

He certainly sounded innocent enough.

"No, you haven't been accused of anything. Not yet, anyway. But if I have any more reason to suspect you were involved in Andy's hit-and-run accident, I'll alert the police that they might want to check your car for any damage. Police labs can do an amazing job of finding evidence, you know."

With Chad just staring at her, Briony turned and left him in the doorway, walking briskly away.

Despite the serene way she had managed to defuse Chad's libido, she found herself trembling and weak-kneed as she retraced her steps in the direction of her office. Perhaps she ought to tell her parents what had happened, ask their advice. Maybe she wasn't really equipped to deal with a student like Chad. What if his inappropriate behavior continued, or even escalated?

But I handled him okay today, she reminded herself.

And just now, in particular, she didn't want her family to know any more of her weaknesses. They already knew about the big one. If she had ever been the type to seek their sheltering wings, it wouldn't be now.

So Briony decided not to tell anyone about Chad.

Carol was waiting for her on the uncomfortably hard bench in the hall outside Briony's locked office, looking like a dark delicate flower against the monastic white walls. Seeing her, Briony had a sudden return of the savage envy she had felt when she saw Carol with Patrick out on the lawn.

Get a grip on yourself! she thought frantically. *This is your sister-in-law. She and Steve are still madly in love, after four years of marriage. She's not your enemy!*

"Hi," Briony murmured in a small voice. "What are you doing here?"

Carol was so obviously relieved to see her that Briony felt heavy with guilt. Her sister-in-law jumped up and met Briony at the door of her office, looking at her with large velvet-brown eyes. "I've been waiting for you, Briney." She used Carly's name for her unconsciously, her voice low and soft. "I've been so worried about you! Where'd you disappear to?"

"I just went for a walk." She unlocked her door and went in to drop down gracefully into the chair behind the desk.

Carol sat uncertainly in the only other chair in the crowded little room. "Honey, you were running when you left!" She leaned forward in her distress. "Whatever is wrong? Is there anything I can do?"

"No." Her answer was clipped. "You're missing lunch, aren't you?"

Carol shrugged. "I don't mind. I'm dieting." She

was always dieting, despite the slightness of her figure, claiming that she tended to be pudgy if she wasn't careful. "I persuaded Steve and Patrick to go on with the brat and meet your parents in the cafeteria." She smiled her sweet smile, showing an impishness that she usually hid behind a demure facade. "They'll have their hands full."

"Oh, well, Patrick can charm her," Briony muttered sarcastically.

"Oh, Carly adores Patrick!" Carol enthused. "He's just great with kids."

"Not quite," Briony corrected her. "He's just great with *females*."

Carol's eyes widened at Briony's grim tone. "Briony, what's wrong with you? I was under the impression you, er, liked him a lot."

"Liked?" She laughed shortly. "You're trying to be tactful, Carol, when everyone has always known I've loved Patrick to distraction. 'Loved' being the appropriate word. Past tense. Or maybe I never really loved him. I don't know." She sighed, leaned back in the chair, and closed her eyes.

"You sound awfully confused," Carol said tentatively, and Briony nodded silently, emphatically. "You know, I think he is too."

When Briony gave a delicate snort, Carol pressed on. "I mean it. I've never had much of a chance to be around Patrick. He was already living in New Hampshire when Steve and I met and got married. Oh, we talked on the telephone every couple of months, and he sent us incredible, funny, wonderful tapes. Whenever one of his letters arrive, Steve and I always listen to it together, drinking a beer and pretending we're out for the evening with Patrick. And laughing! Lord, Briony, his letters make us laugh! I can't tell you how much I've enjoyed knowing him by long distance. But it wasn't like seeing that smile of his that lights up his face and watching the way his eyes try so hard to stay right with you when you move. Of course sometimes they're just a little off, but it's okay. I mean, you have to love him for making the effort. Steve says it would be a lot easier for him just to let his eyes look blind. No one would blame him.

"Anyway, as I was saying, I haven't been around Patrick much, but the little time we've spent together in the past, I really thought he had it all together and knew exactly what he was going after. But *this* time.... I don't know." She bit her lip. "He's different."

"What do you mean?" Briony asked reluctantly, sitting up to look at her brother's wife.

"It's hard to explain. He's quieter. More subdued. Almost as if he's groping, trying to find something he's lost and unwilling to ask for help, or afraid to ask, or not knowing how to ask."

"He lost his father."

"No. No, I'm sure it's more than that. There's a sense of loneliness about him I never felt before."

"Lonely? Patrick? Ha!"

"Seriously." Carol looked grave. "We had a long talk at the *Wurstfest* yesterday. A most enlightening talk. He let down his guard just enough for me to get a glimpse of how lonely he really is. And how remarkably brave. He talked a little about the queasy feeling he sometimes gets in the pit of his stomach when he has to go somewhere strange alone, not knowing for sure if there will be anything under his foot when he puts it down."

That's what his cane is for, Briony thought cynically, and right away felt ashamed of herself for pretending that a cane could compensate for eyesight.

She forced herself to focus on the tender note she heard in Carol's voice, and her bitterness returned. "And when he told you that, you wanted to put your arms around him and protect him, right?"

Carol nodded. "I almost cried, hearing him talk like that."

"If his talk affected you that way," Briony commented dryly, "I can just imagine what it did to Patty. She must have been his for the asking afterward."

Carol looked blank. "Patty? Oh, she didn't hear our talk. She and Steve were off watching the folk dancers perform, and Patrick was nice enough to volunteer to sit with me away from the noise. You see, I got a little nauseated from all the sausage I sampled, and I thought anyway that Patrick might not get too much pleasure from hearing the dancing, although he'd enjoyed the bands and singers earlier."

Sweet, thoughtful Carol. Inventing an upset stomach to rescue Patrick from a situation where he might feel uncomfortable. So it was you alone who got the full benefit of Patrick's magic, and it worked. You fell for it, hook, line, and sinker.

"And I wasn't too impressed with the conceited Patty, and I wanted to find out what he was thinking about you that made him look so . . . so funny whenever Steve or I mentioned your name."

Briony paled. "And did you find out?"

Hesitating for a second, the dark-haired woman finally shook her head. "No, I didn't learn anything definite, but I certainly have my suspicions."

"Such as?"

"Don't you know?" Carol demanded. "Honestly? I think the poor guy is scared to death that he's fallen for you."

No. Carol was mistaken. If Patrick had been falling for her, could he have been so cavalier about shooting her down? *I don't remember asking for your love in the first place. I took your body. I'd have been a fool not to take what you were throwing at me.* And marriage? *It doesn't bear consideration.*

Was that love talk? Not by Briony's standards. Not by the wildest stretch of her imagination, and she tried very hard to convince herself that Carol could be right.

Briony spent the afternoon holed up in her office, not answering the door or the telephone, mostly staring out her single window at the hardy oak trees on the back side of the campus. They still wore their leaves, a fine cosmetic dressing for their gnarled trunks, but not much protection against the coming winter.

Those trees and I, she thought, *are going to be very cold this winter.* Come next spring, the trees at least would be none the worse for their experience. But what shape would Briony be in?

And spring after next?

Glumly she looked ahead to a lifetime of cold winters without even a fantasy to warm her. *How do you cope when you learn your hero has feet of clay?* There was no answer to the question. nothing to comfort her when she thought of the future.

Forcing her mind to other matters, she gave some consideration to whether it was mere coincidence that Chad's car matched the description of the one that struck Andy. She didn't want to believe one of her students could have deliberately hurt anyone like that. But the fear was there, gnawing at her. Should she take a chance on Chad's innocence and ignore her suspicions?

Even as she dreaded doing it, she picked up the telephone and called the Austin Police Department, asking for Tom Clayton's office. When he answered, she identified herself as Steve Hammond's sister.

"Why, hello, Briony!" He sounded pleased to hear her voice. "I'm glad you called. Beth—my wife—and I were just talking this morning about inviting you and Patrick over for dinner on whatever day you visit headquarters. Have you two decided when that will be, by the way?"

"No," she said uncomfortably. "We haven't discussed it. I called about something else." And she related the story of Andy's so-called accident and her fears that Chad was involved.

Tom listened with interest, evidently taking notes as he asked her to repeat herself at several points. When she finished, he said, "I can see how you'd be concerned. Suppose I have a man try to locate this car at school and take a look at the bumper and fenders. I'm not talking about a search, you know. We can't touch the car without a warrant. But the patrolman can see if there's any cause to ask a judge to issue one. If it looks clean and straight, it'll be a load off your mind."

She was already relieved, just having discussed it with him. "That sounds great! Let me know what you find out, will you?"

"Sure. Look, about that tour. Beth is anxious to meet both you and Patrick. Think you guys can make it this week?"

"Uh, I'm pretty sure I can't, Tom. I'm looking at my schedule now and it's just horrible for the next few weeks. Why don't you go ahead and take Patrick around, and I'll call you to set up my own appointment in a month or so? Would that be all right?"

"Sure, no problem." But she thought he seemed surprised. "I got the idea, though, that Patrick would prefer to have you along. The way he spoke of you, it was obvious he's crazy about you."

I don't remember asking for your love in the first place. I'd have been a fool not to take what you were throwing at me.

Briony's chest constricted painfully and she had trouble breathing. After a moment she managed to say casually enough, "Oh, well, Patrick and I are old friends, of course, but I assure you I'm a disposable commodity as far as he's concerned. He'll be just as happy to go without me."

Although he remained unconvinced, Tom accepted her refusal graciously and hung up with the promise to call her if he had any further information about Andy's accident.

Briony ate supper in the faculty dining room at the cafeteria, sitting unhappily at the table with two morose bachelor professors who showed their lack of welcome by glaring at her between bites, angry with her for being a woman and for invading their world of academia. Her appetite hadn't been very good to start with, and after a few minutes of picking at her meat loaf and macaroni, she decided to risk going home.

The Hammond house was well-lit. Dinner was probably under way, with Patrick doubtlessly eating with her family. Parking in the driveway between, she chose the safer of the two dwellings and let herself into the quiet Donahue house.

She turned on a lamp in the foyer and hurried straight upstairs to change into her running clothes. As she came back down the stairs, the front door opened and Patrick stepped inside and paused there in the foyer, his head up.

Briony froze automatically, not ready for another encounter, thinking for the first time in her life of deliberately hiding her presence from him. Even as she deplored the thought, she held her breath, trying not to make a sound.

Patrick had a long-sleeved blue pin-striped shirt and navy slacks, and he held his cane in one hand, gripping it tightly. In the lamplight she could see clearly enough that his face was flushed and brooding.

Did he know she was home?

"Briony!" he shouted, the challenge in his voice answering her question for her.

He listened alertly for a response that she didn't give.

Moving to the foot of the stairs, he turned his head toward the living room, and then the kitchen, and then raised his face as if looking up at her where she stood poised. There was a look of strain about him that gave her the impression he was trying to force his other senses to seek her out, perhaps even willing his blind eyes to find her for him.

It gave her an unexpected pain in the center of her heart, a knifelike stab of unwanted love that made her sigh a little. Not a very loud sound, but enough.

His mouth clenching shut, his face darkening, he put one hand on the newel post. With measured, determined steps he climbed the stairs, keeping that left hand on the banister, the cane in his right. She stood pressed against the wall near the top, wondering if he would pass her by, but two steps below her he stopped and sniffed the air. He probed with the cane and found her ankle, bent over and touched it with his exploring hand, and continued on up her leg, fingering the softness of her warm-up suit.

Abruptly he withdrew his hand and straightened until his eyes were on a level with hers. She saw a smoldering fury in his that made her shrink even further into herself. "I guess that gives you a sense of power, hiding from me like that. It's a very effective way of driving me crazy."

Heaven knew she didn't feel very good about what she had just tried to do. "You found me," she pointed out shakily.

"*This* time."

She gasped. "Are you implying I've done this before?"

"I'll never know, will I?"

"Well, you can take my word for it, I haven't." Her own anger was starting to surface. "As a matter of fact, I don't enjoy a sense of power over you. I just didn't want to have to talk to you. I still don't."

He nodded. "That doesn't surprise me. You made it plain enough over at the college today. But I have some things to discuss with you, and I'd like some straight answers."

Briony stared at his ruggedly attractive features, at the green eyes that gave the illusion of being able to see into her soul, and knew that she was still vulnerable to this man. Dangerously vulnerable.

"Hey, Patrick, I'd really love to sit down and have a long talk with you, but I'm afraid I'm just on my way out to run."

"With Dennis?" he asked tautly.

"Yes!" She snatched at his suggestion with relief. "With Dennis. He's supposed to pick me up any time now."

His smile was cold. "I talked to Dennis just before I came in. I told him you were going to run with me instead. He understood perfectly. Dennis is such a good sport."

"You're lying!"

Shrugging, he took her arm and started upstairs, forcing her to accompany him. "You can wait in my room while I change. I don't want you getting away."

"Why should I do this?" she whispered as he pushed her down onto the edge of the bed. "I don't want to talk to you, and I don't want to run with you!"

"You'll do it because you know I need the exercise and the angel of mercy in you can't resist helping a poor blind man." He turned away from her to find his sweat suit in a dresser drawer and his running shoes in the closet.

The sight of him stripping off his shirt in fluid movements, showing her his wide shoulders and golden brown back, reawakened a torment in her. "I don't have to put up with this," she muttered, rising to leave.

He shifted his head in her direction. "I'll just come after you."

"You could never find me outside."

"Maybe not, but Steve could. Your brother owes me a big one." There was a certain grimness about him as he said that, and she knew he would, indeed, come after her—alone or with help. And either way was unthinkable.

Sighing, she sat back down while he finished dressing.

As it was fairly early in the evening, the traffic when they went outside was heavier than it had been the first time they ran. Briony had to pay close attention to ensure that she didn't run Patrick too far into the street, or into a car parked along the curb. In her present state of mind she found the task nerve-racking.

Patrick didn't seem to be enjoying the run any more than she did. Although he jogged along easily, she thought he seemed tense and preoccupied.

What did he want to talk to her about? Why didn't he get it over with?

The streets were quieter near the elementary school.

"Where are we now?" he asked suddenly, and she told him. "There's still a playground next to the school, isn't there? Let's go sit down."

Briony didn't like the idea for several reasons, the primary one being that she knew they were going to have to talk now. The excuse she gave him, however, was that the little park was poorly lighted.

"Don't worry," he replied wryly. "I remember it from the old days. I'll lead you."

There was a park bench near the merry-go-round, to which Patrick led her with unerring accuracy. He sprawled on one end of the bench, stretching out his long legs, while Briony sat down more gingerly on the other end.

For perhaps a minute he didn't say anything, and then, "Why? Why did you lie to me, Briony?"

The blankness she felt was genuine. "I don't know what you're talking about."

"No?" he sneered.

"No!"

He grabbed her left hand and felt the ringless third finger, then shoved her hand aside in a gesture of disgust, remaining eloquently silent.

"Oh, that," she mumbled.

"Yes, that!" There was bitterness, indignation, hurt pride in his voice. "I wonder how long you would have kept lying to me about it if I hadn't found out from someone else?"

It was Briony's turn to be quiet, not knowing how to answer him.

"And why? That's what I want to know. Why didn't you tell me the engagement was off?"

When she still didn't speak, Patrick pressed on. "Why did I have to find out from your parents? Even though they agreed I had a right to know, they felt guilty about telling me because you had asked them to keep it from me. I was the one person you wanted to keep in the dark." He laughed harshly at his own pun. "It's no trick at all to fool a blind man, is it?"

"I—I'm sorry, Patrick. Maybe I should have told you."

"*Maybe* you should have told me?"

"Okay," she acknowledged grudgingly. "It seemed that there was no need for you to know, but I guess I was wrong. At the time it seemed like a harmless omission."

"Oh. Right. Harmless." She could see his head jerk up and down in the darkness. "Tell me you love me, and give me time to start thinking you really mean it, and then tell me you hate my guts. Let me have your body when it can only get me hooked on you, and then say, 'Tough luck, turkey. Not tonight!' Get me so worked up with my need for you that I can't keep my hands off you—that I all but rape you—and then calmly announce that you've just been to bed with good old Dennis. The whole thing sounds perfectly harmless to me." He was hoarse.

She wanted to think about that for a while. Had she really been so mercurial? "I don't seem to have had much control over myself lately," she said defensively.

"I beg your pardon. I thought you *wanted* to bring me right to the edge of a nervous breakdown. After all, you do it so well."

"Are—are you talking about sexual frustration?"

"That certainly is part of it."

Briony attempted a little sarcasm of her own. "Surely you don't have any trouble finding someone to help you with that problem! From what I've heard of Patty, she'd be more than willing."

Muttering a strangled oath, Patrick stood up and strode forward three reckless steps, then turned to face her, a towering dark figure. "That would be just fine, if I were interested in Patty," he snarled. "But I'm not that lucky. I only want you. And it's your fault. You're the one who made it impossible for me to care how any other woman feels or smells or sounds. Or tastes," he added indignantly.

"I did?" she whispered, shocked.

"Oh, yes, you did. A week ago I could have described six other women who were fun to be with and reasonably sexy too, but tonight I can't. You took them all away from me, dammit, and offered yourself in place of them. And then, when I had no defenses left against your unbelievable sweetness, when I knew you were the one thing that had been missing from my life for the past five years, you withdrew the offer."

She was afraid to believe what he was saying. "What do you mean—I was the only thing missing from your life?" she asked warily.

"Just that. You tantalized me with the knowledge of all you could be to me. Friend, lover, family. My guide. My very eyes. All these years you've been the one who knew what I needed almost before I knew. The one who knew how to help me inconspicuously, so I didn't feel like everyone was staring at me. Here in Austin again, I got to thinking that my whole life had the potential to be how I felt when I was with you: absolutely fantastic."

Briony rose and stood in front of him. "If you felt that way, why didn't you tell me?"

Although he allowed her to slip her hands around his waist and come closer, he kept his arms rigid at his sides. "I'm more afraid of the unknown than some guys are, Briony. I don't want any big surprises. I tend to slow down when I get scared, and this time I guess I just didn't move fast enough."

She pressed her cheek against his shoulder, whispering into his chest, "That doesn't sound like the lover boy my brother described to me."

She felt him stiffen and pull back. "Oh, yes!" There was fresh anger in his voice. "Let's talk about Steve for a minute. It's come to my attention that he might have planted a rather nasty doubt or two in your mind about my character. Is that right?"

Hesitating to condemn Steve, Briony hedged. "What makes you think that?"

"His confession, signed in blood." Patrick finally gave in and put his arms around her, and for the hundredth time she thought how good he smelled, how very clean and male and musky.

"Old Steve began to get the idea he had perhaps been premature to butt in, after he saw the way you reacted, and after he bothered to ask me how I felt. He told me he thought things have gone far enough. Your whole family is worried about you—" Patrick broke off, raising his head.

"And I—"

"Sssh!" he hissed, tightening his hold on her.

Now she heard the footsteps too. She twisted her head to see who it was that approached so stealthily, and felt more annoyance than fear when she recognized the intruder.

"Chad!" Her tone conveyed exasperation and impatience.

"Hello, Briony."

She turned and stood with her back against Patrick, both of his arms protecting her. "Did you follow us here?" She could barely make out his positive headshake. "Well, you've come at a bad time. We're in the middle of a very important discussion, so I'm going to ask you to please just leave us alone. I'm sure whatever

you want can wait until my office hours at school tomorrow.''

''No.''

His refusal startled her. Always before she had handled Chad by being firm with him. With a sudden stab
of fear she remembered her suspicions that Chad had
struck Andy with his car.

''Well, suppose you tell me what you want, then?''
she suggested, her heartbeat quickening.

''You.''

Briony made a small involuntary movement, but Patrick's grip locked on her. ''Shove off, Chad,'' he spoke
coolly, and his voice contained an undeniable author-
ity. ''This is not the right time or place for you to talk to
your teacher.''

Chad came a step closer. ''I'm not interested in her
as a teacher. I want what all the other guys seem to be
getting.''

''Don't you even think about touching me!'' Briony
flashed, pressing closer to Patrick.

The husky student gave a short nasty laugh. ''I'm
going to do a lot more than touch you, and if you relax,
you'll probably enjoy it like I do.''

Before Briony could do more than gasp, Patrick's
strong arms stopped her. ''That may look good to you
at the moment, but think about what will happen afterward.'' He sounded calm and reasonable. ''Surely you
don't want to go to prison for five minutes of pleasure.''

''I've never gone to prison before. They never testify. They're too scared.''

Now she was really frightened. He had done this sort
of thing before! Her heart seemed to be in her throat.
One of Patrick's hands rested on her left side, and she
knew he felt the pounding underneath.

"Briony will testify. So will I."

"Not after I finish with you. I'll get even with you, Briony, for calling the police on me."

"W-what are you talking about?" she stammered.

His face was ugly in the dark, twisted and angry. "You know. Think you're too good for me, don't you? Think you're too pretty for me! I'm not a basketball player like Andy, the creep! I know what you did, though. I saw the policeman giving my car the once-over. He found the dent in my fender, and he radioed in. He left, but I knew he'd be back, and I knew you called him, just like you threatened to do. Well, Miss Hammond, before tonight's over, you'll wish you hadn't."

She was shaking now, and Patrick probably wasn't as confident as he acted. "You don't really think I'm going to let you do whatever you want to her, do you?"

"How are you planning to stop me?"

Patrick seemed to be looking right at Chad. "I'm probably five or six inches taller than you, and twenty pounds heavier."

"Ten pounds," Chad corrected him in a flat voice. "Besides, I've been watching you for days now. You're blind."

Patrick's nod acknowledged it. "I'll fight you, Chad, if that's what you want."

"No!" Briony protested, although she wasn't sure which of them she hoped would listen to her. "You can't fight—"

"Fine," Chad agreed. "Come on. Get out from behind her skirt, or are you hoping she'll protect *you* now?"

Patrick removed her clinging arms and pushed her away from him, listening for a moment and then inching closer to Chad. "You go on, Briony, get home."

"Yeah, Briony," the young man jeered. "Go on home, but just keep in mind that if you do, I'll kill this blind dude before you get back with help."

"I can take care of myself, Briony," Patrick said urgently. "Go!"

Briony was frozen with frantic indecision. There were houses just a block away. They all looked dark, but someone might be at home at one of them. Maybe someone would help them, if she could rouse them to answer the door. What if she screamed to bring help?

But in the faint moonlight she could see the chilling anticipation on Chad's face. He was really looking forward to this, and the more damage he could inflict, the better he would like it.

"For God's sake, Briony, run!" Patrick issued the order with a grim tautness that tore at her, making her want to obey him, to do anything he asked.

But she couldn't. Chad would really kill him. She knew the capacity was there. Too late she realized that his vacant expression didn't reflect the lack of intelligence, but lack of a conscience. He could kill and have no regrets whatsoever. Maybe he already had. . . .

"No, Patrick. I'm not going to leave you."

As Patrick groaned, Chad laughed. "Good. You can stay and watch. I'll show you just how much good a blind lover is to you."

Chad stepped in for the slaughter and asked conversationally, "Have you ever been in a fight before?" There was malicious amusement in his voice.

"Not lately," Patrick responded and swung his powerful right fist without any warning, connecting with the shorter man's throat.

Briony heard a crunch and a cry of pain from the surprised student, and she yelled, "You hit him, Patrick! It was beautiful!"

Chad's hand went to his Adam's apple, and he wobbled on his feet, but before Patrick could find him with another blow, Chad recouped and attacked with the full strength of his outrage. From his hoarse grunts as he went for Patrick, it was apparent that the first strike had done something to his throat.

It was also apparent that Patrick, in spite of his size advantage, was likely to be badly hurt. His arms swung, attempting to locate Chad, but the only hits he made merely glanced off the younger man, who was moving so quickly that even a sighted opponent would have had trouble fighting him.

Once Patrick caught Briony's shoulder and, realizing it immediately, he rasped, "Get the hell out of the way!"

She obeyed, not knowing how to help. Hovering nearby, she kept half an eye on the fight as she searched in the dark for some kind of weapon—a stick or rock or *something* to use on Chad, but she could find nothing. The realization of their vulnerability—hers and Patrick's—shook her, and she sobbed unconsciously. *Don't give up hope!* She sent the silent message to him, praying he would keep fighting. *We have to save ourselves, Patrick!*

But Patrick gave no appearance of giving up. He heard the heavy breathing that identified his assailant and leaned into the fight, jabbing steadily even when he struck air.

Moving in close, Chad pummeled Patrick's face with both fists as he raised his arms to defend himself. On perhaps the fourth heavy blow Patrick's nose opened a geyser of blood that spurted over both of them, soaking their clothes.

"Son of a bitch!" Chad croaked, looking down at himself as if wondering if that were his blood or Patrick's.

"Now, Patrick!" Briony screamed, and Patrick came up with his knee, catching Chad in the stomach.

"Damn!" Patrick swore in frustration, and she knew he was thinking, bad shot!

"Try again," she begged him.

Patrick obligingly kicked, but Chad was ready. Grabbing Patrick's leg, he jerked it out from beneath Patrick and sent him sprawling on his back in the dirt.

Instantly Chad was on top of him, sitting on his chest, pinning Patrick's arms down with his own knees, using both fists to beat at Patrick's face despite the blood that gushed from his nose. Panting, Chad stopped hitting and began a new torture: lifting Patrick's head and pounding it over and over against the ground.

"Stop it!" Briony cried, trying to pull Chad off, sobbing at her helplessness and at the thought of what this must be doing to Patrick. She caught her fingers in Chad's hair and jerked, but he ignored her as he continued his methodical pounding, pounding, pounding.

"He can't even see you!" he muttered between thrusts. "He can't appreciate you like I do!"

"Stop it!" she cried again, slapping at him tiredly, all her energy gone. "Leave him alone!"

Only when Patrick was past knowing did Chad leave him alone. He got to his feet, staggering, his breath a gasping roar in her ears, and took hold of her arm. "Now," he croaked menacingly in his damaged voice, "your turn."

Looking through her tears at Patrick's unmoving body, Briony didn't really care what happened to her now.

Chapter Nine

It was all over. It had been over for some time now. Briony hurt too badly to try to figure out how long she had lain here on the dusty playground where Chad had left her. She thought she must have passed out for a while, but now her head was trying to clear.

As a result of Chad's beating, every part of her body ached, some parts more insistently than others. A knot on her temple throbbed, and her lips were cut and bruised. She was cold in the November night air, cold and uncomfortable and only partially dressed. And tired. So tired she couldn't bother to stir, in spite of the discomfort.

He wasn't able to do it, she thought with a glimmer of triumph. Chad hadn't been able to rape her. Oh, he had tried, all right. And she couldn't have stopped him, not in the shape she'd been in by then. It had been his own body that had failed him. Maybe it had been her inability to fight him off after he hit her. Maybe he needed her resistance in order to be able to perform. Maybe he had simply been exhausted, like her. His breathing had become terribly loud and gasping toward the end, as if he were struggling for air. But whatever the reason, he had finally given up the struggle and crept away into the night, like some evil creature found under a rock.

How many other women had he done this to? Was that why he had left school in the middle of the semester last spring in Louisiana? He couldn't be allowed to get away this time! He had all but admitted having dented his car on Andy. She would tell the police. Patrick had said—

Patrick?

Her tired brain struggled for memory. Where was Patrick? What had happened to him? Was it a dream, or had he been lying by the merry-go-round, unconscious, the last time she saw him?

Unconscious...or dead?

Panic-stricken, Briony moaned and forced herself to sit up slowly, her entire body protesting. It was very dark in the park, and cold. She felt around on the ground and found the rest of her clothes, pulling them on awkwardly, her limbs stiff, her head feeling enormous and heavy.

"Patrick?" She called his name anxiously, her voice sounding strangely weak in her ears. "Patrick, where are you? Answer me!"

She got up on her hands and knees and peered around. She saw the shape of the park bench, and the seesaws and merry-go-round. There was something... but, no. When she crawled toward it, she saw that it was just a patch of long grass away from the playground equipment. The slide was over there, and the swings. Nothing else. No crumpled heap in a bloodied warm-up suit with long arms and legs and a crown of golden hair that caught a ray of moonlight now and then. No sign of anyone.

Had she just imagined that he had been with her tonight? Was that part of it merely a bad dream?

"Oh, God, Patrick, where are you?" she whispered, dropping back down to bury her face in her arms and cry.

A few minutes later when Tom Clayton found her there, she was still sobbing in despair, sick with shock and worry over Patrick. Tom and a uniformed policeman put her into a car and took her straight to the same hospital where an ambulance had just carried Patrick.

While they waited in the examining room for Dr. Travis, Tom put his arm around her and talked to her quietly, gently asking the necessary questions about Chad's attack and filling her in on the parts of the story she had missed. He described how Patrick had regained consciousness and had groped around on the ground until his hands contacted Briony's limp form, passed out near the spot where he had lain. How he had gone for help, disoriented and lost, wandering in circles for what must have been a couple of hours over the block of vacant lots near the school, seeking a house or a passing car and covering the same blank territory over and over before he was finally seen by a lady walking a dog. He heard the woman and called out to her, but the sight of him with his gruesomely battered face and blood-spattered clothes scared her so that she ran back to her house to call the police.

"I got there within five minutes of the woman's call," Tom told Briony. "I had been on the alert ever since the patrolman went back with a warrant to search Chad's car and found that the kid had split from Drey-Bart. We spent a couple of hours scouting around for the M.G., and then Steve called to tell me he was concerned because you and Patrick had been gone from the house an awful long time. My instinct told me it was more than coincidence, although God knows"—his arm clenched around her—"I never expected the bastard to do *this*."

He made a visible effort to calm down. "Patrick

didn't want to go to the hospital until we found you. Matter of fact, we had to pick him up bodily and put him in the ambulance, and he was cussing me the whole time." His laugh was a little shaky. "Even after all he'd been through, he was ready to take on the entire police force because I wouldn't let him lead us back to you."

Briony turned her face into his shoulder and cried.

"Briony, don't!" he begged her. "He's going to be all right."

"How do you know?" she asked, wanting to believe it but not quite daring.

"Because...because he *has* to! Dammit, I'll get the kid that did this to you two," he vowed, suddenly all policeman, his determination clear in the gleam in his eyes and the thrust of his square chin.

"I don't care what happens to Chad," Briony said in a small voice, "as long as Patrick makes it okay."

After the doctor finished with her, Briony begged to see Patrick, but it was very late. "He's sleeping soundly, darling," Esmé told her. "Steve and Tom are with him now, and Steve will spend the night in his room. You can see him tomorrow, when the sedative wears off."

No amount of pleading on her part would convince her parents that she needed a quick glimpse of him to reassure her, to help her sleep better herself. Ryan and Esmé were adamant that she had been through too much to risk the emotional upset of actually seeing him. The thought that seeing Patrick would be a blow to her frightened Briony—just exactly how badly had he been injured?—but she comforted herself with the realization that Steven wouldn't be allowed to stay with Patrick if his condition were critical.

Although she didn't really think she needed to be

hospitalized, she consented to stay overnight for observation because it would keep her nearer to Patrick. Her mother stayed with her most of the night, sitting by the bed and holding her hand. Dr. Travis must have given her something to ease her exhausted mind and body, because she dropped off to sleep almost immediately and slept without stirring for hours.

When Briony awoke the next morning, Steve was reclining in the lounger where her mother had been the night before. Her handsome dark-skinned brother had an uncharacteristically worn look, his shock of black hair falling neglected across his forehead. When he saw her eyes open, he stood up and came to her side, watching her closely, waiting for her to speak.

"How's Patrick?" she demanded at once.

He had to struggle to hide his relief. "Doing just like you." He pretended to scowl. "He woke me up at five A.M. to ask how you were."

"No kidding?" The news gave her a warm feeling that minimized the aches and pains in her bruised body. "But how is he?"

Steve was reluctant to commit himself on that question. "A crew of doctors were with him when I left his room half an hour ago."

"Shouldn't you have stayed to find out what they have to say?"

"Carol is waiting there. She'll come get me if there's any big development. They were getting ready to haul him off for some special kind of test, and the results won't be available right away."

"Is he in a lot of pain?" she asked anxiously.

"Probably." Steve's voice was dry. "He said he felt like a punching bag that has just gone ten rounds with the champ."

She tried to laugh and found that she could without

too much discomfort. "So tell me...how does he look?"

"I've seen him look better." He contemplated briefly. "Remember how he used to run into every tree and trip over every curb on the place, back when he was first learning mobility? Well, just picture all of his black eyes and broken noses and skinned-up shins at once, and you've got an idea how he looks right now."

"I want to see him."

Steve raised an eyebrow at her. "I thought I would discourage you. I'm telling you, he's not a pretty sight."

"He will be to me." Briony plucked at the sheet with one hand, her eyes downcast. "Are you still trying to keep us apart?"

"No, and I never was," he denied emphatically. "He told me before I came down here that he'd rather not have you see him in this shape. Call it stupid blind vanity if you will." Seeing her unhappy look, he added quietly, sounding more humble than she had ever heard him, "I'll admit I made a mistake the other day, warning you off like that, but I did it with the best of intentions. I misread Patrick. If anything, I would have gotten you together a long time ago." He touched her chin. "I'm assuming you two did finally have a heart-to-heart?"

She nodded. "Last night. Just before— Well, just before."

That seemed to satisfy Steve. "I'm a little surprised Patrick didn't tell me about it this morning, since he knew how interested I am. Of course, I don't imagine he's thinking too clearly after having his brain scrambled like that."

She shuddered involuntarily at the thought of the punishment Patrick had taken for her. "They don't think— I mean, his brain couldn't really be damaged, could it?''

She waited tensely, hoping Steve would joke away the possibility, but her brother merely became irritable. ''Now, that's a stupid thing for you to worry about! As if worrying will help.''

Reaching for his arm before he could turn away, she held him beside her and persisted. ''What are they trying to find with that special test you mentioned?''

''I don't know,'' he said shortly. ''You'd have to ask his doctors.''

''All right, I will.'' She pushed the sheet off and sat up, sliding her legs over the edge of the bed. The skimpy hospital nightgown opened to let cold fingers of air run up and down her spine.

''No, you won't.'' Unceremoniously Steve forced her to lie back down and covered her up, every inch the big brother. ''Dr. Travis hasn't said it was okay for you to get up yet. You're not up to par yourself, you know.''

''I'm just fine. I want to see Patrick's doctors.''

More gently now, he explained to her why she couldn't. ''He has the best neurologists in town looking after him, which means they're extremely busy. They don't have time to handle hysterical girl friends.''

''I won't be hysterical.'' She was perfectly calm, on the surface at least. ''Unless you try to keep me from seeing Patrick.''

''Hey, make up your mind. Is it Patrick you want to see, or his doctors?''

Steve was trying to tease her now, but she chose to take him seriously. ''I'd prefer to see both, but if I have to decide, I want Patrick.''

But Steven jutted out his chin and proved how stubborn he could be. ''Not until your doctor gives you permission.''

Glaring at him, Briony felt totally frustrated by the impasse.

If Dr. Travis hadn't come in to examine her a few minutes later, she might have been unable to tolerate the tension that was building within her. As soon as he had pronounced her fit to go home, she sent him out to repeat that to Steven, who waited in the hall.

She put on the soft red wool jersey dress that Carol Hammond had brought from home that morning, and the classic midheel pumps. Trust Carol to know she would want to look her best after what had happened. Studying herself in the mirror, she thought the bruises on her temple and throat looked like faint smudges of dirt that wouldn't wash off. When she stretched her mouth into an experimental smile, her lips stung despite the balm Dr. Travis had applied to the cuts. Her eyes looked as large and luminous as ever, and luckily her beautifully cut blond hair fell right into place when she brushed it.

"I'm ready," she announced to Steve, who looked her over doubtfully.

"Bri, you've had such a traumatic experience—"

"I want to see him!" Her voice was low and tremulous. "Now!"

"Okay, little sister," he agreed, soothing her, putting his arm around her. "Okay."

But outside Patrick's door, Steve hesitated again. "He really made it plain this morning that he didn't want to see you for a while. He wanted to know how you were, but no visits yet."

Her face became thunderous. "Steven!"

Gesturing her toward the room with defeat, he muttered, "He's very likely to kill me for this, but go on in. When could I ever say no to you?"

When Briony opened the door, Carol rose without a

word and smiled encouragement at her, then slipped outside. Briony stood uncertainly, glancing around. The room was thankfully well-lit and cheerful, the draperies pulled wide open to let in the warm sunshine. Patrick lay without a pillow under his head, so completely flat on the bed that Briony couldn't see his face until she moved closer, and then she wanted to cry.

Both of his eyes were, indeed, black and blue, and his crooked nose was taped in place with a strip of plaster across the middle. The jagged edges of a cut over one eyebrow were held together with tiny wire stitches. There were numerous other bruises, on both jaws and his temple, and a long red scratch down one cheek, and his lips were cracked and swollen. His thick fair hair was still matted in spots with dried blood.

Speechless with an overwhelming tide of emotions, Briony stood next to the bed and gazed down at him, her eyes full of tears. She had to clench her hands together to keep from taking his face between them and kissing every inch of it.

From what she could see, the rest of him seemed relatively undamaged. He wore a larger version of the cotton hospital gown she had been issued last night. Aside from a few scratches, his strong tanned forearms were intact, the hairs on the back of them gleaming in the sunlight. Thank heaven his hands had been spared! The idea of his sensitive, indispensable fingers being hurt was unbearable to her.

She sighed softly, and he started, opening his eyes. His taut fingers dug into the sheet that covered him. "Carol?"

"No, darling, not Carol." Bending her head, Briony touched her lips gently to one of the few unmarked places she could find, his chin.

To her dismay, even that light kiss made him flinch. "Briony." He let his held-in breath out slowly. "I wasn't expecting you. I didn't hear you come in."

"Don't apologize for not knowing it was me. Your nose is taking a much-needed vacation."

A reluctant grin flickered over his features and then faded into another grimace. "Please don't try to be funny. Not just yet, anyway." He moved his head a fraction, listening. "Where's Steve? He was supposed to bring me a report on how you're doing."

"I relieved him of that duty when Dr. Travis discharged me."

"Can you go home?" He sounded pleased. "That must mean you're not too badly hurt?"

She stroked his arm. "Patrick, I'm fine. Just fine. The important question is, how are you?"

"Except for the grandfather of all headaches, I feel okay too." Oddly, his eyes stared at the ceiling, for once not trying to find her face. "They tell me you weren't...that he didn't rape you. Is that the truth?"

She took his hand and turned it, then placed her palm flat against his and laced their fingers together. "The gospel truth. Chad wore himself out fighting you, my gallant hero." When he didn't respond to that, she asked, "Would it have made a difference if he had raped me?"

He frowned. "Made a difference?"

"I mean, would you have felt any differently about me? Would you still have wanted me to be all those things you told me I am to you—your eyes, your lover, your family?" She didn't really think it would have mattered, but she wanted to hear him say so.

Instead, he lay perfectly still and silent, his hand suddenly perspiring in hers. "Patrick?" she prompted him.

"If he had raped you," he said, apparently selecting

his words with care, "you would still be very special to me. It wouldn't have changed anything."

She brought his hand up to her lips and kissed his palm. "I love you very much." Now she kissed each fingertip with slow, infinite tenderness.

Patrick swallowed with difficulty, and she saw that his forehead was damp. "Are you feeling worse?" she asked, concerned at his sudden pallor.

"No."

"I've probably exhausted you with all this talk. I just want to say one thing more and then I'll be quiet and let you rest. I want you to promise me that as soon as you're back in shape"—she smiled as she said it— "you'll put a ring on my finger and face up to the idea of having me around the rest of your life."

He shut his eyes, such a look of pain on his face that she released his hand in alarm and started for the door. "I'm going to call your doctor."

"No!" He sat up, reaching out as if to stop her. "I'm okay, Briony," he insisted hoarsely, but even as he said it, he swayed dizzily and groaned, clutching his head in his hands.

She hurried back to his side and pressed against his broad shoulders, forcing him to lie down. Biting her lip, she stroked the wet curls back from his face.

"I really am fine," he said after a moment. "They told me it would hurt more if I didn't stay flat for a while."

Briony continued to caress his hair, raking her fingers through it gingerly. "Did I say something to upset you?"

He got that look again, but this time she waited for him to speak. "I just...I think it would be best if you didn't talk about that."

What on earth...?

"Talk about *what*, Patrick?"

"About marriage. Our marriage." He was staring at the ceiling again, obviously too tired to do anything else.

Her forehead puckered. "Why not? I love you and I want to marry you. Why not talk about it?"

"I thought you might have noticed," he said in a carefully controlled monotone. "I didn't mention marriage last night."

As the gist of what he was saying struck home, her hand froze on his brow.

"But we were interrupted," she suggested, silently pleading with him to stop this nonsense. "We would have covered the subject if we'd had half a chance."

Wearily he shook his head. "You always rush your fences, Briony. You've always been ruled by your impulses and emotions. Sometimes"—it seemed to be hard for him to say this—"you get so caught up in what you're feeling that you don't pay much attention to what other people feel."

"You, Patrick?" She had always liked to believe she was tuned in on a special wave length to him.

"I don't think I'm up to marriage, Bri." He spoke so quietly that she could barely hear him. "I'm sorry. Really sorry."

Withdrawing her hand from his head, she gripped the bedrail desperately. "Then would you mind telling me what was the purpose of our discussion last night? Did you just want me to restore your bedroom privileges?"

He winced, and she took his silence as confirmation.

"I see," she managed. "Well, I certainly misinterpreted you! Stupid, naive Briony has gone and done it again, and after all I said about not throwing myself at you anymore. This could prove to be embarrassing."

She laughed jerkily. "Look, let's just pretend the whole thing never happened, okay? That way we don't have to act all stiff and awkward with each other. All right?" Her voice cracked, and a sob escaped.

As if to shut out the sound, Patrick closed his eyes tight and squeezed out the tears that had suddenly filled his eyes. The sight of the wetness sliding silently down his battered cheeks reminded Briony that Patrick was in a great deal of pain.

"I'm sorry!" she apologized, not really knowing what she was saying. "S-sorry!" And she turned and fled the room.

"I told you not to try to see him today," Steve reminded her grimly as he drove her home. "Obviously neither of you was up to handling the ordeal yet."

"Why should it be an ordeal for us to see each other?" she snapped, her hysteria being rapidly replaced by anger.

"When two fools fall in love, there's always hell to pay," her brother muttered. "It never goes smoothly."

"Oh, but who's talking about love? Patrick never mentioned the word, not once!"

Steve glanced over at her briefly. "I don't remember exactly what he said to me when we talked yesterday, but I know I got the distinct impression he loved you. Not brotherly love, either."

"Yes, well, he's evidently an expert at making it sound like he's talking about love without actually saying the word. How do you suppose he's managed to maintain his freedom all these years?"

"Yesterday he said it was by telling all his women right at the start about the girl next door who was waiting for him to settle down. It used to be his own sort of private joke—"

"Yes, I'm quite a joke to Patrick!"

"It *used* to be, but since he came home this time he realized what you mean to him," Steve continued insistently. "He said he couldn't live without you anymore. I took that to mean he wanted to marry you."

"That's the same mistake I made." She laughed without humor. "Come on, Steve, I know it's hard, but you're going to have to give in and admit you were wrong about your best friend."

He watched the streets now, moodily, not replying to that.

"Anyway"—she didn't notice the hard note that had crept into her voice—"it's no big deal. At least I hadn't started planning the wedding. At least I wasn't that far gone."

From his look of pity, she knew Steve didn't believe her.

Briony was sitting at breakfast the next morning with her parents and Carol and Carly when Steve stormed through the back door, looking wild. He pulled up short at the sight of everyone around the table and glared at no one in particular.

"What are you doing home so soon?" Carol asked mildly. "I thought you intended to spend the day at the hospital with Patrick."

"You'll never believe what that idiot has done now!" No one ventured a guess. "He's gone home!"

Half rising, Briony murmured, "He's next door? Did the doctors discharge him already?" And then she remembered and sat back down. It was nothing to her if he were next door or not.

"No, the doctors didn't discharge him, and no, he's not next door. He's gone home to New Hampshire."

Four adults gaped at him, while Carly played happily in her eggs.

"Are you sure?" Ryan asked, clearly not believing it.

Steve nodded. "He worked his notorious charm on one of the night nurses and got her to help him. She says he took an early flight out of town." He began pacing around the room. "I shouldn't have let him talk me out of spending the night with him again! I should have recognized the signs."

"What signs?" Carol asked.

"Signs of him doing a number on me. He gets just a little too meek and agreeable. Anything to disarm the opposition, and then *whammo*! He strikes a blow for independence. When your back is turned, he goes roller-skating with a girl who can't skate, or does something stupid like this!"

"Well, there's no sense blaming yourself," Dr. Hammond pointed out calmly. "As you said, he's got an independent streak a mile wide. If this is what he wanted to do, he would have figured out a way no matter who was involved."

Esmé fiddled with her napkin, frowning. "I spoke with his neurologist last night, Ryan, and he said they hadn't entirely ruled out complications, perhaps a subdural hematoma or even a cerebral hemorrhage. That's why they wanted to keep him in the hospital a while longer under observation. Do you suppose his injury could account for this irrational behavior?"

"Mom, this behavior is not irrational for Patrick," Briony argued. "It's a pretty typical stunt for him to pull, rushing off without considering the people who— who care for him." She stumbled over that part.

"I can't agree with that," Carol spoke up firmly. "Patrick is usually remarkably thoughtful of others. That's why he jokes so much about his blindness, so people won't have to be sorry for him. I think he may not have been thinking clearly because of the severe pain he was having and—and because he felt so absolutely rotten about what happened. How he hadn't been able to stop Chad from hurting you."

Steeling herself to feel no sympathy for Patrick, Briony almost missed Steven's reply. "That's interesting." He dropped down into a chair beside Carol. "I ran into Tom Clayton on the parking lot at the hospital, and we had quite a talk. It seems Tom suspected from what Briony and Patrick told him that Chad Smith had been injured in the fight, and yesterday he located Chad under an assumed name in Brackenridge Hospital. He had an injury to his larynx, and the swelling that resulted was closing off his air passage. They had to perform a tracheotomy so he could breathe. Tom spoke with Chad's doctor, who speculated that the choking was probably what caused Chad to stop beating on Briony and leave without killing one or both of them. He thought he was choking to death, and went to get emergency treatment."

Looking over at his sister, Steve added, "Tom is in charge of the investigation, and he assures me he's building an airtight case. He's got Chad under close security at Brackenridge, and just as soon as it's safe, he's moving him to the jail infirmary. Tom wanted me to tell you Chad's no longer a threat to you."

"Thank heaven!" Esmé sighed.

"Well," Ryan commented suddenly, "it sounds to me as if Patrick did a damned good job of protecting Briony with that right hook of his."

Steve nodded, and Carol said soberly, "It's too bad Patrick doesn't know that."

"So, what, if anything, are we going to do about him?" Ryan asked.

"I don't like the idea of his being off by himself

when the doctors don't know for sure he's okay," Briony's mother murmured. "Ryan, perhaps you or Steve could go up there and persuade him to come home?"

But Steve vetoed that promptly. "He'd never forgive us, Mom, if we presumed to decide for him that he needs our help. I think that's what this flight is all about in the first place."

"What do you recommend, Briony?" her father inquired.

They all waited for her answer, looking as if she held the key.

She put her hands around her coffee cup, studying the creamy brown liquid for a long minute, trying to be objective about Patrick. Certainly she didn't wish him any harm, no matter how callously he had rejected her. In reality, of course, she knew he hadn't done it callously at all. It had been very difficult for Patrick to be as honest with her as he had. His tears were proof of that.

The idea that he was alone and in pain, possibly still in medical danger, was a torture to her, but she recalled that he had chosen to remove himself from their midst and told herself that medical care was available to him in New Hampshire, just as it was in Austin, Texas. Surely he would be bright enough to know if he needed to see a doctor.

On the other hand, it would be so easy to encourage Steve to go east and pluck Patrick out of his safe, remote environment and drag him back to Texas by the ear.

But what would that accomplish? He still wouldn't love her or want to marry her. She lowered her eyes quickly to hide the glistening drops on her lashes. "I think you should respect his decision to leave us."

Although everyone nodded agreement, no one looked particularly happy with the decision.

Chapter Ten

If anyone had told her the week before that college kids could be such a comfort to her, Briony might have been a little skeptical. But that was just what they proved to be. It was no secret around campus that one of her students, now conspicuously absent from class, had attacked her with the intention of molesting her sexually. The newspaper had done a decent job of downplaying that part of the story, but the potential for embarrassment was still there.

Wanting to submerge herself in activities in order to stop thinking about Patrick and about the huge gap his going had left in her life, she insisted on returning to the classroom before the week was over. Her bruises were still in evidence, and her nerves a little jittery, but she soon relaxed when she saw how the kids supported her.

They were the soul of tact, at the same time that they displayed their usual blunt interest in everything about them, including the now-revered blind professor who was credited in the newspaper with saving her life.

"You promised you'd ask him to speak to us," they reminded her on her first day back. "When is he coming?"

She hated to admit that he wasn't, knowing the disappointed groans she would hear, so she hedged, telling them he would perhaps have time to visit the class after his injuries had healed. Later on, she would have to think up some new excuse for the delay. At least she could be grateful the semester was more than half over.

In their concern, the students tried to mother her and cajoled her into signing up to run in the faculty marathon to raise money for the scholarship fund, and otherwise let her know in a hundred little ways that they were sorry she had been hurt.

At home her family gave her the same message when they forgave her absentmindedness and short temper, and the occasional inevitable self-pity. "You know I really hate to leave you, Bri," Steve told her just before he loaded up his family and drove off on Sunday afternoon. "I was hoping—"

"Yes?"

"Never mind." He shrugged, taking her hands to scowl down at her and pretend to be unemotional. "How about driving up to spend the weekend with us in a couple of weeks? We've got season tickets to the Dallas Cowboys games."

Briony thought that sounded rather nice but didn't commit herself, knowing that in a week it might not appeal to her at all in her present unpredictable state of mind.

"Bri?" Carol muttered nervously as she kissed her sister-in-law good-bye. "I don't suppose you'd give in and call him?"

"Him?" she echoed, although she knew quite well whom Carol meant.

"Patrick. Oh, please!" the small dark girl begged her. "I can't help worrying about him. And I know how much he cares about you. Yes, he does!" she insisted at Briony's immediate denial.

"No. I won't call him, and you'd better get used to the idea of my being an old maid," she announced with forced gaiety. She turned away quickly to receive a smacking kiss from Carly and then stepped back to wave them off.

Lizzie was another unexpected comfort. She was so distressed at the double blow of John Donahue's death and then Patrick's sudden departure, that she dealt with her grief the only way she knew how: by talking volubly about both of them for hours on end. Sometimes Briony would stop by in the morning for a cup of coffee and hear all about the plans John had made for this year he had expected to have Patrick at home with him again. If she saw Liz later in the day, the frizzy-haired old lady would still be soliloquizing, this time about "the dear boy" who had assured her after the funeral that he wanted her to work for him for the next six months at least.

"And he paid my salary in advance," she told Briony at least ten times in as many days.

Every day Lizzie came to work to shine and polish the empty house, always predicting that this would be the day she would hear from Patrick, and every evening she went home undaunted. It was a lesson in faith for Briony, who had to admire Lizzie's complete trust even if she couldn't emulate it.

Somehow the days passed. The foliage was turning in earnest now. Each day the air was just a little nippier than yesterday had been, unlike most Texas autumns, which remained uncomfortably hot until a sudden Norther literally freezes the leaves on the trees.

One afternoon Tom Clayton dropped by her office on campus. He asked her to walk over to the student center with him for a cup of coffee, and in a moment of weakness she agreed. It was the last thing she wanted to do, because she guessed, correctly, that he wanted to talk about Patrick.

Once seated at the table in the snack bar, he went about the task with the air of a police inquisitor. "Something happened between you and Patrick, didn't it?" he demanded without preamble. "Something that caused him to leave town in a hurry."

Briony shrugged. "I guess he left because he wanted to."

"I don't believe that." His voice was flat.

Bristling, she said, "That's too bad. I refuse to take the responsibility for Patrick's whims. I certainly didn't suggest that he leave."

"Maybe not, but I don't believe he really wanted to go. I think he's in love with you."

"Tom," she sighed wearily, "you're not the first one to mistake the situation. Believe me, he looks at me as a sister. A sometimes useful, sometimes pesty little sister. My affection became an embarrassment to him, if you must know."

He swore graphically, and Briony glanced around to see if any students had overheard.

"That's so much crap," he said. "I think it's more likely that *you* were embarrassed."

"At what?"

"At the prospect of getting too involved with a blind man. Besides all the problems that would entail, he could never really appreciate your beauty—"

Briony stood so quickly that her chair toppled over backward, making an unholy racket that caught every-one's instant attention. He rose too and in the inter-ested silence that surrounded them, she whispered, glaring at him, "That's the rottenest, absolutely stupi-dest thing you could have said!"

"No truth in it?" Tom challenged, his eyes meeting hers levelly.

"Not a shred. Now if you're through insulting me, I'll get back to work."

He touched her arm, his voice softening, "Wait, Briony. Don't go—"

Before he could finish, he found himself dwarfed by two basketball players who materialized from out of nowhere and flanked him, looking fierce. "Miss Hammond?" they asked gruffly. "Do you want us to throw this dude out of here?"

"Briony, I'm sorry," he said hastily, withdrawing his hand, his dark eyes appealing to her. "I had to check it out. I had to know if that was the hang-up."

"Well, it wasn't."

Tom nodded. "I believe you. Steve told me the same thing, but I had to be sure." He glanced at her protectors. "Look, I'm not going to hurt Miss Hammond, I assure you."

"It's okay, boys," she agreed, thanking them with a smile for their concern. "This gentleman is a police detective. He's also a friend of mine, although I suppose it didn't look that way." Her smile turned wry.

The athletes left, somewhat mollified, and Briony sat back down, still wary of Tom. "Well, now that I've satisfied your curiosity, what do you plan to do with the information?"

"Briony, it wasn't curiosity that prompted me to come here. I care very much what happens to Patrick, and to you too for that matter." When she didn't say anything, he continued quietly, "Thank you for not pointing out that if I really cared about him, I should have come around twenty years ago. I've told myself that often enough. The only thing I can say in my defense is that I was too damned scared of seeing what I had done to him, of finding out that I had ruined his chances for the kind of life any guy should be able to go for. When I saw you and Patrick together a few weeks ago, it seemed to me that he had achieved that good life, and for the first time in years I could feel good about things. Since he left, I've been afraid again, afraid you dumped him.''

She gave a small choked laugh. "Hardly. *He* dumped *me*. Royally, in fact. I all but proposed, and he let me know in no uncertain terms that he had no intention of marrying me. So you don't need to worry about him. You may have accidentally altered the course of Patrick's future when he was a kid, but I haven't a doubt that he'll get exactly what he wants out of life. He's his own man, and a very exceptional man that is.''

Having admitted that, she felt a little better. All the terrible names she had called him—all the accusations she had made against him in her mind—were ridiculous lies, and Briony thought of herself as a basically honest person. It was a relief to acknowledge to herself that she still loved Patrick—that she probably always would—and to make up her mind to get on with her life as expeditiously as possible.

So when Tom suggested, as Carol had, that she contact Patrick in New Hampshire and try again, Briony shook her head firmly. "No," she murmured, unaware of how heart-tuggingly sad she looked, "I'm going to make it alone. I'm going to be all right, and so will Patrick. Don't worry about him, Tom.''

Briony kept busy with her work, and helping prepare for the Thanksgiving program at the School for the Blind, and running. An attractive assistant professor of biology at Drey-Bart took her to a U.T. drama production of *A Midsummer Night's Dream,* and invited her out once after that, but she declined because she found that he, and every other eligible male she encountered, left her indifferent. She was quite willing to take their friendship if they offered it, but if they so much as hinted that they had something heavier in mind, she bade them a hasty farewell.

Of course her students knew she was no longer engaged, and a couple of them tried to do a little matchmaking, to Briony's secret amusement. It was always some perfectly handsome, perfectly perfect, perfectly boring man with whom they tried to maneuver her into a relationship, but she always resisted, feeling that her rehabilitation program didn't need to move quite that fast.

Andy approached her desk before research class on the Tuesday before Thanksgiving. He was now off the crutches and no longer even limping from his hit-and-run injuries. "Miss Hammond, I have a big favor to ask you. I found out that my cousin is coming to spend the holidays with my family. This is my cousin George who plays baseball with the Astros," he added significantly. "My girl friend and I had already made plans to go to a dance on Friday night, and I wondered if you could maybe come with us, so he won't feel like a fifth wheel?"

Because she appreciated his intentions, she let him down as graciously as she could. "Andy, if I didn't already have plans that night, I'd love to go to the dance with you all. I don't imagine you'll have any trouble finding another girl, though. Cousin George has made such a name for himself, I'll bet half the girls in the senior class would jump at the chance to go."

He gave in good-naturedly and returned to his seat. She was glad he didn't pursue those "other plans" of hers, or he might have learned that she intended to go to bed with a book.

Today Briony planned to compare several different types of sociometric scales and then work with the whole class on composing a research instrument for their project. She perched on the edge of her desk, sorting through her notes as she waited for the rest of the students to get settled down. Her head was bent, her silvery gold hair falling forward to block her side vision. Becoming suddenly aware of the hush that had fallen, she looked up.

"Pardon me," a husky voice spoke from the doorway. "By any chance is this a Spanish class?"

Utterly incredulous, she turned her head, not daring to believe who it was.

But there he stood, tall, handsome, his slightly curling fair hair combed neatly in place, wearing camel cord slacks and blazer over a cream oxford cloth shirt and brown sleeveless sweater, his right hand casually holding the long white cane. All of the facial bruises had disappeared, and his nose was only slightly more crooked than it used to be. His clear green eyes were aimed vaguely at the corner behind Briony.

Her heart pounded with shock, and her throat constricted. It was all she could do not to jump up and close the distance between them at a run, to throw herself into his arms and risk knocking him off his feet with her relief that he was all right, that he was *here*!

"*¿Habla español, señorita?*" he inquired softly, raising an eyebrow at her lengthy silence.

When she heard the faint titters from the class, her sanity returned. This was the charming Patrick, attempting to perform his magic. Well, it wouldn't work this time!

"This is *not* Spanish class!" she said between clenched teeth. "As if you had to ask."

His eyes shifted until they were more on target, only

missing her own snapping green ones by a few inches. "Good. I didn't want to make *that* mistake again." He grinned and used his cane to come another step or two into the room. "Where do you want me?"

"We're about to begin class, Patrick," she muttered in an undertone that all of the students heard. "What are you doing here?"

Halting, he looked momentarily confused—a very appealing kind of look, Briony acknowledged. "You *did* tell me I was invited to speak to your class, didn't you?" He opened his watch and felt the face. "Have I come at the wrong time? I thought you said ten thirty."

"You were asked a month ago!"

He nodded. "Something happened that got me sidetracked. Do your students want to rescind their invitation?"

A chorus of denials from the classroom made it impossible for her to pretend otherwise.

When Patrick flashed an engaging smile in the direction of the audience, Briony groaned and mentally threw up her hands. She hadn't a prayer of competing successfully against him. "Fine!" She stood up. "Here's my desk, if you want to use it."

He found his way to her side with his casual but careful steps, his cane locating the wastepaper basket and the sharp corner of the desk. He stopped when he was near enough to smell her perfume.

Close up, she saw the new scar, not very long but still noticeably pink, that jagged down into his left eyebrow. He had gotten that scar for her, not to mention the latest hump in his interesting nose.

But he hadn't wanted to marry her.

Getting a grip on herself, Briony turned to face the class. They were watching Patrick with something akin to awe, not quite able to believe that the eyes that only seemed a little unfocused as they scanned the classroom were actually blind.

"This is Dr. Patrick Donahue," she announced coolly, "probably one of Dreyfuss-Bartholemew's more colorful alumni. His college career was distinguished by the fact that he majored in girls, but then of course he had an advantage over the sighted students: He was allowed to braille his subjects."

The kids looked undecided whether or not to laugh at Briony's barbed humor. When Patrick inclined his head at her, obviously amused, she felt mean and snide, and set about to rectify the feeling. "Actually," she amended, "he was largely responsible for making the administration aware of how they could smooth the way for handicapped students at Drey-Bart. You may have noticed the braille plates next to the elevator buttons. Those were just one of his suggestions. Others were the wheelchair ramps cut into the curbs, and the Talking Book service at the library. No doubt," she admitted dryly, "if he hadn't graduated in three years, he would have had time to bring about even greater changes. Anyway, I'll let him tell you more about himself."

Briony gathered up her papers from the desk and carried them to a seat against the wall, her heels clicking abruptly across the floor. Patrick seemed to be watching her, following the sound of her movements with his eyes, and when she sat down, he laid his cane across the desk, shoved his hands deep in his pockets, and stood alone before the roomful of people he couldn't see.

"Well," he murmured, "hello." His voice was low and, she thought, a little nervous.

And her next thought was: Impossible! Patrick the ham would be in seventh heaven, given this chance to woo her students.

"When your teacher told me a month ago about your invitation to speak to you, my initial reaction was doubt. Doubt that anything I have to say would be of benefit to a group of sighted kids who will, hopefully, never have any use for the kind of practical advice I could give. I also wondered about your motive for asking me. Did you want to watch me perform so you could be amazed at the incredible way I manage in the dark? Or did you want to confirm what you've always believed about blind people and go away thinking 'Thank God I'm not blind like him'?"

He gave them a wry half smile as if he sensed their sheepish expressions. "I'm still not sure of your motives, or of how much good this talk will do you, but after giving it a lot of consideration, I became pretty clear about what it can do for *me*. I have something to say to someone, and I need a forum where my audience won't be able to walk out in the middle and leave me talking to an empty room."

As Briony puzzled over his meaning, the students sat, enthralled.

Patrick moved back fractionally until he felt the desk against the back of his thigh. After exploring the surface of the desk with a single unobtrusive stroke of one hand, he sat down there.

"Briony suggested that I tell you about myself. I think I won't bore you with that, except to explain that she has lived next door to me since she was born and has seen me at every stage of my life—occasionally triumphant, but more often undignified, clumsy, and struggling. That may have led her to place undue emphasis on whatever success I'm enjoying now.

"People talk in terms of how well I've overcome my disability. The fact of the matter is, I have *not* overcome my blindness. Obviously I'm still blind and

I will be the rest of my life. What I have overcome, or worked my way around when necessary, were the problems that accompany blindness. You can imagine the problems I mean, can't you? Learning to shave without cutting my throat. To dress so people don't wince when they look at me. To eat in public. To get from one place to another without getting myself killed. To live alone if I choose that kind of life. Oh, I didn't overcome the obstacles on my own. I've had a lot of help from some creative people who let me think at the time that I was helping myself. People like Briony and her family, who are very adept at making me feel good about myself.

"Sometimes I've had to accept that a thing is beyond me. Because bills and bank statements don't often come in braille, I have an accountant who handles that for me. And I had to give up my burning ambition to be a jet pilot and settle on a career I could reasonably expect to achieve.

"Which brings us to the trouble I had convincing everyone else I could be a teacher...."

Briony leaned back against the wall, half listening to his witty descriptions of being the only blind student enrolled at Drey-Bart, and later in graduate school in Boston, and then the difficulties of finding a college that would hire a blind Ph.D. to teach history to sighted kids. He explained some of his ingenious ways of getting the job done, using mechanical aids and human helpers to do the things he couldn't manage alone. Since she had heard him talk of this before, she let her eyes drift over the faces of the attentive students, recognizing that he was weaving a spell with his husky voice and his lack of self-pity. The beautiful green eyes fascinated the kids. The occasional smile won them completely. Was it something he did on purpose? She didn't know. All she knew was, it worked. The kids were his on a silver platter. They would leave class today thoroughly convinced that Patrick Donahue was an incredibly wonderful human being, a man among men.

And, dammit, in spite of everything, he was!

Her eyes filling with tears, she closed them and clenched her hands together tightly, feeling her nails biting into her palms.

Don't forget! Don't ever forget again that he never once mentioned love!

So what did Patrick want, if not marriage? She had debated that question often enough since he left town. He had admitted he wasn't complete without her, that she was all that had been missing from his life for the past five years. Had he been planning to suggest that she live with him? And if he had—if he did so now that he had come back—what would she say?

Briony blinked away her tears and looked at him where he sat, leaning forward a little as he talked, his wide shoulders hunched, his hands gripping the desk edge on either side of him. "... ask me what it's like to be blind, and I've never come up with a very good answer. It's *not* like being shut up in a dark closet, because the world I live in isn't limited to four walls. Mine is a huge, complicated, exciting world.

"It's not like the whole world was bathed in blankness, because it's only blank for people who have no memory of sight. For you, the void is filled in with color and form and, most important, faces. I'm luckier than a lot of blind people, because I had vision for ten years. I can remember enough to make up a vivid picture of what's happening around me. It may not be an accurate picture, but it's in beautiful, wide-screen technicolor.

"Being blind is also not like being blindfolded, because if it were that simple, believe me I'd have removed the blindfold twenty years ago!''

When the resulting laughter died down, he went on seriously, ''The best way I know to describe it, and this is far from adequate, is to say that for me it's confusing. Sighted people move along at a speed that scares the hell out of me sometimes. Maybe,'' he conceded with a small grin, ''not all of you are moving so fast, but you certainly seem to. I don't enjoy being confused. I keep wanting to be certain of things, but all too often that's just not possible if you can't see what's around you.

''Sometimes it is possible to clear up the confusion, but there's still the question of whether I want to make a spectacle of myself by brailling a piece of sculpture at an art gallery to see its shape, or feeling around on the ground to discover what it was that just tripped me. It took me quite a while to appreciate the fact that my life is limited enough by my lack of vision, without worrying too much over whether I'll be conspicuous if I explore something by touch.''

''Dr. Donahue?'' Connie spoke up, hesitant to interrupt yet dying to ask something.

Patrick turned his head to the sound of the girl's voice. ''Yes, ma'am?''

''Do you ever, er, touch a person to see what he or she looks like? Or was Miss Hammond teasing?''

He slanted a look toward Briony. ''I think Miss Hammond was exaggerating. In answer to your question, yes, I do sometimes braille people as well as objects, but not very often and only with their permission. Most of the time I have to be satisfied with verbal descriptions of people, and create my own image of what they look like.''

''Would you show us how you braille someone?'' Tim asked.

It was Patrick's turn to hesitate, but only for a second, and then a familiar wicked look rearranged his attractive features into a grin. "I will if your teacher will help me."

Briony drew in her breath sharply. No! She wouldn't. Did he take her for an idiot? She'd have to be one to put herself so literally and figuratively in his hands. Did he want her to break down completely in front of her students?

"Briony?"

She swallowed, knowing that everyone was looking at her, waiting for her to go to him.

"Come on, be a sport, Miss Hammond!" the kids urged her.

As she got to her feet, she found that she was shaking. Her legs carried her slowly, reluctantly, to the desk, and when she reached it, he stood and faced her, his expression that of a man who was prepared to enjoy something.

"I already know what Briony looks like," he confessed in an aside to the classroom, placing both hands on her warm cheeks, "but that doesn't stop me from wanting to 'look' again." Now he spoke directly to her in a quiet undertone. "Are you blushing, Bri?" She nodded mutely. "Good," he replied, to her consternation. "I thought you might be running a fever."

Some of the students heard that and chuckled. They grew hushed once more as Patrick's long fingers began their sensual journey over her face, stirring the usual feelings of need and longing in her as they traced softly over her smooth skin. When they had reminded Patrick of each of her features, they raked for a moment through her shimmering blond hair. One hand paused, took a handful, and crushed it, then released it and stroked it back in place, apparently relishing the silky texture of it.

Briony was having difficulty maintaining her poise as she endured the sweet agony of his touch. She held herself stiff in order not to reveal her tremulousness, and she didn't dare look at Patrick's face as he brailled her, but kept her eyes pinned on the brown cable knit sweater that stretched across his chest.

When he finished with her hair, she began to feel that relief was in sight, a hope that he shattered when his hands traveled relentlessly down her neck to her shoulders and then her arms. "You're wearing a long-sleeved cotton blouse," he observed, a certain tautness in his voice indicating that he wasn't as casual about this as he tried to seem. She glanced up at his face and saw how it had tightened with a kind of grim determination that frightened her. "It has a button-down collar and French cuffs." Despite her frozen resistance, his hands molded down her sides to her hips. "Your skirt is wool and has buttons down the front."

"Patrick!" she hissed. "Please stop!"

He let his hands rest on her hips. "Stop?" he queried in a whisper, seeming to stare down at her. No one else in the room made a sound. It was almost as if they had stopped breathing.

"Please!"

It was a cry from her heart. How could she bear up under this torture any longer?

Instead of releasing her, his hands slid around behind her back and his arms pulled her close, pressing her against him tightly. For a long moment she just enjoyed it, the wonderful feel of him and the knowledge that she was right where she wanted to be, but then she became aware of the delighted murmurs of the students and pushed away from him, horrified.

"Patrick!" she pleaded.

He blinked. "What? Oh. I'm sorry." Moving slightly

away from her, he allowed her a little room, at the same time slipping one arm around her waist and grasping her with his hand so she couldn't move far.

Still holding her, he turned toward the class again. "Where was I?"

Embarrassed, her heart pounding, Briony had to force herself to meet the eyes of the students, and when she did, she saw that they all seemed deeply moved by Patrick's demonstration.

"You were talking about being conspicuous," someone on the front row supplied.

"Oh, yes. Right." Patrick's brow furrowed in concentration. "The only alternative, if I don't want people to notice my blindness, is to hide out somewhere and miss most of what goes on around me. If I choose not to touch, not to ask questions, I'll never find out what's out there. So I've had to learn to feel okay about being blind.

"On the other hand, once in a while it's nice to be able to go places and do things without feeling that everyone is staring at me. To be really sure of where I'm going, where I'm walking. That's a kind of security I usually have only when I'm with a sighted guide. Having a guide who understands instinctively when I need help and when I need to handle things by myself is about as close to heaven as I can imagine."

"Why don't you get married and get yourself a permanent guide?" Tim suggested seriously.

Briony wanted to die. She lowered her eyelashes, feeling the tears start again, and studied the floor in front of her.

"Mmmm...." Patrick seemed to consider the idea. "I could do that. I did once think about getting married, and the lady was certainly all I could want. She was so right for me, in fact, that it was as if a miracle had shaped her into my second half, the part of me I'd been seeking for so many years.''

Knowing suddenly that he was talking about her, Briony turned her head just enough to watch his profile.

"Why didn't you marry her?" a student asked.

His hand moved on Briony's slender waist, almost a nervous gesture. "Because I needed to feel I was bringing something to the marriage, not just taking from it. I didn't want her to think I was only marrying her for her eyes. She's much, much more to me than just a pair of useful eyes. I love her more than I value my happiness.''

Briony's chest constricted with emotions.

"You mean you love her but you gave her up?" the student demanded, sounding disgusted.

Patrick nodded sheepishly. "That's right. Like a fool, I decided to be noble and self-sacrificing. I told myself she deserved more than a man who would come to rely on her more and more every day. Since I made that decision, I've really learned how cold and lonely a bed of pride can be.''

"And?" Briony put in quietly.

"And I've also had it pointed out to me by several concerned bystanders that I can do an adequate job of taking care of my own. I may not be your typical knight in shining armor, but I can get the job done.''

"Is it too late for you to get the lady back?"

Turning his head slowly from the student who asked the question to the flushed, lovely young woman beside him, Patrick seemed to scrutinize her face intently. "Is it?"

"Is it what?" She would make him put it into words, so there could be no further misunderstanding.

"Is it too late for you to marry me?"

Briony didn't answer immediately, wanting to repay

him a little of the torment he had caused her. She just stood there, gazing happily at the strong face that was so full of character, admiring the thick golden hair, the unfocused eyes, the crooked nose, and kissable mouth.

After a moment his expressive features showed uncertainty. "Bri?"

She pivoted within his grasp and encircled his neck with her arms. "This is so sudden. I'll have to think about it."

"Brat!" he growled, his relief obvious. "I'll give you ten seconds."

"I only need five." And then: "Yes, I'll marry you."

As Patrick's head bent and his mouth found hers, she was only vaguely aware of the explosion of cheers, whistles, and applause. After a moment, when the noise showed no signs of abating, Patrick raised his head. "You've been a better audience than I could have hoped for, but you can go now!" He was shouting to be heard. "Class is dismissed."

There were groans of protest. "It's too early! The bell won't ring for another fifteen minutes."

"Out!" he yelled.

"Can we come to the wedding?"

With her eyes on Patrick's grin, Briony nodded. She loved them all. She loved the whole world! "You'll be welcome to come. Bring everyone you know."

"When will it be?"

"Soon," she said.

"Very soon," Patrick corrected her.

It seemed to take forever for the kids to clear the room. When they were finally alone, she clung to his lean hard waist, her cheek pressed into the cord of his coat, breathing deeply of his musky after-shave. "I ought to hate you for going off like that to New Hampshire!"

"I came back."

"But you should never have left!"

"I'll never leave you again."

She sighed raggedly. "I thought you really didn't want me."

"Of *course* I wanted you, but I was devastated to think how close I had come to letting that sociopathic student of yours kill you."

"When really you were the one who saved us both from whatever he might have done."

"But I didn't know that, Briony, until Steve called and chewed me out for leaving. Even then, I thought he was fabricating the story to help me save face. Then your mother mailed me a clipping of the newspaper article, and when my neighbor read it to me, I started to think and hope. I've been thinking for weeks, trying to get up my nerve to come back and face you."

"What finally decided you?"

"Tom Clayton paid me a visit."

"Did he, now!" she exclaimed. "And what did Tom do to lure you home when the entire Hammond family hadn't been able to accomplish that?"

"Oh, he claimed he was there just to get away from things for a while, but he kept dropping subtle hints about how bad you were looking. He pretended he didn't know there was anything wrong between us, but I thought I knew what he was up to so I ignored his little tidbits. Finally he mentioned very casually that they were going to have to let Chad Smith go, because you were afraid to testify against him at the trial. Unless someone could change your mind, or unless I was there to testify, he said the chances were pretty dim that they could get a conviction against Chad."

Why, Tom Clayton! she thought, smiling to herself. *How devious of you! And how brilliant!*

Patrick seemed to be studying her very seriously. "Knowing how brave Briony Hammond is, I still suspected Tom was conning me, but when I called Steve to check it out, all he would say was that you hadn't been yourself since you left the hospital. So"—he gave a mock shrug of defeat—"that left me no choice but to come back here and take care of things myself. Tom and I flew home yesterday, and I spent the night at his place. Just before he drove me over here this morning, I got a confession out of him that you hadn't really said you wouldn't testify."

"Are you sorry he tricked you?"

"Are you kidding? Sorry to be holding you like this?" He threw back his head and laughed, tightening his arms around her. "Honey, I was ready to come back. One way or another I would have made it before very long. Tom just gave me an excuse to speed it up."

Suddenly grave, his clear green eyes met hers so squarely she could have sworn they could see her. "It's not important, is it? That I'll never really know how beautiful you've grown up to be, except by how you smell and feel?"

"And sound and taste?" she added. "I've been madly in love with you for most of the twenty years you've been blind, Patrick, and you're the very center of my life. If I knew for sure that you would never love me, I don't think I'd care much about anything else. Does that answer your question?"

"Yes, it does, thank you." Patrick nuzzled her with satisfaction, nibbling at her neck and flooding her with delight, but then he stopped abruptly and lifted his head. "I'm afraid your parents may not be so pleased with the idea of me as a son-in-law."

"What are you talking about? You're already as dear as a son to them."

He gave an almost imperceptible shake of his head. "I've sensed your mother's reluctance for us to be together. Every time you show any affection for me, she seems to become more withdrawn and unhappy."

"It's only that she's been so afraid you would reject me. As long as she knows you truly love me, she'll be just as thrilled as Daddy and Steve and Carol." Something else occurred to her then. "Do you know, I'll bet I can name someone who is smiling right now with sheer contentment." At his questioning look she murmured, "Uncle John. He'll be glad I kept my promise to him."

"Did you promise him we would get married?" Patrick asked, laughing again. "When he died, he must have had plenty of peace of mind, because I promised him the same thing that morning."

"You!" Briony was astonished. "But you were so outspoken against it!"

He shrugged off her accusation. "Only on the surface. Underneath I found the idea an intriguing temptation."

Briony laughed and hugged him tighter, and his response was immediate. His sensual mouth began at her forehead and worked its way down to her soft rosepetal lips, experiencing her beauty by touch and taste, increasingly hungry for more. He parted her lips and feasted on the sweetness within, until he had to raise his head, shaking with need.

"Oh, Lord, Bri," he muttered hoarsely into her hair, "I've wanted you so badly these past few weeks! I couldn't believe how lonely it was in New Hampshire without you."

"I was lonely too," she assured him. "That was a dirty trick—teaching me how wonderful it can be to share yourself fully with another and then deserting me cold turkey. If I weren't so stuck on you, I might have tried to find satisfaction with second best."

"That works both ways, you know. But speaking of satisfaction, how soon can we...?"

"Go home? To your house?"

"To bed. *Our* bed."

"But it's the middle of the day!"

"Is it?" Patrick pretended to look around. "Are you sure? It looks just like midnight to me," he said persuasively.

Giggling, Briony caught his face between her hands and pulled it back down for another kiss. "We can go right now if you like, but Lizzie will be there."

"We'll give her the rest of the week off for Thanksgiving."

"She'll be so happy to see you, she'll cry all over your shirt."

He sighed in resignation. "I guess I can put up with it. As long as I have you around, I can put up with anything." His lazy eyes looked right at her chin. "I love you more than life, Briony."

"Oh, Patrick, I've waited so long to hear you say that! Let's go home."

A few minutes later they walked out into the sunshine of the chilly November day, a handsome man with his hand on the arm of a very pretty woman, a golden couple oblivious of everything except each other.

HARLEQUIN
PREMIERE AUTHOR EDITIONS

6 top Harlequin authors—6 of their best books!

1. **JANET DAILEY** Giant of Mesabi
2. **CHARLOTTE LAMB** Dark Master
3. **ROBERTA LEIGH** Heart of the Lion
4. **ANNE MATHER** Legacy of the Past
5. **ANNE WEALE** Stowaway
6. **VIOLET WINSPEAR** The Burning Sands

Harlequin is proud to offer these 6 exciting romance novels by 6 of our most popular authors. In brand-new beautifully designed covers, each Harlequin Premiere Author Edition is a bestselling love story—a contemporary, compelling and passionate read to remember!

Available wherever paperback books are sold, *or* through Harlequin Reader Service. Simply complete and mail the coupon below.

Harlequin Reader Service

In the U.S.
P.O. Box 52040
Phoenix, Ariz., 85072-9988

In Canada
649 Ontario Street
Stratford, Ontario N5A 6W2

Please send me the following editions of **Harlequin Premiere Author Editions.**
I am enclosing my check or money order for $1.95 for each copy ordered, plus 75¢ to cover postage and handling.

☐ 1   ☐ 2   ☐ 3   ☐ 4   ☐ 5   ☐ 6

Number of books checked_____ @ $1.95 each = $ _____

N.Y. state and Ariz. residents add appropriate sales tax $ _____

Postage and handling $ _____ .75

I enclose $ _____   TOTAL $ _____

(Please send check or money order. We cannot be responsible for cash sent through the mail.) Price subject to change without notice.

NAME_____
(Please Print)

ADDRESS_____ APT. NO. _____

CITY_____

STATE/PROV. _____ ZIP/POSTAL CODE _____

Offer Expires June 30, 1984.

PA-W

31256000000

A Harlequin
ROBERTA LEIGH
Collector's Edition

A specially designed collection of six exciting love stories by one of the world's favorite romance writers—Roberta Leigh, author of more than 60 bestselling novels!

1 Love in Store
2 Night of Love
3 Flower of the Desert

4 The Savage Aristocrat
5 The Facts of Love
6 Too Young to Love

Available now wherever paperback books are sold, or available through Harlequin Reader Service. Simply complete and mail the coupon below.

Harlequin Reader Service

In the U.S.
P.O. Box 52040
Phoenix, AZ 85072-9988

In Canada
649 Ontario Street
Stratford, Ontario N5A 6W2

Please send me the following editions of the Harlequin Roberta Leigh Collector's Editions. I am enclosing my check or money order for $1.95 for each copy ordered, plus 75¢ to cover postage and handling.

☐ 1   ☐ 2   ☐ 3   ☐ 4   ☐ 5   ☐ 6

Number of books checked_____ @ $1.95 each = $_____

N.Y. state and Ariz. residents add appropriate sales tax $_____

Postage and handling $ .75

                                               TOTAL $_____

I enclose_____

(Please send check or money order We cannot be responsible for cash sent through the mail.) Price subject to change without notice.

NAME_____

(Please Print)

ADDRESS_____ APT. NO._____

CITY_____

STATE/PROV._____ ZIP/POSTAL CODE_____

Offer Expires June 30, 1984.   31256000000

RL-N